The CODE of the HUMAN SPIRIT

A WINDOW ON THE SOUL!

A NOVEL BY

DAVID R. GRAY

DEDICATION

This Book is dedicated to my loving and lovely wife Kathi. Without her encouragement and enthusiasm, it would not have been started nor completed. Thank You!

Love, David

<u>Work Of Fiction</u>

COPYRIGHT NOTICE

Table Of Contents

PROLOGUE

Alexandria, Egypt

285 – 240 BCE

On this day, Ptolemy I stood with his son, soon to be Ptolemy II, before the Library of Alexandria which was now reaching a most exalted status within his kingdom, and gaining the same level of recognition within the known world. He could not help thinking back to the year 332 BCE and the first moment that he stood at this location with his king, Alexander the Great, the eventual conqueror of the world. Since then, so much had happened that it was like an ongoing dream playing thru his mind. His beloved Alexander had died and the Empire had been divided; and in the course of time, having been one of Alexander's closest friends and leading General, he had received Egypt as his share of the Empire. Afterward, he had taken power, declared himself 'Pharaoh,' defended Egypt from attack and in time advanced its power through war and the taking of surrounding areas. However, for now, all was quiet and peaceful.

Even so, he had never forgotten Alexander's dream and plan that this location and city should be the center of the ancient world. And just as importantly, that the Library at Alexandria, along with the accompanying museum and lighthouse (Pharos), would be the worlds cultural center and focal point. It would be truly international and universal in character and scope, serving as the center of knowledge for the civilized world. And now, even with all that had transpired since then, he had held true to his word, in that the Library structure was now largely complete and being filled, almost daily, with more and more of the greatest works of knowledge from the past as well as the present by current thinkers and scholars.

Ptolemy I Soter, now savoir of Egypt, was especially proud of this accomplishment, among the many that had taken place during his life. But now, having reached the age of eighty one, and knowing that even with his status as Pharaoh he could not live forever, he wanted to impress upon his son, his planned successor, the importance and magnitude of this Library. He wanted him to know how much it could aid in his rule as Pharaoh and benefit the whole of Egypt. He also wanted to set the tone for what he expected his son to follow upon his death. And, he wanted to brag a little, just to feel good about himself and give momentary relief to the ravages of age upon his body, from the many injuries suffered in the never ending battles he had fought throughout his days. And finally, as always, he loved spending time with his son, for in his early manhood, he was tall, handsome, mature and a pleasure to be with on these outings.

Ptolemy I, was a physically large man, strong and athletic, able to fight and ride better than most, and well educated for the times, having been in 'school' with Alexander as a youth. Together, they and a few others had followed Aristotle around and about the Lyceum in Athens, listening to him talk, lecture and philosophize as they walked under the covered outdoor pathways. He was the kind of man that loved to be with his colleagues, engaging each other first hand, arguing and learning from such discussions. This inevitably led him to need to be with and among his men as he grew into the leader he became. He always had or made time to talk with or listen to his men no matter their rank or complaint. He knew many of them personally no matter their position within the organization under his command. Furthermore, when he wanted to know what they were thinking or feeling, he would do a 'walk around' to gather the sense of it. He never abandoned this practice as his success grew and even did this as Pharaoh, traveling throughout the northern and southern areas of Egypt, hearing from one and all.

Today, with his son, would be no different. He wanted to reinforce in him the importance of 'being with his people.' To this end, and to once again see the Library, they walked over the extensive grounds greeting and talking to all. Over several hours, they walked under the colonnades, admiring the hanging plants and flowers, moving into and out of the gardens, constantly speaking with the gardeners, asking about existing and planned varieties, looking at the fountains, and complimenting them on their results. This went on all morning and he was pleased when his son introduced him to many of these people. Ptolemy's son, at an early age, had been given gradually increasing duties and responsibilities at the Library. Toward midday, they went to the shared dining room, joining others there for a luncheon, eating the same food and drinking the same wine as all attending. They made a point to go around and exchange greetings and personal comments.

Afterward, they went with the head librarian and a half dozen assistant librarians, past the meeting rooms, past several separate reading rooms and a couple of lecture theatres, then thru the many hallways that held the shelves with stacks and stacks of papyrus scrolls, which were steadily increasing. This entire area was done in marble quarried in Egypt, abutted by many columns. In the center, was the main hall, with the floor, columns, and walls all surfaced in marble, more grand and beautiful than the surrounding storage hallways. In the center, was statue of the God, Sarapis, combining the Egyptian God Osiris and the Greek God, Zeus. This was surrounded by many specially designed and built upright platforms used by patrons to layout scrolls and study their contents. And, adjoining and around the walls were many palm trees and subtropical shrubs, adding further grandeur to this key location. It was all very special, indeed.

On the way back to the Palace, Ptolemy emphasized the future of the Library as a center of knowledge, and equally important, as a place for a 'community of learned men' in a setting that could do the most good for Egypt. And, by the end, arriving at the crux of the matter, he recognized that if one were to rule, as was his sons destiny, it was essential it to understand ones people. Knowing that, and given the isolation of being a Pharaoh, he observed that by obtaining and translating their books, i.e. the scrolls, he would gain the insight needed about the nature and thinking of his subjects that he should heed in ruling.

———————

With the passage of time, Ptolemy II followed his father as Pharaoh, inheriting a strong, prosperous and generally peaceful Egypt. The Library at Alexandria went on to great heights of literary splendor for this time. An acquisitions department was established that aggressively obtained hundreds of thousands of papyrus scrolls. A unique cataloguing method was instituted and its stacks were filled with works on mathematics, astronomy, natural sciences, geography and many other subjects. Great thinkers and scholars were hosted and supported in their studies, including Euclid, Eratosthenes, Homophiles, and of course Claudius Ptolemateus, who founded early cartography. Moreover, Library scholars conceived and practiced new ways of thinking via the scientific method, thus using empirical measures as well as textual criticism. By the end of his reign and as intended, the Library and Alexandria had become the economic, intellectual and scientific capital for the Greek dominated world.

One of the most prestigious positions at the Library was that of head librarian. This was a great honor and in most cases it was given to one of the famous editors of the period. At the Library, they had established a well known reputation predominantly by working on Homeric texts. It was customary for the head librarian as well as his assistants to work in the acquisitions department, located near the rear of the main building and facing the harbor. The other major department was for cataloging the many scrolls and placing them according to a specially devised system on the shelves within the various halls surrounding the great hall. As the years had gone by, and the collection of papyrus scrolls had grown to hundreds of thousands, the importance and size of these departments was substantial.

During the reign of Ptolemy II, there were literally hundreds of assistant librarians and clerks working under the direction of the librarians, resulting in a highly organized structure.

One can easily imagine, given the varying sources for the scrolls, especially from varying countries that were home to the authors, the many languages used and found by the library staff while indexing them for the stacks. These languages varied considerably and included Greek, Hebrew, Aramaic, Egyptian Hieroglyphic and its later Hieratic version, Nubian, early Arabic, and dialects from many tribal peoples and places, etc., etc.. From this diversity there evolved, under the Ptolemy's, a Greek influenced version of the Egyptian Hieratic type of Hieroglyphics, known as Demonic. Over time this became widely used in Egypt for administrative and commercial purposes. It was a well accepted compromise considering the Greek influence and Pharaoh rule at the time. Clearly, this was the language used on a daily basis at the Library.

One of the head librarian's chief assistants was a young man from a good Jewish family in the suburban Alexandria area. His first name was 'Jacoby.' He was a third generation Jew, in that his grandparents, as the result of the Ptolemy I conquest of Judea, were among the one-hundred thousand captives taken to Egypt. These captives were given a separate section of Alexandria and integrated into the culture over time. Many had become traders and merchants, settling in this Mediterranean seaport and accepting the city as their home. Jacoby had excelled during the education he received as a boy and was fortunate to become a library apprentice at a young age. With the showing of a good attitude and an abundance of energy, various librarians had advanced his education and career, bringing him along rapidly within their system.

Jacoby's specialty was in the area of languages; grasping, learning and translating many with an ease seldom known or seen by his superiors. Physically, he was of average size, with dark curly hair, a ready smile, and deep brown eyes that just seemed to invite anyone talking with him to like, trust and want to work with him. He had a small room at the side of the acquisitions department where he constantly received, reviewed and classified the text of new scrolls. In his work, he was always one of the first to see and work upon languages that differed from those generally found in most arriving scrolls. Because this work had so much variation from day to day, he was challenged most of the time to know to understand what he was looking at and reading. It was at about this time that the strange events took place that would gave rise to what become a Legend, about an inscription, whose meaning over time was never been fully grasped.

As this story goes, the events happened in the middle of the night during the latter part of the reign of Ptolemy II. It was late summer this year when a storm of unimaginable magnitude came upon Alexandria and Upper Egypt. A combination of things took place during that night. First came an ellipse that lasted for hours, darkening the night sky, pitched with blackness, and followed by an eerie calm. Next, relentless winds blew in from the hot outlying desert, depositing sand in quantities that only occurred about five centuries earlier. And then, if this were not awesome enough, off the Mediterranean came a gale carrying very high winds, brief in duration, but destructive in force, crashing immense waves on the shore, twisting boats of all sizes from their moorings, and slamming them to pieces on the shore and jetties. The accompanying rain turned the accumulated sand into heavy concrete like mush, destroying the roofs of many structures and forcing families out of their homes. The devastation was wide spread and caused its share of damage to the Library, although luckily, the roof held.

Jacoby, who still lived at home with his parents, rose early the next morning, and decided to see what happened at the Library, after realizing his home had fortunately been spared. Despite the chaos in the streets, he worked his way the several miles it took to reach the Library. Coming upon the scene, it was easy to see that the gardens were in great disarray and that sand was piled up against the building everywhere. He managed to get to the door that he usually used to enter the building. In that he often worked late into the evening, he had a key to the crude lock and was able to enter the building. Everything was quiet, totally quiet, which was wholly different for the building than on normal days. He realized that he was alone there and this made him nervous due to his minority status. He decided to look around to see if any damage had taken place, but he would not touch anything, to avoid potential blame should there be any. All went well until he came into the long hallway adjoining and within sight of the Grand hall. About mid-way, lying on the floor, was debris. He had seen this kind of debris before and knew from the materials that it was not from the storm; it looked like the type of pieces that occur from the carving of stone or marble. Instinctively, he looked up, and there it was, an inscription freshly carved in the marble on the wall above the shelves and stacks of scrolls. He knew it had not been there the day before. It said:

"The Place of the Cure of the Soul."

This carving was not in normal everyday common language, i.e. Hieroglyphic, Hieratic, Demotic, Greek, Hebrew, etc., etc.. However, sure enough, Jacoby could and did read it. It was in a language that had evolved from Demotic, and he knew the words, because he had recently seen them and worked with its symbols from writings that had arrived from southern Egypt. This new language had come into regular use by these people and tribes and in this area.

Even so, he was stunned; how could this have happened considering the extreme and unusual night that had just taken place. What should he do? What does it mean? Why is it there? Why now? Questions? Questions? With no answers.

Jacoby hurried out of the Library and went over to the nearby quarters of the head librarian. They were both well acquainted having worked together as master and servant on some translations. He banged on the door until the head librarian arrived. Excited beyond belief, Jacoby could barely talk and virtually drug him over to the Library. He too, was stunned. No one had been authorized or instructed to do such a thing. Was it a desecration or was it from the Gods and to be revered?

And if from the Gods, was it the Egyptian God, Osiris or perhaps, the Greek God, Zeus? Or even, another God. And what did it mean? What should it mean?

He could not even read its language. He relied upon Jacoby for the translation. But even with that information what did it mean? Was the referenced 'Cure' based upon something in the present and ongoing collection of knowledge and scholarly works? It would seem so. This would be the logical implication. Or was it? Perhaps, because of the word 'Soul,' its intent and purpose more elusive? Who could know? Who would care?

He would bring Ptolemy II here as soon as he was available. They would decide what if anything should be done about it?

Apparently that would be nothing, because so far as is known from history, the inscription stayed there as long as the Library continued to exist. And, of course, with the later destruction of the Library, it has been totally lost to the world, rendering the inscription to be a insignificant footnote in history.

Sometime after the night of the storm, we know not when, Jacoby memorialized this carving in a scroll he prepared for his Jewish church. He did this writing in

Hebrew, describing the entire event, the carving and its words, in detail. In that it was his own parchment, he volunteered a simple explanation for the inscription. He credited the words and the act of placing the inscription on the Library wall, as well as the incredible weather events of that night, to be the acts of his one and only beloved God, *Yahweh*, the savoir of the Jewish culture. When finished, he titled this narrative: The CURE OF THE SOUL: THE PLACE & THE LEGEND.

He opined that no one could know for sure what the words were intended to mean. He refused to believe that it was solely related to the Library and the growing body of knowledge it contained. *Yahweh*, he thought, was giving insight and inspiration to something deeper and far beyond what he and all others of that era could comprehend. Even though the inscription was quite vague, it appeared to him to be a puzzle or riddle. He felt and said that the answer to its meaning was likely somehow included within the inscription itself. He knew not what that might be and thought it presumptuous for him to even guess. He would leave that to the future to make clear.

Thereafter, this LEGEND was lost with the destruction of the Library at Alexandria and the passage of centuries and millennia; only to be rediscovered and interpreted in a new and meaningful way by and through the story that you are about to read!

PART 1

THE DISCOVERY

CHAPTER 1

  Barney could not stop shaking. He couldn't help it. His hands and arms moved uncontrollably. As he had grown older, Barney's hands had gradually, but steadily, become worse. He had the same condition as his mother--- it was diagnosed and known as Essential Tremor (ET). Genetically, he had inherited it from her, even though his sister did not have the same condition. Not everyone related to the person with the gene was subject to its effects.

Barney first noticed it when he was around age 45. Upon consulting Doctors, and taking some tests, he learned that Essential Tremor often occurred as people aged and that more than five (5) million people in the United States suffered from the condition. He was relieved to learn that ET was not a precursor to Parkinson's disease. It was not life threatening but it did impact all aspects of his life as he got older. He was now sixty (60) and it was really bad. His medication no longer did much good and gave Barney diarrhea regularly. It had degenerated his body substantially.

He had worked most of his life as a customer service representative. His condition was now so bad that his employer no longer wanted him to interact, face to face, with customers and had moved him back to the warehouse. He could hardly write down legible notes from customers calls! He could barely take care of himself and lived alone; his wife had divorced him years earlier. He dressed poorly, looking as if his clothes came from a rag bag, wearing tattered and torn jeans, tee shirts, and an old camouflage vest. His face was haggard and unshaven most of the time. Overall, he was a mess but he just could not help it. He could no longer cope under the circumstances.

In fact, Barney's condition was so bad that he had been qualified and approved for surgical treatment. His neurologist had reviewed and advised him on different possible procedures. The focus was upon the thalamic part of his brain because this is the area that coordinates and controls muscle activity. The neurologist referred

Barney to the best neurosurgeon he knew, Dr. Janice Westphal. She was about 41 years old, with deep mahogany hair, eyes that sparkle, attractive in the conservative way of a professional, quite energetic and personable, and highly qualified, having been trained in all types of brain operations at the acclaimed Johns Hopkins Medical Center. Her actual experience in the operating room as the surgeon in charge extended over ten years.

The procedure planned for Barney was known as Deep Brain Stimulation. Dr. Westphal had successfully performed this procedure many times   During a four to six hour operation, a small electrode would be placed through his skull into the thalamic area. This electrode is then connected to a programmable pacemaker type of device implanted under the skin in the shoulder area. The operation would be on the left side of the brain and would affect the right side of his body benefiting this arm and hand, being the areas most in need of help. The left side and hand would have to wait in that, as with all brain surgery, dangers, risks and hazards were always present.

Barney was prepped and ready. He was in the campus Hospital being prepared for the surgery. His entire head had been shaved. Earlier, he had undergone a Magnetic Resonance Imaging (MRI) scan to carefully map his brain. MRI scans provide a high contrast image of the soft tissue being studied. Dr. Westphal had used this information to specifically target the route and area for the implant placement. The anesthesia Doctor had reviewed with him the drugs and practices to be used. He had met the recovery room nurses and been told what to expect as the drugs wore off. Next, Dr. Westphal arrived, dressed in her surgical scrubs, and reassured Barney that all things were ready, that the electrode had been tested and retested, that she had done this procedure a number of times, and that he could count on her to see to Barneys care through the operation, the recovery room and the subsequent follow up, right up to the time of discharge. Shortly afterward, Barney was wheeled down the hall and right into the operating room.

Dr. Westphal began by applying a special anesthesia to the area where she would drill the entry point. Then, exceedingly careful, the opening to the brain was prepared. Next, tenderly and delicately a passage was slowly made and expanded, deep into Barney's brain, all the way down to the thalamic region. Now the task was to prepare the base, being the area upon which the electrode would be placed.

It was at this point that Dr. Westphal encountered an abnormality at variance with all the training and experience that she had had over the years in performing this procedure. There was a tiny piece of unusual brain material protruding at the very spot that would be the place to settle the electrode. She had seen this protrusion during other such procedures but it had not interfered at those times. In this case, it was a problem because of its abnormal size and the direction of its interior attachment. Searching and preparing for a different placement was impractical and contrary to the guidelines for this procedure. The practical alternative was to snippet; otherwise the operation would have to be aborted. Dr. Westphal chose this alternative, confident that if something fundamental was at issue, it would have been established long ago and known to her via her training and the medical literature.

So, continuing, she did the snippet, slipping the material out of the passage and, by signaling the attending chief nurse, placed it immediately into a lab transfer container.   She then finished the placement of the electrode and completed the operation in the normal manner.

In finishing up, she instructed and saw to it that this snippet of brain material was transported right away to a close colleague at the Medical Research Center (MRC), being an adjunct of the Hospital. Dr. Westphal didn't like surprises of any kind in her work, and being a diligent taskmaster, she wanted to see what she could learn from finding this piece of protruding material in that part of the brain.

Little did she know that this action would lead to one of the most profound findings ever made in the field of medical- science, a Discovery from within a part of the human body of immense importance, eventually recognized the WORLD over.

CHAPTER 2

Durham,
North Carolina

The Medical Research Center, located next door to the Hospital, and not far from other parts of the University, had become a premier lab facility for genetic research. In fact, it was so renowned, that it was one of the leaders in the fields of genetic manipulation, gene re-engineering, cloning and other genetic development. Their specialty delved into determining the human traits related to specific genes. In other words, if a persons DNA disclosed a specific gene, it would follow that this person would either develop a "particular" disease, and/or, reflect a "certain physical and/or personality characteristic." This included grant based cutting edge research on behalf of many non-profit organizations for specific diseases as well as projects for pharmaceutical companies, foundations, and other institutions, including government agencies, needing aid in genetic studies. In addition, over the past ten years, it had been a major participating organization in the Human Genome project, as it moved through its various stages and on to completion.

Even so, it came as somewhat of a surprise to receive a lab sample from Dr. Janice Westphal in that,

considering her field of specialty and local practice, she seldom needed to use anything other than the Hospital's in house pathology department. However, in this case, this unique sample came directly to Dr. Eric Rhodes, a long time friend, associate and romantic partner of Dr. Westphal. Their relationship dated in various ways all the way back to their University days together on this large multipurpose campus. As a key Project Research Manager for the Medical Research Center (the MRC), Eric was in a position to see that the sample material received the kind of attention Dr. Westphal would want to take place. Straight away, he knew that Dr. Westphal must have felt the sample to be important for some reason.

Moving immediately, Eric carefully prepared the sample to determine its DNA content. In that the snippet was quite small he had to handle it delicately. Even so, he followed the Center's standard dual processing format which allowed for subsequent testing of the second part of the sample should that become necessary for any reason. The preliminary processing steps, were now all performed by sophisticated biomedical equipment, that removed proteins, fats and other cellular material to avoid their interference with the DNA. Then, the sample was further purified by treatment with lab reagents, all designed to release the DNA as the end result. A robotic machine did this procedure many times a day with consistency, reliability and precision.

Next, the sample went to a machine that amplified the DNA across several orders of magnitude, thereby generating thousands and thousands of copies of the particular DNA sequence. This technique, discovered and

developed in the mid-eighties, is known as Polymerase Chain Reaction. It provides a quick method for reproducing specific portions of the DNA molecule for analysis. This string like object is long and narrow and must be sequenced to determine its make up, by and through listing the basic building blocks designated for DNA, being the four letters A,T, G, and C. Literally, these strings of letters go on for great lengths, and are determined and spelled out by a third class of machine, being genetic analyzers. The MRC had many of the best and latest versions of this type of sequence machine.

Eric had performed this procedure many times over the years. At this point, he finished, with the entry of the sample into the gene sequencer(analyzer) and activated its operation. Even though this equipment was state of the art, the processing would take all night, and part of the next day, being a twenty-four hour process. This machine would produce a lengthy tracing, listing much information, but most importantly, detailing the applicable DNA code related to the test sample.

Afterward, the piece would be referenced and preserved. If for any reason questions arose, it would then be reviewed within a sub-atomic electron microscope by a specialist at a later time. This was all quite routine for the Medical Research Center in that DNA process samples were initiated each day, being an essential part of their ongoing projects. When the 'results' were in, Eric and/or his colleagues would read and interpret what had been found by and through the analysis. This was assisted by the findings of the many cases that had already been completed and the data published by the Human Genome Project as well as information made available by other research centers. In fact, databases with such information were used constantly by professionals in the 'genetics' community.

At this point, being late in the afternoon, Eric had had enough for the day. Even though he often worked late, especially when he had a special project underway, he was ready for a break. Taking and putting on his high tech walking shoes from his backpack, he prepared to enter what he called the 'Church of the Walking Feet.' This was his solace. His escape to a place of peace. He would leave the trials and tribulations of the workplace. It was the long walk home but it meant a lot to Eric. It allowed him the 'right way' to move away from the pressure packed activities of this work and relieve his mind for a while.

As he walked thru the park, past the large serene lake, his tension would ease, laying aside the struggles of the day. In this setting, the pleasure became all his, as he soaked up the beautiful surroundings, viewed the ducks floating around and about, their coming and going on the lake, and watched the people moving between the different parts of their lives. Sometimes, at this point, he would take a park bench, and watch for a while the activity and, in many cases, the lack of activity. He would see and smell the flowers in bloom and listen to the birds around and about him. This was the way to end a busy but good day.

Eric appreciated Mother Nature in all of its variations and expressions. He never ceased to be amazed at the complexities and intricacies of the endless number of species that exist, whether they be plant or animal. Even though he was a man of science, and knew and understood many of the underlying processes, at moments like this, he just liked to feel the wonder of it all and did not need to rationalize any particular meaning.

Within him, he felt that even with the why's and wherefore's of natures creativity being understood, there was much more lying beneath the surface that man has yet to know let alone understand. It was a never ending question in his mind, how could all the beauty reflected within Nature, such as the sunsets, the bird's coloration, the blossoms of spring, the hues of fall and so on, be so magnificent yet so transitory. He visualized a supreme artist creating never ending masterpieces with nature at his fingertips and then just throwing them away, having served the artists need for exquisite displays.

Instinctively, he realized that the act of making the masterpiece was likely the answer in and of itself. While appreciating the result was desired, it was not the objective, for the masterpiece provided satisfaction enough. He felt that his life and the lives of others were constantly enriched in these beautiful ways and days.

Sure, as a scientist, ready explanations were there, but to Eric's way of thinking, they were just narrow minded and hollow within themselves. How could anyone ever really know the true essence of it all?

Yet Eric was not a rabid environmentalist, although he did feel strongly in favor of conservatism. Caring for and preserving the 'best' of the earth's natural beauty and landscape seemed worthwhile to him. However, being so occupied and deeply consumed with his work, Eric studiously avoided involvement in most organizations beyond the scientific realm related to his profession. He considered himself to be a 'scientist', first and foremost. He just did not want the entanglements that came with the 'point of view' advocacy groups. He had more than enough to fully occupy his life. He was not searching for a new agenda.

He never suspected that his work and where it would take him, would move him in a special direction. That what he was about to discover would lead him in ways well beyond his wildest imagination.

CHAPTER 3

Eric Rhodes had become a remarkable man. A bit introverted, yes, but nonetheless quite exceptional. Growing up as the son of a Christian pastor, he developed a sense of duty and responsibility earlier and more deeply than his contemporaries. Oh sure, he loved to play as much as his pals, got in trouble from time to time, but in the end he always did the right thing. He studied hard, earned top grades and became a class leader, especially as he moved through grade school and high school.

From the beginning, he was fascinated by the first chapter of the bible, namely 'Genesis.' Creation was a story so big, so huge, and so large in all of its magnitude, that Eric found himself rolling it over again and again in his mind during his youthful, dreaming, idle moments. He always wanted to know 'why' this happened or 'why' that happened in the world around and about him. Inevitably, this led to a youth consumed with understanding Nature and the science of the processes that lie within Nature. His father and mother were of little help because theology could not sufficiently answer the kind of questions he would ask. Yet, he always felt the answers would be there if somehow the right questions were asked.

All through high school he excelled, taking as much science as he could and getting all 'A's.' Well ahead of going to college he was buying, reading and comprehending books explaining the underlying science in various aspects of Nature. From mammals to bugs, from fish to amoeba's, including their evolution, he wanted to know, and came to know and understand how it all worked. However, from these efforts, in the end he realized that within all organisms, it always came down to the make up of their cells, to understand what was happening.

Thus, it was no surprise when he enrolled in the study of microbiology at the nearby University, being a top school in this field in the United States. Fortunately, the University was within his same community, so he did not have to move away and leave all of his friends, family and loved ones. And, important to him, he could still attend his father's church, as he had done his entire life.

Physically, by this time, Eric had grown to be about six feet tall, slim and lanky, with dark unruly hair, and a small patch of white hair behind his right ear. It was a strange kind of birthmark. He was not athletic and was actually somewhat awkward and uncoordinated. Being so studious, he did not have a wide circle of friends. At this point, his friends mostly came from those attending his father's church and included adults as well as some youth, not necessarily his own age. Even though he was above average in looks, he had not had any ongoing involvement with the opposite sex.

The college years were exciting for Eric in that he was constantly challenged, intrigued and further fascinated with his studies, if that were possible. Meanwhile, during his second year, he found Vanessa and engaged in his first deep romance. This became the most passionate and emotional time of his life in that they engaged in sexual liaisons frequently. He was sure this first love would become an ongoing part of his life.

Also, during this time, he was deeply saddened when, at the end of that sophomore year, his mother passed away after struggling with breast cancer for three years. While grieving for her loss and trying to console his father, he drew closer and closer to him, gaining a deeper appreciation and respect for his faith and his abiding belief in the presence of God. Through him, he once again faced the 'Creation,' not just as it is described in the bible, but additionally, as it lived and existed all about him. For now, having grown, matured and reached greater heights of understanding in the underlying science, he was able to step back for the first time in a long while and take in its magical scope and grandeur, and see ever more than he did before. He felt inspired to continue down this road for his future.

Towards the end of that summer, Eric was attending church as usual when his father, Joseph Rhodes, launched into the Sunday sermon. However, for some reason unknown to him, he was struck deeply by his father's words on the human spirit and values. His message elaborated on the Church's acceptance that a persons Soul is one and the same as their Human Spirit.

But that the Soul and body, each receiving separate nourishment and exercise, develop to the point of being known apart from each other. And furthermore, he had not known until that sermon, that the language of Genesis was in some circles interpreted to mean that man had become differentiated from animals by God bestowing a Soul upon Adam and Abraham. This 'breath of God' made all the difference in the making of mankind.

Afterwards, while driving and at home, they continued to discuss the "Values' part of the sermon. Even though it seemed a little silly, they decided to reenact an exercise that they had done many times in Eric's youth, and name as many values as they could. In fact, they were surprised to name so many, that they came to realize that the list of human values may well be unlimited, depending upon the sense and culture of the person naming them.

And, by the same token, there were always 'Opposites and/or Negatives' for a Value, depending on one's point of view. Then, continuing, they played at assigning a ranking to a particular value, based on perceived importance to mankind. This clearly showed that no matter what, depending on who was doing the prioritizing, the rankings would vary considerably.

This went on well into the evening and resulted in much give and take discussion between them. The bottom line, they summed up, was that ones values were essential in thinking about the Soul for they were no doubt one and the same, at least in part.

By the time Eric was a College senior, his academic acclaim was well recognized within his department at the University. Furthermore, to the extent available, he had become deeply involved in the study of genes. In labs, he would use the equipment to look at specimens of all types, animal and human, gaining further insight into the cells that define all being on earth. This type of inquiry had become the central driving force within his life.

With graduation came honors and most importantly a full scholarship and admission to the Doctorial program for genetics at the University. The head of the genetics department had personally come to him and asked for him to apply for the scholarship. This was definitely unusual but had been done because his case was so outstanding. And, it was not a minute to soon, in that his father was retiring and could no longer afford more education costs for Eric.

And, Vanessa was still the central lady in his life. But in this area it was not all smooth sailing, for she had a strong mind of her own. They had many ups and downs but still cared deeply for each other. On the other hand, she had no desire to go on to graduate school and was anxious to move out into the world. She did not delay, and by the time they graduated, she had found a good job with a pharmaceutical company. Eric and she agreed to stay in touch and be together from time to time. Even so, this seldom happened.

The study of genetics at the graduate level entirely took over every aspect of Eric's life. His courses, his professors and the constant lab work occupied every hour of the day. He especially concentrated on the genetic code of the Nucleotide Triplets for various amino acids and how they related to different parts of the body. One of his classes at that time included some medical school students and this led to his meeting the future Dr. Westphal, an attractive and very intelligent young woman, dark eyed, and definitely nicely built, even with her conservative dress. She exhibited an unusually strong ability to associate and connect cell structure and how it would bear on her prospective patients; she planned to become a brain surgeon. Both were very serious students, but when they needed a break they would call each other and hang out together for a few hours. Her real name was Janice

Westphal, she stood five feet, six inches tall and had a quiet but pleasant personality. Men found her attractive but she could not be bothered for her focus was solely on medical school and the specialization years to follow.

Midway thru this graduate program, Eric began work on his thesis and what would become an award winning paper and a seminal study recognized throughout the field of genetic research. He spent hours and hours, days and days and his entire second summer on the

research for this project. In doing so he learned and tested various intricacies on all the lab machines that analyzed cells and presented the chains and elements that comprised the double helix genetic structure.

And, expressing his brilliance, he chose to go further in certain ways than prior research had done in this area, namely defining and redefining the genetic make up of particular body parts, their likely development as fetus, and the triggers that would bring about their malfunctions leading to disease. He dedicated his own computer to this effort, diligently entering all the bits of information into detailed databases, and constantly reviewing the information in different ways alone in his room. In the end, a separate program was put together by him, associating data more in the ways that he had observed it. In turn, this led to revelations and conclusions and supporting proof that gave his Doctoral thesis its credibility and acclaim beyond the University.

Completing his Doctorate in genetics was the most exhilarating accomplishment Eric had ever experienced. The week before the graduation ceremony was frantic with preparations His father and other family friends would be attending. And, his friend, the new Dr. Janice Westphal, would be receiving her medical degree concurrently. It was all very exciting. They knew and acknowledged by then their strong mutual attraction to each other. Shortly beforehand, however, Dr. Winston Jones, the dean of the Department of Genetics, summoned Eric to an unscheduled meeting in his office. When Eric arrived he was shown into Dr. Jones office and introduced to Mr. Richard Johnston.

Mr. Johnston, after opening pleasantries, explained that he was Chief Administrator for the Medical Research Center and had been briefed about Eric and was well acquainted with his successful thesis paper.

Mr. Johnston then said:

"Eric, we do not want to lose you! We want to keep you working in this medical-science complex. So, I am here today to convince you to stay. Our Center is offering you the immediate position of Project Researcher at a substantial salary. We hope that you will look favorably on our proposal."

Eric was taken aback by the suddenness of this proposal, not anticipating this prospect by anything that had happened previously. Eric answered:

" I don't know--- what would I be doing at the Center--- what would be the future prospects--- this is so new and different than working for a drug company?"

Mr. Johnston: "This situation is also quite unique for us--- but I can promise you this: the Center has secured a multi-year Grant for a project that is in essence an extension of your thesis. You, of course, would define, structure, find staff and carry out the project. There is plenty of money for your salary, and bonus money for achieving milestones on the timeline for the project. In

many ways, it is almost a blank check for you to continue doing what already inspires you."

Dean Jones added:

"I recommend you take it Eric--- its tailor made for you--- I have no doubt that this will bring credit and recognition to you, as well as the Medical Research Center and this University."

And so, with all of that having been said, Eric accepted, and moved easily and naturally from the academic world to the Medical Research Center, being a transition for which he was surely destined, no matter what.

CHAPTER 4

The gene sequencer had run all night and much of the next workday on the sample piece of material from Dr. Westphal. Dr. John Howard, Eric's chief assistant at the Medical Research Center (MRC), was the first to remove and see the tracing from the machine. What he saw was both surprising and confusing to him. It was not normal DNA or for that matter genetic code of any kind. It was 'blank,' completely and entirely 'blank!' Something that Dr. Howard had never seen before in looking at cell tissue from a human body. There must be something wrong with the machine or the sample preparation, or even the nature of the material being tested.

Dr. Howard had started working for Eric about a year after he became a Project Director. The MRC had only two Project Directors; this being a major position with responsibility for the management and results of numerous ongoing Grant funded projects. Dr. Howard had come to the MRC after receiving his Doctorate in genetics and microbiology from a major northeast university. Dr. Howard was of medium height, with dark complexion and nervous eyes that appeared to others almost uncontrollable.

Nonetheless, he was knowledgeable, skilled and attentive and generally quite helpful to Eric. On the negative side, however, he was not that well liked by others he worked with due to his constant need to push himself up on the back of other Center personnel, pushing them down for whatever reason he could find. From sidebar discussions with these MRC personnel, Eric was aware of this situation but had not taken any steps about it. He wasn't sure what to do, but he did realize that this same thing would likely happen to him should Dr Howard get the opportunity with Eric's superiors. He had decided to be careful with how much rope he would give Dr. Howard.

Stepping into Eric's office, Dr. Howard said:

"You're not going to believe this, something must have gone wrong with the preparation of that sample you had running. There is nothing there --- it's 'blank,' just plain 'blank!' I can't read anything from the results." And with that, he placed the resulting print-out on Eric's desk.

Looking a little bemused, Eric indicated he would take a look at it in a few minutes. After finishing the task at hand, Eric began looking at the print-out. In the portion that would normally list the important DNA triplets, being the genetic code, none were specified.

Mystified, Eric went to the checklist he had filled out in doing the procedure before placing the material in the gene sequencer. Nothing appeared to be out of order. He had followed these steps a thousand times. So next, he decided to check the machines he had used. He did this by running their internal diagnostic programs. This was also a dead-end; all functions and other elements were showing normal operational status and well within there limits. The sequence analyses tester was just fine.

Then, he decided to look at the sample under the sub-atomic electron microscope to get some idea why the DNA sequencer produced a 'blank.' Eric carefully prepared the snippet and placed it in the scanning electron microscope. What he saw shocked and amazed him. It was a cell all right. But, it was only the shell of one, otherwise it appeared entirely empty (except for a submicron thin center fiber or nerve that likely connected back to the thalamic brain region). Otherwise, there was *NOTHING*. In all of his experience, having looked at literally thousands, and thousands, of cells over the years, he had never seen anything like this. A *BLANK, BLANK* hollow cell!

He tried turning up the magnification, but found little to focus upon, other than traces of three faint lines. Seeing traces were not something that would normally grab his attention. Beyond that, there was nothing, leaving only the 'blank' space within the cell. Sitting back Eric thought about it for a while. Still mystified, he decided to try something else. This would be unusual, but that didn't bother him, he had done such things before. So, he took the prepared sample over to the Hospital Radiation and Imaging department, found the manager with whom he was well acquainted, and asked him to run the prepared snippet through the MRI. He then left the

Hospital, indicating he would pick it up along with the image tomorrow.

Until that point, his service at the Medical Research Center, totaling almost sixteen years, had gone quite well. He had moved through the ranks to become one of only two Project Research Managers, taking on sizeable projects, interfacing with grant making institutions and leading the research direction at the MRC. Without question he had become a 'star' at the MRC, known nationwide in important matters related to genetics. He had also managed the Centers participation in the Human Genome Project, by overseeing the in-house team and presenting reports and data to fellow scientists at meetings where they worked on pulling it all together.

And additionally, there was Dr. Janice Westphal, his girl friend dating back to their University days during graduate school. They had stayed in touch over the years as Janice went through medical school, neurosurgical specialization and the residency levels for her certifications. When it came time for her to establish her practice and join the staff of a Hospital, Eric had encouraged and introduced Janice to the officials and leaders of the huge Hospital adjacent to the Medical Research Center. They were both quite pleased when she was named to the staff at the Hospital. And, during the ten years since then, she had become a highly successful surgeon with a splendid reputation within the medical community.

But that was not the full story. Shortly after she joined the staff of the Hospital and started her local

practice, Janice and Eric entered into the romance they had long delayed as their professional lives developed. During these early years, as their affection and love blossomed, they took every moment they could get to be together. They became known and accepted as a couple socially. And, their vacations with each other were glorious. Without a doubt, all that knew them expected there would be a wedding.

Furthermore, Eric and Janice themselves, expected to marry.

As time went by and they constantly discussed how to deal with their highly demanding professional careers, the prospects for their marriage dimmed. Janice did not see how she could cope with having a child after having worked so long and hard to become a neurosurgeon. And Eric, was constantly under demanding circumstances and pressures at the MRC, quite often working until 11:00 P.M. for weeks at a time. Yet, without question, they often acknowledged their love for each other in many ways and at many times.

So, they did the pragmatic thing after a long talk one evening. They agreed that during the weekdays, each would live his or her professional life as needed and to its fullest extent. However, they would go to great lengths to protect and preserve the weekends, holidays and vacations to be with each other the entire time. Each would continue there own separate residence, and they would take turns staying at one place and then the other. If, as time went by, should either his or her situation change markedly, they would marry at that time. And that was how their life

was conducted right through the time of Barney's operation for Essential Tremor.

In the long run, this loving partnership would endure despite the twists and turns that were about to take place.

CHAPTER 5

      Shortly after returning to the Medical Research Center, Eric decided that he had had enough of this workday. Nothing seemed to go right all day long. Occasionally, there were days like that. And, he still could not get over the sample Dr. Westphal had sent over. He could not believe that he might have somehow erred in preparing the test sample. It was just not like him. How could human tissue from any body location, even the brain, fail to have DNA? In itself, this seemed to be an impossible thing physiologically speaking.

However, if Eric was anything, he was responsible and dutiful and so he stuck by his normal routine. Being Thursday, this was the day he stopped by and paid his respects to his late father, Joseph Rhodes. He had passed away about five years after Eric had become a Project Researcher at the Medical Research Center. After Eric's mother died, he and his father would talk daily, often meeting for meals at a favorite local restaurant. Over dinner, it was not unusual for them to touch upon faith and science, their chosen lives, and discuss to what extent they were interrelated and consistent or opposite and non reconcilable.

Often times during these exchanges, due to ongoing media reports about school districts dilemma's on teaching human development, they would touch on evolution. To them, it was not a matter of evolution versus creation, but more in the direction of the development of the many structures and mechanisms within the processes of Nature. They refused to be drawn into the endless creation versus evolution debate, considering it to be artificial and useless.

They just accepted that when Creation took place, and the processes began for what is known by all as Nature, evolution was simply included as an underlying element, much the same as the weather and climatic changes within the planet. The how, when and why such pathways came about were just matters of speculation and debate between them? They enjoyed their intellectual jousting; and it brought them closer together.

When Joseph Rhodes died it came as a surprise that his Will directed that he be cremated and his remains placed in the Sunset Hill Cemetery and Mausoleum. His wishes were carried out and the urn was placed in its own separate locker. Other than the cemetery office, Eric was the only other person to have a key to this locker. As per Eric's usual practice, he would open the locker and speak in a low manner of the things his dad would surely like to know and as typical, tell of things happening in his life, ending with some favorite words they both shared from the Bible. Eric always felt better afterward for taking the time to do this act of respect, much the same as he would feel after attending church on Sunday.

Eric lived alone. He didn't exactly plan it that way; it just sort of happened given his arrangement with Janice. Like many academic's, he was a man consumed by his work and his condo showed it. Aside from a small kitchenette and eating area, there were two rooms. His bedroom and most importantly, the main room, being a large study/library/living room, that spoke volumes about this man. It had a huge ornate desk, a couch and reading chair, a TV and sound system, and a substantial computer system that gave him a window on the world. But the most outstanding thing about this double tray'd ceiling room was its multi-level library on the exterior walls, all of which were lined with books and more books.

The main wall concentrated on biology, microbiology, and genetics and included reports and studies related to the types of research being pursued. Another wall was filled with books on Nature and especially a set of volumes detailing the unique characteristics of various species and their development. Likewise, included there were books on evolution and creation, with publications covering the academic, religious and popular views from the literature of the day. When one looked around the room, it was easy to see where Eric put the considerable earnings that he received.

Surrounded by all of this knowledge, Eric sat down that evening, troubled and perplexed about the 'blank' tracing on the sample material he had received from Dr. Westphal. In his own mind, he knew that there was no error by the machine or by him in preparing and initiating the sample within the sequencer. However, the most striking part of the whole thing was the empty shell

within this snippet. Clearly, from his knowledge of genetics, he had seen no precedent for this empty tube. It must contain something. Everything in the body is there for some reason. At this point, he settled himself and just concluded that he would leave it for tomorrow and try to sleep .

      With that, off he went to bed, hoping that it would all straighten out the next day.

      Little did he know that this MYSTERY would only grow deeper.

Chapter 6

The next day, in the morning, Eric was back at the Hospital Radiation and Image Department picking up the sample and disk with the images from the MRI test. This time the results were better, so to speak, showing a clearly contrasted outline of the sample and interestingly, three separate internal lines. The resolution for this image was high and clear but still unintelligible. Eric decided to blow it up on the powerful computers at the Center.

Working with the Centers top computer technician, they increased the resolution five thousand fold, making adjustments as they went to sharpen the result, yielding at the end a clear image. The result was most unexpected. In fact, it was down right amazing. It showed three separate lines each with a strange Code, something they had never witnessed before. Eric knew right away that it was not genetic for his entire career had been based on all matters genetic, and this was definitely not genetic. On the other hand this was definitely a Code, a strange Code to him, and it set him back on his heels, bewildered. Shocked! Amazed!

He did not know what to do, but he did know enough to swear the technician to secrecy, to talk to no one of this finding. He did not want this to become news spread all over the Lab. It was up to him to decide what to do, being the Project Director and leader. At that point he dismissed the technician. He also decided not to share this finding with Dr. Howard and to keep all post Lab results, being the MRI disk, to himself.

He then printed out two copies of the magnification and burned a disk that he kept with his records. He then deleted the magnified images from the common computer they had been working upon. Next, back at his desk, Eric began concentrating on the strange Code. He was looking for patterns and/or consistent elements within the three lines of Code. When viewed over all, he found that each line broke down into three elements; each having a singular group of characters at the beginning of the separate line; then a space, followed by many sub divisions, with each subdivision followed by short sub areas. However, the characters and symbols comprising the Code, made no sense to him and were in fact, not any of the code known in established DNA syntax.

And, surprisingly, the short sub-areas were quite simple, being slashes, grouped first in a forward direction and then more slashes, grouped in the opposite direction, i.e. backslashes. All very strange, indeed, especially the slashes.

Furthermore, the characters and symbols, were not like anything he had ever seen before. He did not know why, but they gave him a sense of an old, ancient language. But, why would he even know to think of that? He had no idea why.

Eric was puzzled to say the least.

Even so, at this moment, he did not have the luxury of continuing to think about it, for he was meeting Dr. Westphal, the neurosurgeon and his 'significant other' for lunch. They did this at least once a week as part of their arrangement.

They met in the senior staff dining room adjacent to the cafeteria that provided food service to the Hospital and Medical Research Center. It started off in a jovial mood for they were always happy to be in each others company.

"All right Janice, what did you send over to me ---- if it was sent to stump our lab --- you have succeeded?"

Janice deadpanned: "Maybe it was from my patients farm --- has it given you problems?"

"It sure has --- but I could tell if it was animal matter --- and this is far from that!"

At this point, the tempo changed and Janice became serious:

"I'm not sure what you are talking about Eric, that snippet was a tag of inner brain material that struck me as unusual. Why are you so roiled up?"

"Well when the results came back from the DNA sequencer, it showed a 'blank,' being different from anything otherwise known in genetics and the human genome. It is not understandable. So, I ran the snippet in the Hospital MRI. And, you will not believe it. The result, when magnified five thousand times, clearly shows a strange Code, totally unknown to any medical science that I have ever seen."

"I'll have to come over and have a look --- but believe me I am not up to any funny business --- it was a serious sample. I want a report on it."

The lunch continued and finished as normal, catching up with each

other. In parting, Janice said: "Oh, by the way, I should probably mention that the patient, from whom the sample was obtained, died the second night after the operation."

Eric returned to the lab and busied himself the rest of the afternoon with his usual duties. Even so, he sensed an uneasiness within himself but did not search for its meaning.

Later, that evening, he focused on this "uneasiness" and finally realized that it flowed from learning that the patient died the second night after the operation. This would have been after obtaining the strange Code from the sample of brain material. The more he thought about it in this light, he realized that he was SHOCKED by the whole episode. Because of this, he decided to test the 'blank' snippet sample again, to see if by chance any change had occurred.

The next day, Eric immediately took this snippet sample back to the Hospital and had a second MRI run on it. He then went back to the Center and as promised, Janice showed up shortly thereafter. She studied the results from the DNA tracing and then the enlarged MRI image and was just as mystified by this strange Code as

50

Eric had been. She had to leave then for a scheduled procedure back at the Hospital.

Friday, the next day, once again Eric hurried over to the Hospital and received the second MRI image, now available. He looked at it right away in the presence of the MRI manager. It did not take much of an increase on the resolution on the computer to see that while the outline

of the sample was present, the three lines of Code had completely disappeared! By now, Eric was so used to finding strange things relating to this piece of brain snippet, he was not overly surprised as he walked back to the Center somewhat in a daze of disbelief. Upon arriving, he had the same technician blow up the image in the same manner as the day before. The result showed the three lines of Code to be gone notwithstanding the outline of the snippet itself. All very puzzling. He called Janice right away and left a message.

Later on that day, while driving to the coast for a long weekend, Eric and Janice discussed the situation further. Neither one of them were inclined to pass off their involvement or findings as just an anomaly that could be disregarded. After all they were a man and woman of science and did not take lightly coming upon something as unusual as this.

Thinking about what had happened, Eric asked about the possibility of further samples of this tag of brain material? He explained that other samples would allow him to see if something new had been discovered and take steps to determine what had been found, if anything? He also wanted to dismiss the possibility on some type of error taking place.

Janice said that she had already talked to some of her fellow neurosurgeons and they had encountered this same

tag of inner brain material while performing the implant procedure for Essential Tremor patients. However, they had made no inquiry about it. Even so, she would have to inquire about the propriety of taking such snippets. Nonetheless, she felt sure the standard Surgical Waiver would cover this tag material; and, she knew that most patients would cooperate if asked and assured that removing this tag material would not adversely affect them or the results of the operation.

Little did they know of what would be the full meaning of having further samples of this tiny piece of brain material.

Generally, Eric and Janice, avoided 'shop talk' while enjoying their 'private time' together. They were on the way to Beaufort, North Carolina for a three day weekend and a relaxing getaway. By the time they arrived, it was late and they were tired. The next day was spent in just recharging their batteries. After sleeping in, they spent the next few hours in some 'heavy breathing exercise,' cleaned up and went out for lunch along the interesting waterfront. Afterward, Eric was in need of one of his long walks, so they went arm in arm around and about the streets and town. Returning to their room, the rest of the day was spent entwined with each other, enjoying being alone, laughing and loving their time together.

The next day, they caught the ferry over to Ocracoke, North Carolina and went sightseeing along the Cape Hatteras National Seashore. The day was beautiful, the sky was blue, filled with passing clouds and the ocean was a joy to behold. The surf was great, the people were fun to watch and all in all it was a magical day for these two lovers. They finished by catching the ferry back to Beaufort, having dinner at a fish house, and falling into bed, to finish off the day in delightful ways with each other. Truly, they were deeply in love.

In that the next day was a holiday, they took their time returning home, stopping in New Bern, N.C. to have a look about. This took a few hours and then they were on their way back. At her apartment, Janice made a light dinner for them and they polished off a bottle of wine. While sitting there they could not help touching on the strange case of the Code from the brain snippet. In the way of a woman who knows and loves her man, Janice realized that Eric would not give up on this situation until he got to the bottom of the mystery.

She knew that she would help and would see that more samples would be found. Moreover, she promised herself that she would see to it that it was done in a highly ethical way.

It had been a magical weekend

CHAPTER 7

Time passed quickly that Winter. By the following spring the 'side' project to define the 'blank' was well underway. Eric had met with success when he talked with the Dean and Medical director of the Medical school. This was not the first time they had cooperated on a research project. It turned out that obtaining the needed snippets was not all that complicated. The school was able to build this into some final work by the medical students graduating that year. In fact it was quite interesting and informative for them and advanced their knowledge and understanding of Essential Tremor.

Furthermore, just as Eric had surmised, when the samples were processed by the Lab, the sequencer results were 'blank' as with the other decedent samples. The same was true with the images from the Hospital MRI. The medical students were pleased to have a pro like Eric show them other DNA testing samples, the nature and structure of DNA syntax, and talk about what was taking place, and what was likely to happen as the science of genetics advanced. This part of the student study program had been easy for a change.

Furthermore, over the last nine months, his 'significant other', Dr. Janice Westphal, had been

successful, via herself and other neurosurgeons, in obtaining and immediately transferring to Eric at the

55

Medical Research Center, further snippets of the tag brain material from patient's thalamic region. Eric saw to it that each snippet was handled immediately and very carefully. Utilizing the same practices and protocols followed on the initial testing, the piece of the tag brain material was prepared and placed in the gene sequencer. Afterward, by arrangement with the Hospital Radiation and Image Department, the piece was then run through the MRI and the resulting image (and supporting disk), and test sample, were returned to him at the Center. Where the patient had died shortly thereafter, for whatever reason, the MRI testing would take place again.

By summers end, work on two of four additional 'live' snippets, had been completed.

Sure enough, the resulting tracings from the gene sequencer, were 'blank,' being the same finding as the testing of the initial sample from Barney. In addition, and more importantly, when the snippet was run thru the MRI, being the second test, the image that resulted, when magnified, once again disclosed the strange unrecognizable Code.

In like manner, this strange Code had three separate lines, each having a heading, then a space, then many sub divisions, each followed by short sub areas. And, as before, these sub-areas, following the different sub-divisions, were confirmed to be slash marks, some forward leaning, followed by a space, then some by backslashes. In each case, the slash marks varied in number.

However, in these separate cases, the sub divisions were variable, in that the coded words were 'different' because the coded characters (i.e. letters) were not the same, most likely being other words; and in the few cases where they were the same words, they were in a changed position relative to each other. It was all very mystifying, indeed! The good news, however, was that neither of the patients had died shortly after the MRI results were complete.

The third snippet, arriving a week later was more problematic, right from the start. The patient had died right on the table as the operation was in the process of completion. This was not the result of the brain operation, it came from heart complications which the patient had been warned about beforehand. Nonetheless, Eric and his team went right to work on the sample. It turned out that the testing results for both the gene sequencer and then the MRI were the same ---- they produced 'blank' results, no DNA nor three trace MRI lines. All being consistent with the findings on the very first sample from Barney after he had passed away.

The fourth sample was the one being completed today. It had arrived two days ago, right after the patients operation. The next day DNA test results from the gene sequencer showed the same 'blank' as found in the three additional recent snippets as well as the first snippet from

Barney. This was immediately followed by the MRI testing, yielding once again the three separate lines of

strange Code, similar in all ways with the previous 'live' samples.

However, while Eric was studying this latest image, Dr. Westphal called and reported that the latest snippet donor had died just an hour ago. This set Eric into immediate action. Right away, he walked over the returned fourth sample and had it run once again thru the MRI. Because the sample was small, it did not take long before he had the resulting second image. Quickly, moving back to the Center's Lab, he had this image magnified, and could see immediately, the three lines of Code within the outline of the sample were gone. Clearly, once again, he found that when the sample provider dies, the strange triple Code lines disappear. This was a phenomenon that he was at a complete loss to understand.

"But why? Where did they go? How could something physically remote from the patient change following their death?" This seemed to be an impossibility. At this point, he had only questions with no answers.

Eric immediately called Dr. Westphal and reported the results from the second MRI.

Janice: "Eric, I don't know what to say. This defies logic and all the training and experience we have had. It's just the same as our first case with Barney."

Eric: "I know, I know. I 'm just as dumbfounded as you. Are we still here on earth or is this other worldly? What are we missing? How can any of this make sense?"

Janice: "Not counting Barney, we now have test results from four separate snippets of "live" tag material plus 'blank' results from the five medical school cadavers --- what are your results telling you --- have you been able to make any sense of this strange Code?"

Eric: "Well, Janice, there is a definite pattern --- where the patient survives, the strange unrecognizable Code appears in its three part form within the MRI image; however, where the patient dies, even if it happens during the gene sequencing or the MRI retesting, we get totally 'blank' results."

"Eric, can you tell anything about this strange Code --- you're the scientist --- what can we do to make sense of the Code --- the test results should start to add up to something by now."

Eric: "Janice, before concentrating on a theory, I want to summarize the pattern. Then we can start to put together some explanation."

With that, they ended their conversation; Eric would review, list and summarize the facts which had now been established by the various tests.

Later that day, Eric gathered together the various
test results from the ten different patents, and listed their
common points:

1) Sample material: a snippet of tag brain
material, from the thalamic region, where the
electrode must be placed and settled, treating
Essential Tremor;

2) Test Protocol: the same for each test --- the
snippet sample was first prepared for and processed via
the gene sequencer; next, it was   tested via the
Hospital MRI; then, the image was greatly enlarged at the
Center lab; and finally, if the patient expired, the snippet
was   retested with a second MRI; except, for the
cadaver samples, where the snippet was processed solely
by the MRI, with a retest notbeing needed.

3) Samples: Test Results:
   Patients:
   1 (a)   DNA blank   Code   Alive (Barney)

(b)	retest	blank		Died
2 (a)	DNA	blank	Code	Alive
(b)		Alive (no retest)		
3 (a)	DNA	blank	Code	Alive
(b)		Alive (no retest)		
4(a)	DNA	blank		Died
(b)	retest	blank		Died
		Died		
5 (a)	DNA	blank	Code	Alive
(b)	retest	blank	blank	Died

Cadavers:

6-10 (a)	DNA	blank	blank	Died

4) Characteristics: the Strange Code:

    a) three major Code lines; the line always begin with the same Code word, in the same relative position;

    b) Followed by, separate sub divisions per Code line; many, many sub divisions; sometimes the same Code word within, but generally different Code words; relative positions always different;

    c) Sub areas, per Code word, following each sub division; each with slash marks,

both forward and backward, always
varying in number;

5) Pattern(s): the Conclusions:
    (a) Where the patient survives, the strange
        Code is present solely in the MRI
        image; with the first Code word
        always being the same;positioned at
        beginning of each separate line;
    (b) Followed, within the line(s) by many
        sub divisions and sub areas, differing
        in number and placement for each
        patient, including the number of sub
        area slashes;
    (c) When and where the patient has died,
        the results show   'blank' DNA and
        MRI results for the tested brain
        material; for Code from the MRI
        image, the patient must   still be alive.

Being a scientist, Eric carefully prepared and
documented these conclusions with copies of all actual
test results as well as all Hospital records for each patient,
keeping a master copy for himself at home; a second copy
with Janice; and secretly, on one of his Thursday visits, a
third copy, in an envelope, placed within his fathers
locker at the mausoleum.

Over the years, he had learned from fellow
scientists how anxious one's colleagues could become to
claim credit for another's findings and breakthrough's.

Should he be able to establish this Discovery, he wanted the records to be clear on his part in the matter.

By now, he knew that this substance, the snippet sample, was not genetic in its make up, in that no DNA was there. In addition, he knew that finding Coded words in the samples via MRI's was an incredible Discovery in and of itself. Yet, lacking an explanation for 'what' had been discovered, let alone a translation for the Code, made the entire matter incomplete. Hence, likely a big 'yawn' in the academic community and of little or no interest elsewhere.

Eric would have to get to the bottom of this Discovery, no matter what.

CHAPTER 8

Meanwhile, the testing of the various snippets of brain material had caught the attention of Dr. Howard. Actually, as much as anything, the DNA 'blank' results were known generally within the Lab and were of particular interest to him. While he didn't have the full test results for this project, he was able to follow along with the regular entries the technicians made in the computer database at the Center. Beyond that, he did not know of Eric's MRI tests, which were kept separate and apart from him.

Even so, and more importantly, he realized how extraordinary it was that tissue from a human body would fail to show DNA upon sequencer testing, resulting in just 'blank' readouts. This was beyond all scientific education and training that he had ever received.

When he went home for the Thanksgiving holiday that year, he could not help mentioning this strange project to his father. For them, shoptalk was not unusual, in that Dr. Alex Howard was a well known and highly regarded microbiologist and geneticist. Dr. Alex Howard was a physically large man and could be quite intimidating should one choose to disagree with him. His eyes would seem quite large and intense, and slightly red, on those occasions when he was angry. He dressed in a tweedy New Englander way, appearing professorial and acting with intellectually superior manners and ways. In fact he had been a full professor at the university where Dr. John Howard received his degrees.

While in that position, as a side venture, he had started a vanity press publishing business, mainly for his colleagues and comrades doing research and writing technical Articles. One thing they all had in common was their dedication to the advancement of evolution science through the science of genetics and any other theories and methods. He also used this press set up to promote views from his own 'scientific' research.

As Dr. Alex Howard became older, this publishing enterprise became more and more successful, and he gradually phased out of the University. He was now regularly publishing full length books that were increasingly being used in high schools and colleges as textbooks, on natural science, and especially on advancements in 'evolution science' since the time of Charles Darwin.

Additionally, this had led to the founding of a nonprofit association for the advancement of 'evolution science' with a large membership among the academic and education community. Not surprisingly, Dr. Alex Howard as a founder, board member and first president, was the leading force for this group. And of course, his publishing company produced their monthly newsletter and quarterly

Journal for all members and others interested enough to subscribe. All in all, this whole effort had become very lucrative for him and he was now a wealthy man.

Over the years, Dr. Alex Howards notoriety and efforts on behalf of 'evolution science' became known and recognized nationwide. This occurred because of his appearance and testimony in various court cases in the ongoing controversies between creationism and evolution. Each time he appeared he was a strong advocate on behalf of 'evolution science.' So much so, that he presented the image and views of an overwhelming zealot, tailoring, turning and twisting academic 'facts' well beyond the extent to which they were creditable.

Consequently, when his son described the so called 'blank' test results from the DNA tests on the snippet of thalamic brain material he reacted that something must be wrong, because "that was just not possible." While John kept reassuring him of the facts he knew to be true, the father remained doubtful, emphasizing that he knew of no such thing in the scientific literature, but that he would make a check nonetheless.

He also admonished his son to keep him advised and up to date of any further developments.

Dr. Alex knew full well how widely respected and advanced the Medical Research Center was in the field, after all he had been instrumental in seeing that his son went to work there. John promised to do this and at the same time indicated that his boss, Dr. Eric Rhodes, was not disclosing or sharing with him developments on this project and seemed preoccupied with the entire matter.

John guessed that Eric had done other things with the samples, but that he did not know what or if there were any results. They left it at that for the day, but it was clear that the father was greatly interested and wanted to be told of any further actions or events.

Dr. Alex Howard, although being disturbed and unsettled about the 'blank' body tissue, never in his wildest imagination, had any idea what could and would come from learning of this Discovery at that time. Nor that, it would eventually remake his life.

In his study, night after night, Eric pondered the strange, mystifying unexplainable Code and the results from the lab tests. His gut told him that they were on to something, but *what*? He felt as though his entire life, given his education, training and experience, were all a prelude to the challenge of making sense of this DISCOVERY. And if it really was a discovery, just what had been discovered? He had to know. *HE HAD TO KNOW.*

The more Eric thought about all of this, the clearer the question became to him: whether this could be a whole new part of the make up of the brain (i. e, the human body) and if so, what was its purpose and function? At

this point, after all the review and work completed, he was becoming fairly certain of such a conclusion because of the consistent pattern from the tests. However, he knew he could not put forth a theory or conclusion, nor name it, until he knew just what had been found. This was still a mystery to him and Janice and they had no answer at present for what they had found. Furthermore, he also knew that in order to find an answer, and confirm any theory, it would first be necessary to decipher the Code to show its meaning in human terms.

It was now Sunday, and Janice had left after a delightful Saturday night. Winter was in the air, and in keeping with his usual practice he had been to Church that day. His pastor, much like his father, had given a marvelous sermon, talking of the Holy Spirit, and how it had touched various personages in the Bible. The pastor had gone on to talk of the Human Spirit (synonymously, one's Soul), that resides within each of us and then goes to God upon our death. It was a far reaching sermon and was highlighted by scripture relating to the conversion of Saul to Paul. Pleased, Eric was happy he attended that day.

When it ended, Eric went home by way of the 'Church of the Walking Feet.' Only this time, feeling

refreshed, he did not take the most direct route. He felt very good for some reason, as if a major burden had been lifted from his shoulders. He did not know why, it was just there. As he walked, he enjoyed more than ever his surroundings and the small animal and bird life around and about him. He smiled thinking that Nature held the same love for birds and animals as well as man. That Gods charity was so great that it included all creatures.

Then, he sat by the lake for a good while, taking in its beauty and especially the reflections of tree's and buildings upon it surface. At about that time, a small wind came up and made its presence apparent on the lake surface. Though chilled, Eric couldn't help but reflect upon the pastor's point that the Human Spirit was like the wind, changing and growing at the core of ones essence throughout life. He was at a loss to grasp or connect why that should mean something at that time. But, he had just felt it and that was enough for the moment. Not long afterward, he finished his walk home, greatly invigorated by attending Church and those special moments on the walk home.

Later, that evening, he was sitting at the desk in his study thinking about the coming week. Automatically, his mind shifted back to the subject of the brain tag snippet and the strange mystifying Code. It had been such a good day that he could feel a struggle within himself, that he did not want to go there. "Why spoil it?"

And then, it HIT him, like a bolt out of the blue. "That was the answer. It is the HUMAN SPIRIT, OUR SOUL!" This feeling exploded within him --- instantly, he knew that this was right. It was an HA HAH moment.

An EPIPHANY. a REVELATION, a sudden BREAKTHROUGH, an insight that dazed and amazed him for a few minutes.

Then reality set in? "Could it be? Could there really be a place within the human body that housed the

Human Spirit? He knew of no such place --- but could it be there? Or, could some part of it be there?"

Certainly, the human brain is not fully understood --- he knew this from having worked with the medical community for so long. Turning back to logic, he realized that it would make sense here. The Bible makes it clear that upon one's death, the Human Spirit (the Soul) leaves the body. He believed that there may even be scientific studies on this point. Clearly, this explanation would be consistent with the change in the test results of the samples, turning from the strange Code to a 'blank,' following the death of the patient. That made total sense.

"But, could it be --- and if so, what does the strange Code mean if, in fact, it is the Human Spirit or a part of the Human Spirit?"

That night, by the time he turned out the light on his desk, he felt quite shaken by the whole experience. His mind was in utter and complete turmoil.

Eric could not and did not sleep that night. He was profoundly shocked by his conclusion and did not know what to do about it. He was so taken back by this that he just called in sick to the Medical Research Center the next day. As the morning went by, he calmed down and became an intelligent rational person once again. He gradually realized that if he was right about finding a physical connection to the Human Spirit (the Soul), there was more at hand here than just scientific findings.

Being the son of a Pastor, he knew automatically that this kind of finding added issues related to the transcendental, supernatural and metaphysical. He concluded that he would have to solve the Code in order to prove this conclusion. The content of the Code for the four 'live' samples of snippet would identify and support the conclusion of a connection to the Human Spirit (the Soul). Figuring out how to do this would be challenging, but it would be the only way of providing a solid foundation for the Discovery.

On the other hand, he did not even know if the Code itself had a 'key' to decipher the words, and if so, whether it would be intelligible to human beings. After all, given the possibilities, it may or may not be a language known or understood by human beings? This was enough to make one's head hurt. So he took a break.

With that, Eric laid down and rested for a while. Later, he called Janice and told her that he had to see her that night; their had been some developments on the Code.

CHAPTER 9

As promised, Janice came over early that evening. She had her own news for Eric that had her smiling from ear to ear. The Hospital administration had asked her to become the Assistant Medical Director, Department of Neurology. This would put her in line to become the Medical Director for this Department in a few years when the Doctor currently holding this responsibility retired. And, this new position would not interfere with her ongoing practice as a neurosurgeon. All in all she viewed it as a nice promotion and a step up in her professional standing. Furthermore, besides receiving a modest salary, this position would also qualify her for a nice pension in her later years. Being a surgeon, she knew from others, that a doctor only had a limited number of years where they could do this kind of delicate surgery before their physical dexterity declined and it would be necessary to move on to something else. She was pleased and happy and she physically showed it with an upbeat attitude and new striking hair do.

However, when she looked at Eric, she said: "You look terrible, what's wrong, what's happened?"

Eric did look bad, disheveled, tired, worn out and unshaven. Janice said: "I called the Lab for you today and was told you were sick. What's wrong?"

Eric: "It happened last evening. I was working on the strange Code and all of a sudden I knew the answer. It just hit me --- sudden, beyond belief. I have been shaken by it ever since. It's way beyond anything we, as scientists, would ever find. But, I know I am right. I just feel it."

Eric went on to tell Janice what happened on Sunday evening. He described the day and then the moment of the EPIPHANY. He told her all the reasons why this made sense from their tests.

Janice's loving reaction: "Oh, Eric, a theory like that is well beyond what we do as medical and genetic specialists. That is such a huge leap, to go from science to the supernatural, from the physical to the metaphysical."

Eric: "I know, I know, that's why I had to see and talk to you this evening. You're the only one I can talk to about such a thing. I would be laughed right out of the Medical Research Center to conclude such a thing on a project. We have both worked too long and hard for our reputations to be jeopardized with such a finding. After thinking about it last night and today, even feeling as bad as I do, I can see that the only way to go forward would be to actually prove these findings to be the Human Spirit or at least a part of the Human Spirit."

Janice, with a sympathetic look; "I agree, but that is not as simple as our normal lab based efforts. We would be two scientists, used to working with empirical facts, trying to establish a supernatural connection. How do you do that? I don't know; I don't have any idea of how to even approach it; it's well beyond our fields of knowledge. And, most likely, everyone's field of knowledge."

Eric: "Yes, that's true, I know. But consider the magnitude of what we have found. Several things are most striking. First, how and why is it possible for something that comes from a human body to be totally lacking in DNA? This tissue is from the human brain, yet it lacks any signs of normal genetic make up. This is more in your field, with your expertise in all areas of the brain. Have you ever seen or read anything about any part of the brain failing to have DNA cellular material?"

Janice: "No, but on the other hand, before I say that it is impossible, I'll need to do some checking, because this is not something neurology would normally concentrate on. But, I will have a look at my source literature and let you know right away if this has ever been found by or within our field of expertise."

Eric: "The other thing that strikes me as rather incredible is finding

Code, actual communication code, with letters and/or symbols of some sort, within a part of the body. This is entirely different than the letters assigned to the DNA triplets. As you already know, they simply represent the underlying nucleosides and proteins at the sub atomic levels of a cell. I know that it was unusual for me to run the snippet through the MRI, but I had no other choice when it failed to show any genetic composition. I thought there must be something. So, I did what I have done on other unique situations, I had it run by the MRI."

"And I' am glad I did. There was nothing there but three simple lines. Most likely, this would have been thrown away --- but in this case, being a digital image, it only took a few minutes to increase the resolution many thousand times. And there it is was, spread out before us (my technician was there), characters and/or letters of some kind; spread out in a specific pattern; which has all been repeated in like circumstance in a consistent way via our other "live" samples. Now, tell me, how does an alphabet based Code get into the human body? I don't know and I dare say that no one else does."

Janice: "I can't say much about that, other than it seems utterly impossible for a real alphanumeric type of code to exist within a human body, instead of being an interpretation of the genetic make up, as with DNA. How did it get there? And furthermore, what does it mean? The whole thing just plain scares me, and I am not sure why?"

They looked at each other with blank stares. Janice looked up and volunteered: "Lets do this Eric; lets just roll it all over in our minds and sleep on it for a

couple of days and meet as usual this Friday evening at my place and go over where we stand with it at that time. I'll take on the search of the 'blank' body part for a precedent and you figure out what you want to do on the strange Code. How's that sound Eric? "

Eric: "Sounds good to me. But, there is one other thing that you and I must do with this entire matter. We must agree to keep the whole thing completely secret, not sharing it with anyone at your place or mine, not even our day to day working colleagues. From the Center's point of view, I will see that this project is closed and filed away, with a simple 'inconclusive' finding in the file and the ongoing data base. There is no telling what would happen if others came to realize the direction this project seems to be heading."

Janice: "I agree; I will be very careful with my project papers."

At which point, Janice stood up, walked over to Eric, pulled him up, gave him a big kiss, and said as she pulled him toward the bedroom: "Now, I think there is something else that you need to 'sleep 'on." And then she gave him a big smile.

Meanwhile, Dr. Alex Howard sat back in his library at home. After having had a busy day, he still could not dismiss the thought that a part of the human body, especially arising from the area of the brain, could fail to show DNA code, in any combination. He was already checking his major source indexes, literature and Journals on this subject. He had found nothing upon which to proceed. This left him puzzled, baffled and in denial. He was at an impasse and didn't like it one bit. In his view, he was not a man to be trifled with.

Few people knew, including his family, that he had grown into a fundamentalist, and hardliner, etc. on all matters related to the science of evolution. As he had pressed forward on these beliefs and views, his 'teaching' classes at the University had moved to various extremes, so much so that some of the graduate students had secretly complained to their Deans about the things Dr. Alex Howard was doing and requiring. Within two years it had become so bad, that the academic Dean and the University President forced him 'out' under the usual cover of "spending more time with his family and pursuing other interests." In this way both the University and Alex saved face, but set loose upon the academic world a man capable of acting in all kinds of ways, and becoming a force that could and would do extreme things to serve both his financial and 'zealot' views.

As time went forward, this paranoia would and did drive him to act in severe ways against those who might jeopardize 'evolution science.'

CHAPTER 10

The next day Eric went back to work. His mind was now clear again. He had recovered from the turmoil brought on by the sudden 'Epiphany' of Sunday evening. He was back to his old self and on an even keel once more.

He spent the whole day catching up on outstanding project business. He was always amazed at how much accumulated following just a single sick day. In the back of his mind, he thought that maybe he had neglected some matters while pursuing the strange Code. With that possibility, he set about moving ahead on the many matters that were in process. His staff wondered what had put such a fire under him.

By mid-afternoon, Eric had collected the entire file on the Centers lab work on the brain snippet from Barney (forwarded by Dr. Westphal), as well as the other samples that had been obtained. As he had promised Janice, he then prepared and signed an internal order closing the project as "inconclusive,-- no significant findings." This would also be placed upon the computer records. Officially, this action ended the project at the Center.

However, all of the MRI results and the magnifications of the three lines per 'live' sample were not included in this file. This work had been done at the Hospital and the only person privy to and in possession of such images was Eric. He did not intend that this Discovery be made part of the Center records; for it could have either a positive or negative outcome on its reputation should anything result from his further independent inquiry. It would be kept secret unless more definitive conclusions could be reached.

Later that evening, Eric sat at his desk and turned his mind once again to the strange Code and the breakthrough he had made over the weekend. For the moment, he choose to relax and not be so scientific. He just wanted to contemplate it all on a more down to earth basis. In doing so, he began to think of people he had known and did know now. And, more indirectly, he was trying to relate the spirit he had observed within them to how it could be codified within their brain. And, if so, what was it that would be codified and why. Everyone was so different, it all seemed impossible. Yet, without scientific development, the understanding of human genetics would likewise seem impossible. Answers were never easy.

Eric sat back and thought about some special 'characters' he had known over the years. In this mode, he first went back to his high school days, being among the best of his lifetime. Jerry, his friend and pal, sat two seats behind him at that time. He had to chuckle when he recalled how Jerry always had lame excuses on why he didn't get his home work done. The answer was simple but Jerry would not say it. Jerry did his paper route after school and never got around to schoolwork because he then went home to work on his hot rod Ford. Nowadays, Eric and Jerry would meet for lunch occasionally, have some good laughs, and that was about it.

Next, he thought of Rick, his neighbor down the street, and a constant thread through out his life. They had played and grown up together and shared many good times. Eric turned out to be quiet and somewhat introverted whereas Rick was the opposite, being an athlete and leader of the High School football and basketball teams. In keeping with this 'big-man-on-campus' image, he was also the darling of several cheerleaders. But, with all this going on he remained Eric's good friend, and quietly 'backstopped' Eric when some of the other 'jocks and muscle men' thought it would be fun to pick on him. These days however, Rick was not doing well, having failed in an early marriage; he now had an overall dissatisfaction with life in general. Eric made a point to go to lunch or dinner with Rick regularly but it had become more and more difficult as time went bye.

He went on to think about his University days and there highlights. Immediately, Vanessa came to mind. There were many memories of her, some sweet and some quite sour from when it all ended. She had introduced him to 'sex' in a very tender way and he was ever so grateful. The sour part came as she moved on after college and eventually turned to another lover. Nonetheless, in the context of his present thinking, her spirit was enduring, and Eric realized how special it still was to him.

Going further, Eric harkened back to his mentor and eventual colleague, Dr. Henry Johnson. When they first met Eric was the student and 'Hank' was the professor and later, the Dean of the Genetics Department. But all that was only titles, because they became fast friends, with the Dean recognizing the exceptional talent in Eric and his sound character. In the summers, Hank and Eric worked day to day on state of the art research projects, completing and publishing major papers in their field, with Hank always seeing that Eric received as much credit as him. For this Eric would forever be grateful. However, presently that was all a given, for now he was focusing upon 'Hank' and his character. In doing this, Eric started to list the qualities and values he saw in this man, but then stopped abruptly, feeling that in doing this he was somehow demeaning this mans spirit and that was the last thing he wanted to do.

Noting that he could go on for quite a while with these recollections, Eric sat back and let his thoughts run onward. After a bit, he knew that such an exercise would be fruitless and likely not help in what he was trying to get at. All of this just went to show him that the 'Spirits' of each individual were separate and unique, identified to them, with no end to the variations that may exist. And that this could also include negative areas and omissions in much the same way. This clarity became Eric's bottom line. He could see that having a Code may well make it possible to see through the actions and omissions of individuals to get at their true *essence*.

Another point that he struggled with was whether one's character or personality, probably being one and the same, should be considered as part of the Human Spirit (the Soul), or whether they were so different as to be just incidental traits for each individual. He could see arguments for this both ways. On one hand, for certain people, they were such 'characters' that these traits totally dominated all thoughts of them. On the other hand, such traits within their 'personality' were so minimal that they did not stand out in that way. Furthermore and beyond that, didn't it make more sense that one's Spirit or Soul, being their very essence, should be more substantive and fundamental than what were often fleeting 'traits' and 'idiosyncratic' ways. Perhaps, he thought, if he were ever able to figure out the Code, he would have the answer to these questions and likely many others.

Arriving at this point, jogged Eric to switch back to his scientific inquiry. He tried to figure out what to do next?

Turning to scientific and deductive reasoning, he would start by setting certain basic assumptions. He knew that they may or may not be correct, but at least they would provide a beginning point. Furthermore, even if they proved incorrect, that alone might led to the right direction.

He stated and listed:

First, that the Code, found within the brain snippets, was the key to determining if his revelation was right; that it was in fact, the physical location of the Human Spirit (the Soul), or at least a part of it.

Second, that this Code was entirely unique within the world of medical science in that it showed an image of language and/or symbols instead of normal DNA.

Third, that the language and/or symbols found are from ancient human times; He guessed this to be as far back as the Hebrew tribal periods, perhaps even within the Egyptian kingdoms and early Israel occupation. This he considered to be a reasonable assumption because established history reflected that early language development occurred at or before that time period. Moreover, bible history that he had been taught by his father, the Pastor, reflected God's active involvement with the prophets and kings of tribal Israel at and before such times. He had no doubt that only through the hands of our Creator, could the development of man and mankind include the placement of a language based Code within the human body. Surely, this must be for some transcendental purpose or reason.

Fourth, given the appearance of the language and/or symbols, it may or may not be encrypted. That would be something to look for.

And finally, given the nature, manner and placement of the Code, clearly it was intended to be hidden from mankind for many, many centuries; perhaps never to have be known or discovered; all adding up to and supporting an other worldly or heavenly purpose. Who could ever really know?

That would be enough to get him started. With that, he reached over to his computer, brought up the Internet and went to a major search site. He typed in "ancient language and writing," pressed the go button and watched the output. Sure enough, there were many items listed; but it became immediately apparent that they were dominated by developments related to the Dead Sea Scrolls, discovered in 1946. He read that in1991, the Israel Antiquity Authority, after much international consternation, had finally made these scrolls and translations available to scholars, the press and the public under controlled conditions. Eric read on and on until late that evening and finally went on to bed, mentally and physically exhausted.

Janice, meanwhile, was able to focus her attention, during some open time she had at the hospital, on the question of whether there was any existing precedent for a 'blank' DNA body part, especially pertaining to the brain. After all, she had started all of this when she sent over to the Centers lab, the snippet of brain material she removed from Barney. Her task was much easier than Eric's in that she had full access to medical reference literature via the Hospital library. And importantly, the question at hand was more objective and could be directly answered.

Her research, on and off Tuesday thru Thursday, came up with nothing on point, And that was the answer in itself. Because, nothing had ever been observed, tested and/or recorded, showing any human language and/or symbol of any kind, within any part of the body. Human tissue was just that, human tissue, notwithstanding its location, with nothing having been written within its make up being recorded. That however, did not mean that it was not there beforehand, because the tools, means and mechanisms, especially machines, now made things possible that never could have been imagined years and years ago. Perhaps it had been there all along, but impossible to discover, without today's modern technology. Who was to know, new things come along almost every day.

And that would be her report back to Eric.

By Thursday evening, Eric had read and read the many articles on the Web about the Dead Sea Scrolls and the caves at Qumran in Israel. On the one hand, it was helpful because they related to a period in time that would seem to make sense with the issues he was looking at given the nature of the Code itself. On the other hand, it became frustrating because he could not look upon the actual writing in the Scrolls in a way that allowed him to specifically compare one to the other; Scroll to Code, Code to Scroll.

Being an ingenious person, highly motivated to find the answer to the strange Code, it came to Eric that he should just go there and follow this search to whatever end he may find. Financially, he could handle it because he had saved quite a nest egg from his high salary. And academically, he was confident the museum authorities would allow his inquiry, even though a cover story might be needed.

The main question was how he could be absent from his position as a Project Director, at the Medical Research Center, for say, four months, guessing at an estimate of how long he might need to be away. The answer, actually, was right there, in that the Center had a policy permitting sabbatical leaves of up to six months, at half salary, after five years prior employment. This was something Eric had never done or even thought about though he was now in his seventeenth year of employment.

To him, it was always the matter of the time away and how it would affect his work, so he had never requested such a leave. In this instance, however, he knew he would risk it because the Code had taken over his life, both professionally and personally; so he thought he would just ask for such a leave. He was confident that the request would be approved. He just had to know the answer and therefore, he had to go. He would try the idea out on Janice this weekend.

CHAPTER 11

Friday nights were always a delight for Eric and Janice. Their rigorous schedules for the week were over and it was time to relax, enjoy life and their special time together. Oftentimes, one would surprise the other with a small gift, a novelty or something plainly out of the ordinary. Tonight, Eric did just that, having made a dining reservation at a darling little Italian bistro. They were both anxious to share their investigative results following their Monday night meeting. But it became agreed that such discussion would have to be delayed to the next day while they found gratification between themselves as lovers. It was a wonderful dinner and a delightful follow up between the sheets well into the wee hours.

Late the next morning, Janice went first: "Eric, your suspicions were right, I found nothing in the medical literature pertaining to an absence of DNA in human tissue in any part of the body, let alone the thalamic region of the brain. We have to conclude, as you thought, that this is a 'new' medical Discovery, or something that no one had ever thought to test, which is the most likely. Also, advances in technology, may well have made the difference here, because finding a 'blank' in living tissue is off the charts. Consequently, it's hard to know how long this has existed, but from what I know of human development, it has to be a very long time. "

"I thought so, and I am thankful to have confirmation of this, especially given your expertise." Eric allowed.

"I dare say Eric, no one else I know, would have taken the time to run a MRI on such a small sample; the 'blank piece' more than likely would have been trashed. How could you do that?"

"Easy, I have done it before. I like having an image for the Lab file, since the specimen deteriorates quickly and there is nothing physical left. The shocker here was the three parallel lines, and their apparent orderliness. I just had to see what they looked like so I magnified them. Each time we upped the resolution it became more unusual and exciting" Eric went on.

Janice: "Where did you come out with your review?"

At this point, Eric went over his meandering about people and how different their 'Spirits' must be. He even volunteered that the Code could be a means to track 'life' events of each individual, assuming of course that he was right about a connection to the Human Spirit (the Soul). Then he went on and spelled out the assumptions he thought to be fundamental to what ever must be the next steps. Janice agreed with these points, curious on what would be next. And now was the hard part for Eric, who said:

"I have some good news along with some bad news for us. My research has shown to me that the logical next step will be to go to Israel and see if the Dead Sea Scrolls can shed any light on the strange 'Code.' I have found an announcement dating back to 1991 making them available for public inspection? And, from my reading, the authorities are well along with most of their translation."

"Oh Eric, how are you ever going to be able to do that and how could that help? How long would you be gone and what about your work at the Center? Now, I see what you mean about bad news, I am already starting to feel lonely."

"The reason is that they are ancient documents that relate back to the Old Testament and history of the Hebrew tribes and their communication with God. I am not so much interested in their religious disclosure; but, the various languages used to write the scrolls. I am confident that the MRC will grant me a sabbatical leave of absence and that I would only be away about three to four months. I have never taken a sabbatical even though this practice is used all the time by our Lab personnel. Besides, I just can't seem to find any other way to access these ancient writings. In this situation, I believe the older the writing, the better the likelihood of finding a 'key' to the Code."

"But Eric, is this thing so important to you that you will risk all the possibilities that could happen from being absent so long?" Janice said.

"Janice, I have weighed and thought about it; and yes, I must do it; I just can't let it go. I love you deeply and will miss you terribly; but this has become something I must do. Eric answered.

"All right then." Janice said: "I will do all that I can to back you up and support your efforts; you can count on me."

And they embraced, kissing each other in a long deep passionate way.

Over the years since Eric had started work at the Medical Research Center, he had become well acquainted with its Chief Administrator, Mr. Richard Johnston. Indeed, Eric had become one of his 'stars' during his tenure, bringing both honors and prestige to the Center via many Grants and the related Projects. He was not surprised that Eric stopped by that Monday, for they often had impromptu catch up exchanges. After normal pleasantries, Eric said:

"Mr. Johnston, I need a favor at the moment. I want to take a short sabbatical leave, I estimate to be about three to four months. There is some foreign travel I have in mind with study included at the location. I know this is unusual for me but it is something I really want to do."

Mr. Johnston was in a good mood that morning and easily answered;

"No problem Eric, you're long overdue for a break like that. And, I don't recall any pressing overriding Projects at the moment. However, there is one thing I always I insist on with such leaves, and that is making clear arrangements to cover your responsibilities while being away. I imagine you have given that some consideration?"

"Yes, I have. I will have my assistant, Dr. Howard, substitute for me. He should be able to cover on the current Projects. One other thing, if I may: would you be kind enough to give me a letter of introduction accompanied by a statement of credentials that I could use at certain museums I plan to visit? There are some archives I plan to look into that may not generally be available to the public and knowing my academic background should help ease the way. I will write a short draft of what I am requesting for you to use in the preparation."

Mr. Johnston: "Ok, sound fine to me. Your absence will give the MRC a good opportunity to see how your assistant works out and judge his potential future here. I'll have my secretary type up the letters you want. Just tell me and coordinate with Human Resources on the timing of your absence. And, if I may say so, have a good time on your leave; you have earned it long ago."

Later that day, Eric and Dr. Howard sat down together for their typical short meeting at the beginning of each week. After reviewing the outstanding Projects and the related actions to be taken, Eric said:

"John, I am going to be taking a short sabbatical leave soon to do some foreign travel. If you agree, I will name you to be in charge in my absence. I have spoken with Administrator Johnston about this, and it is acceptable to him. Would that be acceptable to you?"

"Yes, of course, Eric. When will you be going and how long? And where; and will I be able to get in touch with you, if I need to? We will need to review the projects in more depth so that I understand where and what to do with them, depending on developments. This is all so sudden."

Eric: "Sure, don't worry; you will have the grant files for the Projects that make all of that clear. And, I will see that you receive what you need to get in touch with me via e-mail. We will make all of this happen."

With that, their meeting ended. Eric was pleased that it was so easy to gain the freedom and opportunity to follow his thoughts and instincts on 'breaking' the strange Code. And, Dr. Howard, more than anything, was pleased to have the chance to prove himself at the MRC, away from the shadow of Dr. Eric Rhodes. He could hardly wait to tell his father.

CHAPTER 12

That evening, at home, Dr. John Howard did not waste any time before calling his father and telling him the news that Eric was taking a leave of absence and that he would be in charge of the continuing projects. John was excited with this vote of confidence and the opportunity to show his abilities and leadership. He did not particularly focus on why Eric might be suddenly taking such a leave; he was simply pleased with the big news and wanted to share it.

While his father's reaction was pleased with his son's advancement in responsibilities, he wanted to know about what Eric was up to:

"John, did Eric say why the sudden leave, where he was going, or any reason for doing this?" Alex asked.

"No, he wants to do some foreign travel and promised he would give me the means to stay in touch with him while gone."

Alex again: "What about the project with the 'blank' results from the DNA testing? What did he tell you to do about that?"

John: "It's over; its not a project any longer. Eric closed it out about a week ago. Marked it all as 'Inconclusive: no findings.' I won't have to do any work on that."

Alex: "Even so John, keep me up to date on Eric and where he goes. And, I am proud of your interim appointment. It's a good chance to improve your odds of moving up at the MRC. Remember, you represent one of the leading genetic institutions in the United States. Pay particular attention to its participation in the Human Genome Project for it is at the cutting edge and will have a huge impact on the future."

"I will Dad. I will make sure to actively interface with our outside liaisons and our participation here at the MRC. More later on Eric, I have to go now, love you Dad."

After that call, Alex went immediately to his study. Sitting at his desk he thought about the news of Eric's plans. He lamented that John did not have the guile he had and did not see any potential link to the closed 'inconclusive' project.

His son did not know about the work Alex had done in reviewing the 'blank' results from the DNA tests.

Actually, Dr. Alex had made a through review of the medical literature and found nothing that could come even close to explaining such an anomaly. Either the machine was wrong or the sample was improperly prepared or this was an aberration never known or discovered before. If the latter was true, and this appeared likely, considering the number of samples tested and the quality of the work at the Center, then Eric was on to something. But what?

The more he thought about it, a Discovery of this kind would mean that a part of the human body would be lacking an evolutionary basis and connection. This would be a disaster in itself, not to mention the additional importance that the samples had originated from a part of the brain. What should he do about it, if anything? He was not the type to sit around and wait for what happens; he wanted a part in any outcome and would strive to make sure that it served his purpose(s).

With all of this in mind, he decided to hire his favorite 'consultant' for an investigative assignment including a little 'black bag' work. He had done such things before involving certain litigation and been successful in getting 'results.' His man was a former CIA operative that still had access to modern surveillance devices. Dr. Alex planned to have Eric, and his lover Janice, telephones bugged, their e-mail hacked, and their personnel computer files copied, in order to keep an eye on them.

Upon contact, this operative indicated that he was available right away, and they made arrangements to meet the next day at Boston's Logan Airport. The operative lived in the Washington, D.C. area and it was easy for him to catch a short commuter flight to Boston.

They met outside the gate where the operative arrived and sat down in an adjoining passenger waiting area. It was the first time for them to actually be together. It was quite a contrast given Dr. Alex's large physical stature, his professorial appearance and his intense dominating eyes, sitting beside the diminutive looking 'operative,' a man of less than average size, with a common everyday appearance and unremarkable eyes, that tended to turn away when someone looked upon him. He had been trained to not stand out in any way in order to avoid 'recall' at a later time should that ever happen. He prided himself on being 'inconspicuous' in public. He was good at this.

He recognized Dr. Alex by way of his advance description of himself and the clothes he would be wearing. He walked right up to him, made a brief introduction and they moved aside and sat down. Quickly, they touched upon their prior association almost as if it were a means of identification, together recalling a few particulars only they would personally know. After that, Dr. Alex gave him the basic facts on Eric and Janice, including their addresses, where they worked, the phone numbers, etc., etc.. Then, he went over what he wanted to start with from the operative. Also, he allowed as how this might eventually need to get 'rough' and asked if the operative would be up to such an assignment and what the price might be?

The operative used the name 'Charles', would not give his real name or address and would only use an e-mail address for communications between them. He indicated the telephone 'bug', break-in and hacking with copies of the computer files would be easy and that he could and would do this right away. As for the potential 'rough' stuff, he may or may not do it, and that he had an associate that would take care of it if necessary. Depending on the level of 'roughness', the price could go as high as one million paid in advance to a Swiss bank account. This last amount would be for a 'final' result. Dr. Alex nodded approval to all that was said and then did the most important thing and reason for their actually meeting that day; he handed over twenty-five thousand in cash to have him move ahead ASAP. Charles made it clear that he alone would do most of the communication and that Dr. Alex should minimize 'contacting' him. They parted after having been together for only an hour.

  That week Eric got busy making preparations for his trip. He had his travel agent obtain fares and travel information to Israel, especially the availability of a tourist visa. He took steps to place copies of all of the data and research, including the MRI's and their follow up magnifications, with Janice and secretly within his father's locker at the mausoleum. He had his attorney prepare a comprehensive Power of Attorney, a Last Will and Testament and a Living Will, all in favor of Janice. Eric believed in being prepared for all eventualities. After all, he was going to a part of the world that lived in constant danger of bombings and other tragedies.

He made arrangements with his condo managers and cleaning personnel to pay for interim expenses and to keep an eye on the place. Days later, he learned that a six month travel visa would be issued in short order after their U.S. Embassy quickly looked into and verified Eric's identity. Eric then instructed the agent to call him right away and book the ticket and some hotel reservations in Jerusalem as soon as approval was received. The pace of things became quite busy.

Unknown to them, Charles, (not his real name), Dr. Alex's operative, had started watching Eric and Janice on alternating days. As with all people, he caught on to their daily habits and routines quickly. He was in a hurry and under pressure from his employer to get as much info as fast as possible. With the ease of a longstanding pro, and on the very same day, he had quietly entered their apartment and condo, placed 'bugs" on their telephones, copied their home computer files, and discovered the passwords needed to access their e-mail. For people that were not usual targets for surveillance, all of this was not difficult at all. Charles had done it many times beforehand. In short order, he now had his first delivery ready for Dr. Alex.

It wasn't long before Eric had almost completed final preparations. He decided to be careful and minimal on all things he took. He had heard about and knew of the in depth inspections and reviews it took to pass thru Israeli customs and immigration. With that in mind he packed only what he needed in clothes, keeping to his professorial look, and he limited his papers, making sure not to reveal much about his real purpose and objective.

Pertaining to the Code, he settled on taking only one page, but likely the most important one, listing the repetitive first Code words per line on each MRI image from 'live' samples. He placed this page in the middle of the one thick file he was taking. For her records, he also e-mailed Janice this single page. He would have her send it to him in Israel if need be.

This is the important page he included:

The CODE: Line Headings

Top line: ɯ ɵ d ɣ ʏ ꞓ

Middle line: ı ɴ ⊥ ɘ ʏ ʏ ɘ ɔ ⊥

Bottom line: ɯ̃ ɣ ʏ ⅄ ɘ ꞓ

This Code appears at the beginning of each separate line on each live sample (per MRI images magnified x5000).

He went on to add to her e-mail a Creed; actually the Creed he intended to follow, in his continuing pursuit to find the key to the Code. He had thought about this and decided it would help keep him from becoming distracted by all the new things he would see. It was simple and designed to avoid getting hung up on the potential supernatural issues and pitfalls that he and Janice were concerned about. He stated:

1. I am a scientist, first and foremost.

2. I have no advance agenda.

3. I will go where the facts and modern science takes me. And,

4. Otherwise, I am mainly interested in adding to the knowledge and advancement of mankind.

And with that as an ending, he sent her the e-mail. Eric knew that Janice would let him know if she took issue with any part of this Creed.

Shortly, the phone rang; Eric was at work; his travel agent informed him that he had been successful in obtaining a tourist visa allowing him to stay up to six months in Israel. With that Eric authorized his ticket to be booked. He also instructed this agent to find and book him for three weeks at a mid-price hotel in Jerusalem near the Israel Museum and the Shrine of the Book. He figured that by then he would know about how much more time would be needed and would find another place that would meet his needs, if necessary. Concurrently, the Chief Administrators office sent back signed copies, in triplicate, of the Credentials and Letter of Introduction Eric had prepared for himself.

A little later, the phone rang again and he was advised by the travel agent that the ticket was now set and Eric would be leaving in ten days. Eric quickly typed up his notice to the Human Resources department of the dates he planned to be gone on the sabbatical leave and a short note of this to Mr. Johnston. Eric was becoming very excited and anxious to go. Now he would have be with Janice, his 'lovee,' and do his best to make their parting as tender and considerate as possible.

He would and did spend as much time with her as he could during these last ten days. She did the same for him spending every night together at his place. They tried to fit in all their favorite activities and things, joking and carrying on as if Eric was about to drop off the end of the earth. They even laughed at each other about the way they were acting, after all it was only to be a three or four month absence. In the end though, it was clear that they both were deeply touched and concerned about parting. They had not been separated from each other for any length of time for at least five years. During these last moments, they were sad and melancholy, doing the best they could to comfort and reassure each other. However, the time to depart had arrived, and that's what happened, with their last moments being spent together in each other arms at the airport.

Eric had no idea of how important a role she was about to play in what would happen next in his life.

PART 2

THE SEARCH FOR THE KEY

CHAPTER 13

Jerusalem,
Israel

By the time Eric arrived in Jerusalem, Israel, it had been the longest day of his life, even though it was still only noon, local time, the next day. Traveling from west to east, the time had changed six hours. He had left from New York in the early evening, and begun a new day during the overnight travel. He was quite tired even though he tried to sleep on the airplane. He had been fortunate that his travel agent was able to connect him at Frankfort Airport, Germany, with a non-stop flight direct to Jerusalem.

The worst part of it all had been the extensive preflight check-in procedures with Air Israel. They were thorough, very thorough, at both New York and Frankfort. All of his bags had been carefully searched, some products disposed of, files and papers looked over, and so on. Next, he had to remove all of his clothes which were immediately screened. And, in an almost totally naked state, his body was looked over for scars and injuries.

Next, he was interviewed by an immigration agent. Their conversation went on for almost an hour. Eric was a tourist, pure and simple. He was asked about his plans and he made it clear that he was there to focus upon the Dead Sea Scrolls, a matter of ongoing public interest. He indicated he would travel to see the caves at Qumran on the west bank of the Dead Sea by way of a tour. And that he would spend time at the Israeli Museum and especially the Shrine of the Book. All of which was true.

And as a typical tourist, he would no doubt visit the 'Old City' to see the shrines located there. They had heard it all many times before and did not find any reason to disbelieve him. He was passed on with no problem. They even called his hotel to confirm his reservation, which was in order. And, they were most curious about the fact he had a six month visa instead of just a simple usual stay of one or two weeks. He explained and they accepted that he was also an academic and that he intended more than a cursory view of the information on the Dead Sea Scrolls. This explanation, along with his credentials and references, all of which had been pre-checked, was sufficient to complete their questioning. He then cashed some traveler's checks for local currency that he would need. And, with all this finished, along with his bags, he walked out and summoned a cab to his motel.

Being dog tired, Eric was thankful that the ride was short, across town, in the heart of Jerusalem, to the Iztik Motel, in the Neve Granot area. Purposely, it was situated within walking distance of many of the cities major sites, and particularly the Israel Museum. He knew that this venue would likely occupy much of his time. After check in, it being mid-afternoon by that time, he laid down and took a short nap, followed by a light dinner, and off to bed for a long nights rest.

Meanwhile, Dr. Alex Howard, once again back in his office for the evening, dressed in a soft luxurious emerald jogging suit, was going through the first 'drop' of information from his agent, Charles. He had found the information on their computers helpful from a background point of view, but even so, it lacked the depth he desired to get to the bottom of what Eric and Janice were really doing. He read it all very quickly. He went on to review their habits from a daily living point of view, and found nothing all that interesting, except that he could tell they were deeply devoted to each other and always 'hot' to be together. He also got a good sense of Janice's qualifications as a Doctor and the depth of her medical knowledge.

Dr. Alex became excited and pleased to find Janice's notes on the search of the medical literature pertaining to the mysterious 'blank' DNA test results. While this effort matched his own and arrived at the same

110

conclusion; namely, the utter lack of any confirmation that this phenomenon had ever been found before. The most important thing this effort showed was that while Eric and Janice may have closed the file at the MRC, they were still actively looking for some explanation for the underlying test results. He quickly realized that the "Closed: Inconclusive Finding" was a ruse and that further action was taking place, likely via Eric. Dr. Alex was certainly happy that he had engaged Charles, his operative.

Next, he turned to the e-mail accounts that had been reported to him. Knowing that Eric was now on his sabbatical leave, he tried the e-mail account, carefully entering the password that was given. Sure enough, the account came right up. Eric had received nothing beyond the file copies he had already read. In that it was getting quite late, he failed to check for messages Eric had sent. But, he went on to check the e-mail account for Janice and was glad that he did. There, on the screen before him, was the last e-mail Eric had sent to her. Alex focused on the three Code words and their strange letters/symbols and was stunned, literally stunned.

"Code; What Code; this is the first I'm hearing of any Code; was my son holding out on me; and what MRI images; they must not have been in the project file, or John would have told me? Where are these images?"

And next, he read the Creed that Eric intended to abide by. Oh yeah, he thought, sure, sure he will. He concluded that Eric was indeed naïve, but dangerously naïve, considering Alex's point of view and interests.

With that, Alex quit for the night, perplexed, tired and troubled, definitely troubled.

CHAPTER 14

Eric awoke the next day to the sounds of the city beginning a new work day. His head was still foggy and his back ached from the motel bed. Quickly, he realized he was in Israel and that it was time to do his thing, begin the search for the key to the Code, that strange Code, which had become his singular 'mission.' He showered and dressed in everyday tourist clothes and went off to breakfast at the Motel café. It wasn't much but at least enough to get him started for the day. He stopped at the front desk to ask about an internet portal that he could use. They advised of an internet café just down the street. With that he left for the Israeli Museum which was only a short walk away.

In no time he was there, and moved immediately on to the Shrine of the Book, the symbolic building complex and international landmark for the Dead Sea Scrolls. Its striking architecture, intended to express spiritual meaning, was quite impressive to Eric. Its white dome is placed to reflect within a surrounding pool of water across from a tall black basalt wall. The dome is in the shape of a lid styled like those that covered the earthen jars within which the scrolls were first discovered in the caves in and around the Qumran wadi in 1947.

The complex is designed to evoke imagery important to the Essenes sect and their beliefs about the war of the "Sons of Light Against the Sons of Darkness," symbolic of good versus evil. The Essenes began their worldly exclusion approximately two-hundred-fifty to three hundred years before the time of Jesus Christ.

In the lobby of the entrance to the Shrine, Eric noted that a tour was leaving in two hours to visit the

Qumran cave area, so he immediately signed up, since the area was only thirteen miles eastward.

Afterward, as he worked his way down the cave like Shrine hallway, Eric was struck with awe by the sense and feeling the passageway provided; it portrayed the setting within which the scrolls were found. The lighting and stone walls included various informative exhibits that were deeply set and outstanding, capturing ones attention with their information. Upon reaching the end of the passageway, he arrived at the circular hall that is the focal point of the exhibit. The ceiling is done in a way that one's attention is immediately drawn to its many sculpted ridges and recessed lighting. From there, ones eye is drawn to the enclosing circular walls and the varying floor levels for exhibits, all of which are encased by beautiful stone and magnificently lighted.

The first archaeological masterpiece that Eric viewed was the Temple Scroll. It received this name because more than half of it relates to the construction of the Temple of Jerusalem. It is by far the longest scroll, with 66 columns of text and measures a little over 26 feet. It was found in Cave 11. It was stunning to view.

Moving on, other exhibits presented parts or portions of various biblical scrolls; but ones attention could not resist being drawn to the center point of the exhibit, being the most prominent display within the Shrine itself, the Great Isaiah Scroll. Upon viewing this breathtaking artifact, one soon learns that it is the only complete book of the Hebrew bible discovered in its entirety. While the Scrolls comprise over 800 documents, with some complete or nearly so, there are many, many fragments, numbering in the thousands. While looking at this exhibit, Eric could not help but look up at various times at what he came to realize was a lid handle affixed to the dome ceiling directly above the Great Isaiah Scroll. It was most interesting in the way it had been done in a tasteful manner.

Even though he could have spent hours studying the Shrine in detail, Eric left, went to the restroom, and was ready for the Qumran tour. He would have plenty of time to return to this place and gain a deeper appreciation for its many displays of ancient history.

As the tour bus worked its way out of Jerusalem, Eric could not miss the dry, arid, stark landscape around and about the route of their travel. Even though his native North Carolina, USA, was warm and quite hot in the summer, it was nothing like this. He could not imagine spending a lifetime in such an environment.

In addition, and again most striking to anything he had ever known, Eric found the contrast between Israeli and Palestinian neighborhoods to be wholly different. On the one hand, the Israeli areas were typical to city and suburban parts of the United States with the styles of housing adjusted for their surroundings. On the other hand, the Palestinian areas were the opposite. Houses were partially built with laundry hung on uncompleted second stories. The houses were spread well apart and quite haphazard, strung out on twisting turning streets, lacking an orderly arrangement. Upon asking why so many houses were only one story, yet obviously prepared for a second

images that you had prepared for the 'blank' DNA snippets, where you found the strange Code. Our Department Director put him off saying that he would look into it, and called me instead because my name was also on the authorizing paperwork. What do you want me to do?"

Eric: "How did he ever learn about this; you and I are the only ones that have any info on these images?"

Janice: "I don't know, but I don't like it--- aren't we trying to keep this all confidential?"

Eric: " Yes, Yes: Lets do this, have the Director tell John that he will have to wait until I return, since they are under my name and control per the paperwork. Under no circumstance is he to release this info to anyone other than you or me. I will need to think further on this and what it means."

Janice: "Ok, I don't think that will be a problem. I'll tell the Director to handle it that way. Anyway, how is it going over there? I miss you already. I want you back. My time is so boring without you."

Eric tried to console her and went on to tell her about his day and coming plans. At that point, they decided to keep it short due to cost reasons, and their conversation ended.

As he lay in bed that night, Eric knew that someone else had put Dr. John Howard up to making the image request. He knew that John did not initiate such things. He wondered who and why as he drifted off to sleep after a long day.

CHAPTER 15

By the time Eric awoke the next day, his mind had already solved the question of how Dr John Howard was 'on' to the MRI images at the hospital. He had related back to the last time he sent a message to Janice on this subject and knew right away that it had been a personal e-mail to her home computer. This meant that somehow, someone had gained access to either his or her e-mail and then put his chief assistant, Dr. John Howard, up to trying to get these images.

It also meant that whoever was doing this now knew about the Code and the three words that had been written in this e-mail. Furthermore, that their attempt at security had been broken and the Discovery of the Code was now known to someone. It was hard to know whether it had been 'hacked' or someone knew their passwords. That left the main questions of 'who' and 'for what reason' for later, but he vowed to get to the bottom of it and not be blindsided again.

Therefore, while on his way to the Israeli Museum, Eric decided to warn Janice of this suspected snooping by using her hospital e-mail. He did this by stopping off at the nearby internet café. It was to be the first of many visits to this small shop.

Eric utilized the institutionalized hospital e-mail address knowing that its security was much better than for their personal computers. He felt that her unique password on the Hospital system would make it safe. Also, since he was there, he sent brief e-mails back to Mr. Johnston and his assistant Dr. John Howard, advising of his location in Israel and how to get in touch with him should the need arise. He had promised to do that and was relieved to have attended to that detail.

In addition, Eric did one other thing that was wholly unusual for him, but nonetheless, something he considered to be a good move under the circumstances. He prepared and posted a letter to a former high school friend that had become an investigator. His name was Justin Avery. Justin had been employed by the F.B.I. for over twenty-five years right out of college. He had taken an early retirement and opened a small office not to far from the complex that housed the Medical Research Center.

Writing to him in confidence, Eric spelled out that he was working on a Discovery that he hoped would be of some major importance and consequence, and that he needed Justin's help due to the irregularity that had taken place resulting from an e-mail he had sent. The e-mail was to have been quite private and confidential; however, it had somehow led to an inquiry by Dr. John Howard for certain documents, the e-mail mentioned. Eric went on to describe the entire matter in some detail.

In the end, Justin was tasked to look into Dr. John Howard and whatever connection(s) that he might find that could explain his snooping. Eric insisted that any reply be directly to him in writing, not e-mail, at his motel, and that Janice was the only other person he was authorized to contact during this investigation on Eric's behalf. Eric enclosed a check for three thousand dollars and sent the letter right away. This entire effort took a while and by the time he was finished it was almost noon; nevertheless, Eric continued on to the Israeli Museum, having lunch on the way.

Upon arriving and making inquiry, he was directed to the Dead Sea Scrolls Information and Study Center (the DSSI&SCenter) donated to the museum by the Dorot Foundation. This underground facility, was quite large and the primary location for scholars and other parties interested in the review and investigation of the actual scrolls. Given their fragility and sheer volume (over 800 documents as well as thousands of fragments) they were, of course, not physically available themselves. The demands over the years since discovery for observation and detailed review had necessitated careful handling by the Israeli Government and preservation in protected vaults.

Special laboratories had been developed and manned by highly competent personnel responsible for their conservation and display. After all, they do provide the oldest copy of the bible still in existence, because they date back as far as 250 B.C.; and they present a time period lasting thru 60 A.D. Without a doubt, they set forth the best insight into Judaism just before and during the life and times of Jesus Christ. Accordingly, the actual viewing of a particular scroll or fragment is severely limited.

Instead, for people like Eric, making an independent investigation for his own reasons and for undisclosed purposes, they are given access to microfiche files of the scrolls, which are highly indexed and accompanied by the necessary readers with photocopies being available. Furthermore, this source is supplemented by an ever expanding and growing digital file version of the same information. This, in turn, is made available in translations in various languages, all done in a very high quality, sophisticated, manner. And this, of course, went to the crux of Eric's mission to Israel, unscrambling the strange Code found in the 'live' patient MRI images.

His prior research had established and he knew that the scrolls themselves were written in three languages: Hebrew, Aramaic and Greek, and not surprisingly, dominated, by Hebrew. However, more important to Eric, his research had found that the scrolls also included many non-biblical parchments and books, in other languages, most of which received minimal disclosure, identification and/or translation. And, just as important, some of these non-biblical documents provided further mystery and challenge, in that they were obviously encrypted in a manner and method in keeping with the times within which they were written.

He carried the 'key' to this entire effort in his back pocket, being a twice folded page of the words of Code that began the three major parts and/or "regions" for patients MRI results. The point being that these words were the *same* for each patient, even though the rest of the words (i.e. the Code) and their placement may be different. As he had done countless times, Eric looked at them again and thought to himself, how am I ever going to do this?

He didn't know for sure, but somehow he was going to make it happen. And then, for no particular reason, he went over to the copy machine and made several copies. Next, he borrowed a pair of scissors, and sat there cutting out each separate letter of each word. Then, he sorted them, setting aside any duplicates, and listed them in a vertical sequence on a blank page, affixing them to the paper. He then made several copies of the list that he could now use in advancing his inquiry. Afterward, thinking about what he had just done, he chuckled to himself. He had always been a spatially oriented person, especially as a child, realizing that old habits do die hard. Then he moved on to the task at hand.

He decided to use this new page in two ways. First, it would allow him to keep his main word page secret in his back pocket; and secondly, it would give him a 'tool' to ask questions of museum personnel and others, on whether they recognized any letter and/or the related language. Even so, this would be something he would not do right away. He was vitally concerned about keeping his 'search' confidential and wanted to try to find a 'match' document on his own. By 'keying in' on the suspected language first, he could control the scope of his inquiry. From his own years in the academic world, he knew how helpful staff and fellow scholars liked to be; proud of their specialized knowledge. And, he knew as well, of the ongoing interest in making any 'advance' on one's own. Perhaps, he thought, he was just being paranoid.

The next thing to happen was a loud bell that rang. This signaled the end of the day at the Study Center and Eric had to leave. Eric was a little peeved at himself; he had not even looked at any part of a scroll or fragment yet. He could not shake a disappointed feeling --- there was so much to be done.

CHAPTER 16

While Eric slept peacefully at his motel that night, back in the United States, in an early evening time zone, Dr. Alex Howard fretted and fumed over the mistake his son had made. He was just plain livid that John had been so stupid and lacking in guile, as to personally ask the hospital for the results of the MRI tests learned about via the intercepted e-mail. He knew that this would alert Eric for sure, and most likely Janice as well, that an unknown third party was deeply interested in the "closed" project that had given rise to the strange Code. Dr. Alex could only hope that nothing would come of it; that Eric would either be so involved with his activities in Israel, or that he would otherwise dismiss it as simple curiosity from perhaps an extra or errant copy of the e-mail to Janice. He viewed Eric to be a naive academic who would let something like this slide and do nothing about what had happened.

In any case, Dr. Alex decided not to give up on trying to get the MRI results referenced in the e-mail, and just as important, to figure out what these strange Code words were in the unknown language. Personally, he had struggled in his own mind as to why he should be so alarmed by the entire matter. However, instinctively, he knew that finding a human language based Code within a part of the body was clearly at odds with all scientific findings and theories relative to evolution. And that, if such a revelation was factually established, it would undermine his life's work and destroy the basis for his "association" and his publishing enterprise. In other words, most aspects of his life would collapse and that would clearly be *unacceptable*.

With this in mind, the next day he met with Charles, his operative. He had hastily arranged the meeting upon learning that Eric was taking a leave of absence and had traveled to Jerusalem, Israel. In addition, even though he had instructed and 'used' his son John to try to obtain the MRI images, he had been careful not to disclose to him his alarm about Eric, the strange Code and the use of an operative behind the scenes. He would try to keep the 'dark' side of his nature hidden from his son and others as long as he could.

During this meeting, Dr. Alex briefed Charles on what had been found through their e-mail snooping activities and that this had all become much more important to him. Dr. Alex told him that Eric was now in

Israel searching for the key to the mysterious Code and that he only had three of its words with no idea of their meaning.

He then authorized and instructed Charles to go to Jerusalem, Israel, to do two things. First, he was to break into Eric's motel room and search for and copy or steal the MRI listings of the strange Code. In his mind, he just had to see for himself what this Code really looked like from the 'tissue' of a living being. This would make it authentic for him and he could stop worrying about whether he was over reacting; or alternatively, making the right moves to protect his interests.

And secondly, to plan, prepare for and be ready to 'take out' Eric if Dr. Alex should give him the signal in any manner, i.e. phone, cable, fax, e-mail, etc.. In case this should go that far, and to further confirm his directive, the sum of one million dollars would be deposited in a Swiss bank account in 'Charles' name.. The signal word that Dr. Alex and Charles agreed upon was '*barbeque.*' Charles would be requested to attend such a function on or before a so called 'drop dead' date. Dr. Alex told him that he did not know if this would be necessary, but wanted to be prepared just in case. With that agreement, their meeting ended and Dr. Alex provided twenty-five thousand dollars 'traveling' money. Charles agreed that he would prepare and travel to Israel except that this would take up to two weeks. Dr. Alex was not pleased with the delay but:

"It would have to be alright. He doubted that much time would make any difference anyway."

When Eric awoke to the new day he was ready and anxious to get back at it, so he did not waste any time returning to the Israeli Museum. Quickly, he went down to the Dead Sea Scrolls Information and Study Center and the huge index and library files. Sitting down a few minutes to compose himself, he focused upon how he would go about finding his way in breaking this strange Code, what his strategy would be. Being a scientist, he would set aside the substantive aspects of the scrolls; namely, looking into religious 'biblical' areas pertaining to the Human Spirit (the Soul). To his way of thinking, this would put aside the 'leap' he had made during his 'epiphany' and would allow the search to focus at a more objective level, being the language.

Next, he was able to spend a few minutes with one of the librarians on how to use the index system. That was followed by a demonstration of how to move and view a microfiche selection on one of the many reader/viewers available. Then, he learned that the scrolls, and the many fragments, are arranged and indexed by the cave where they were discovered. And finally, he was instructed on the numbering sequence within the index system.

The librarian also showed him an example of how the scrolls and fragments for the non-biblical books and information were separated and marked within the index system. Eric naturally paid particular attention to this information as a likely source for the language he was searching. And then, at the end of his time with the librarian, he took the list of letters out of his back pocket that he had prepared the day before and asked whether she recognized that language or any of the letters included. The librarian had no idea of what alphabet they may be from and pointed out that she was not trained in such things. She thought it would be best if he consulted a translator.

With that introduction, Eric actually, and finally, began looking at indexed selections via the viewer/reader. All in all, there were scrolls and fragments from eleven separate caves, with some cave findings being much more extensive than others. In that Eric was not reading anything, he simply searched for a writing that contained letters and/or words that matched the style, shape or any other characteristics consistent with either the letter list or three word page he kept in his back pocket. Consequently, when he brought up a selection on the screen, the review would go quickly and the document would be dismissed if it was recognized as Hebrew, Greek or even occasionally Aramaic.

Eric had learned to readily recognize these languages and knew that they did not contain any of the letters he was looking for. For those rare other documents, Eric would quickly print a photocopy, mark the index reference and take the copy with him to study against his two references at a later time.

For the first day, Eric followed this routine making his selections on a random basis. Other than a few rest breaks, the day went by surprisingly fast. As he walked back to the motel, Eric only had four pages for careful review and study that night. If he hadn't been so tired and mentally rung out, he would have been disappointed. As it was, he was pleased that he had finally started. He knew it would be a struggle to find this 'needle in a haystack.' He would fight against being bored or discouraged. As he had always done, he would work long and hard to find and arrive at the answer. He would not give up. He felt that he was right on how to do this and that he was in the 'right' place to make it happen. He would not accept failure as an option.

CHAPTER 17

The next day Eric was quickly back at the Dead Sea Scrolls Information and Study Center. Last night, when he looked at and compared his selections from the day to his "back pocket" pages he knew that he had found nothing of value. Nonetheless, now that he was back at the Center, Eric decided to try the page reference on a selection and pull up the translated document. He wanted to see what it would show and make available to him.

This introduced him to the digitized version of the microfiche selection he had made, and then in turn, the translation. Immediately, he could see a major improvement in the clarity of the digitized version of the underlying piece of scroll and/or fragment. Additionally, the speed of accepting 'for further study' or rejection of the document improved significantly when viewing the translation. All of this convinced Eric to always use the digitized document version where available, which was facilitated by the index system as well. In a sense, this was a breakthrough that would move along his search in a faster way.

Moreover, when looking at the translated document, there was always a notation in the upper right-hand corner of the language found on the piece of scroll or fragment and the name of the translator. This in itself, eliminated many documents instantly. Eric knew this would be helpful if and when he actually found the writing that included the alphabet letters of the Code or even language that appeared close. Time would tell how all this worked out. He knew intuitively, that if our Creator had included the Code within ones Soul, its roots in 'language' would more than likely have dated back to well before the time of the Dead Sea Scrolls, but may have played some part in the foundation for these historical writings. He shuttered to think that perhaps the Code might not have any basis as a human language. If that were the case his efforts in Israel would be meaningless and the whole inquiry about the Code would no doubt fail. Surely, God did not need humans to create a language to be used internally. Not wanting to go there, Eric stopped letting his mind wander and turned back to the work at hand.

Now that Eric understood the layout and underlying process, he immersed himself in the search one-hundred percent. Throughout the rest of that day, the next day, the day after that, and so on for what was now over three weeks (almost a full month), he worked at making selections and then viewing and distinguishing them. It was tedious, mind numbing and boring work. The kind of thing that would so discourage the average person, they would give up in frustration.

The only relief Eric allowed himself was an occasional visit to the many tourist venues in Jerusalem. This had led him to some of the famous shrines, namely the Church Of The Holy Sepulcher, the Wailing Wall and the nearby Al Aqsa Mosque & Dome of the Rock complex. However, these were only short lived diversions to him. His mind was always on whether he was doing the right thing in the right way to find the key to breaking the Code.

With this picture in mind, Eric moped his way back to his motel to end another long day, lamenting all the dead ends he had encountered. Upon entering his room, Eric was *shocked* at what he found. It was a complete mess. Everything had been pulled apart, thrown on the floor, all drawers of the chest and desk emptied, bed ripped apart, etc., etc.. Even the articles in the bathroom were in total dishevel and destroyed. Nothing was as it should be. He had been burglarized. No doubt about it, **BURGLARIZED**.

The manager was called and he immediately turned around and called the local police. He apologized and apologized. He swore that this kind of thing had never happened before at this motel. He promised to do all he could to help Eric recover from this burglary. He professed that their security was sound, and that they would redouble their efforts for their guest's protection. Housekeeping quickly put his room back together especially because there were no other rooms available at that time. The police forensic team gathered up many of Eric's things and tested them for fingerprints. Meanwhile, Eric was questioned at length as to why someone might be 'interested' in him. It all seemed to Eric to be basic procedure and indeed perfunctory.

He just needed to rest and end this day. It was becoming too much. Why would anyone do this? Was it the Discovery? How could anyone know? And even with the little there was to know, it all had little import unless 'someone' was deeply involved in the same kind of scientific endeavors as him. On the other hand, could it have been as simple as an everyday burglary? Was someone after his traveling money? He doubted it; even he did not know how much he had left and he always carried this money on him.

Bewildered, he just turned in for the day and tried to sleep.

CHAPTER 18

As Eric walked back to 'work' the next day, he could not stop thinking about yesterdays break in to his room at the motel. He knew, of course, that the intruder could not have found anything on what Eric was doing, because he alone carried the two 'key' pages for this within his back pocket. Nothing had been stolen, because there was nothing of any real value in the room to steal. Maybe, it was some petty criminal looking for whatever he could find of value. Even so, he was now, more than ever, pleased that he had engaged a detective back home and he would update Justin Avery on the break in ASAP. No matter what explanation, this event was unsettling to him for he could not reconcile how his potential Discovery, and search for the answer to the Code, could be of value or threatening to anyone, if that was what it was about.

Due to all of this, Eric could not help looking over his shoulder from time to time and from street to street. Sometimes he would pause ten or fifteen minutes, moving behind a corner, watching those who would pass, trying to identify anyone that might be following him. He even bought a digital camera and was ready to snap a picture or stop and ask any likely prospects, why they were following him? It was haunting and Eric wanted to get to the bottom of it. However, at no time, did it dawn on him that he might be in danger. The situation did not seem to be grave enough to warrant such suspicion. Nevertheless, later he would purchase clothing typical to those worn by the Israeli people. This might give him some cover should anyone be following him.

Today, at the study center, Eric was again working on the huge number of scroll fragments found in Cave 4. It was commonly known that this was the most productive of all the Qumran caves. Following his practice during the preceding days and weeks, he randomly selected and reviewed indexed microfiche and digital fragments for the language he was seeking. This process was wearing on him now that it had gone on so long. The way he was doing this search was just plain boring and his patience was faltering. This, plus the break-in at his motel room, as well as the absence of his friends and colleagues and especially Janice, made it hard to concentrate. His mind would easily drift, causing a loss of focus and inattention to detail. It was time to try something different. After all he did not have forever to unravel this Code.

During lunch that day, Eric thought more about the situation. It wasn't hard, so he simply decided to loosen up his approach. He would spend this afternoon in a different way. Instead of focusing on language, he would turn to two key words that could possibly lead him in the right direction if his theory was right. After all, being here in Israel came from his solid belief that the Code was tied into the Human Spirit and/or the Soul.

Drawing back on his memory, he understood that the Human Spirit and the Soul were one and the same. From his Pastor father's Sunday sermons, he knew that under Christian theology they were considered synonymous with each other. He had no idea if this was the same in the Jewish religion. But he would go on anyway, taking comfort that there was at least some metaphysical connection by and between the Holy Spirit and the Human Spirit (the Soul). With that thinking casually in mind, he would have a look for the words Spirit and/or Soul in the index and see where it would take him. The diversion would relieve the boredom that was setting in.

Surprisingly, as he looked and listed references on these key words, their were not as many as one might think. He found about twenty and went on to their microfiche and/or digital pages for review. Most he could tell right away were nothing and he dismissed them immediately. In particular, he spent several hours running down the Essenes thoughts related to duel Spiritualism and their views related to light and dark, good versus evil. From a language point of view this went no where and by the end, substantively, it was unrelated and internally oriented. Another dead end.

Moving on, near the end of his list, he came upon a digital document, originally translated from Hebrew, that mentioned a legend regarding the Soul. Despite the language not being of help, it was well worth looking up. So he did and found and photocopied this single page:

The Cure of the Soul: the Place & the Legend

by: Jacoby, Assistant to the Head Librarian,
Library at Alexandria

most Holy Rabbi: thank you for having confidence in me; asking that I put in words; what is now widely talked; but quietly, at Library; some even say, now, a

Legend; being most humble servant to Head Librarian;
me do not know or judge-for sure; can it be Legend?
years back (maybe 25); in me young time work there;
work on many scrolls, written many world places; maybe
you remember; the great storm; its damage, big; BIG!!
that night, moon went dark, but for little part; next, big
winds dumped much, much sand everywhere; last, huge
wind from sea, with much, much rain; hour and hours-
rain; next day; damage all over; many roofs fall in!

I hurry to Library; outside area crushed; gardens
swamped- torn out; walkways no more there; walls
toppled; huge mess! I enter Library - it seem good;
papers blown about; but not bad; head librarian arrive;
upset and worried; we go about Library quickly;

suddenly; at Great Hall - find - high on wall- new
carving; scrap pieces still on floor; I translate:

The Place of the Cure of the Soul

head librarian cant talk; stammering; shocked; did not
order carving; who did it; why; later, no one know; much
happening; talk, talk; no answers; Osiri ?; Zeus ? Isis ?
talk, talk;, no answers; no action; it stay on and on; still
there.

*me think it **Yahweh:** the night and carving; left*
mystery for all; me no know answer- me guess; answer
inside words; within carving.

your servant; Jacoby;

Eric, did not know what to make of this? What did it mean by the word 'cure?' And, what about the 'place?' Being the Library at Alexandria. He knew from history that it had long, long ago burned down, destroying an incredible number of scrolls by early thinkers and scholars. He read it again and again. His instincts told him to give it more consideration. Connecting the words Cure and Soul with a place, actually the *Place,* he knew to be the pinnacle of ancient learning and thinking. This should tell him something. He would have to think about it himself and look further at it to see if there is anything that might help.

Since it was late in the afternoon, Eric decided to call it a day. He tucked this new page in his back pocket along with the letter list and the three region word list. He wasn't sure if he had or had not made any progress, but still in all, he felt some sense of relief from the 'weight of the world' cares he had earlier that day. Now, for the other task he had set for himself. He would buy new clothes so that he could look like an Israeli and blend in with the crowd. This would make it harder for anyone 'tailing' him to follow his movements. Quietly, he wondered whether he was just getting 'paranoid' or if in fact someone was really there? How to know? Besides, no matter what, it would be helpful to get a couple of new packs of underwear.

Walking briskly, Eric moved down the hill and on too the business district. A department store was nearby and he went in, located the men's department, tried on a few things; bought a nice but modestly priced pair of pants and a couple nondescript shirts, all long sleeved. He also purchased a pullover vest sweater, light weight, but good enough to get him thru cooler mornings. On the way out, thinking ahead, he slipped into a changing room and put on the new clothes. Shoving the other 'clothes' he had been wearing in a shopping bag, he went out the door, down the front street and around the corner, stepping quickly into a small Cafe, the second door on his right.

He sat down by the window and ordered a cup of tea since the waitress was there immediately. All of his attention was fixed out of the window to see if he could spot any person that might be following his movements. He also studied the people across the street. That could also be a possibility.

As he watched, several American looking men went by within the next few minutes, maybe looking about, maybe not, he could not tell for sure. Then, his tea arrived and he took his time drinking it in that it was very hot. It wasn't long before, when he looked up, he could see across the street one of the American looking men that had walked by just after Eric had ducked into the Cafe.

This man was looking about, up and down the street in front of the Cafe. He even went a little further down that side still searching for someone or something. It was hard to tell. Eric carefully looked over the distance at this man. What could he say about him and the way he looked? Immediately, he realized that was a hard question. He wasn't big or small, only normal to a little undersized; he didn't have a beard or mustache, glasses, tattoo's or physical abnormalities. he appeared in all ways normal. But then, for just an instant he saw something small, that may in this situation be meaningful; he had on a pair of high tech jogging-running shoes. They had the big Nike swoosh and some bright blue trim, just enough to stand out. That was all; and he was now gone; who knows where.

Certainly, Eric did not know for sure whether he was on to his 'stalker' or not. At least, he had one possibility. Should he see this man again any where near him, it would confirm 'who' was watching him.

Could it be the man that broke into his room? Could this man be threatening to him? Would he be in danger if he were to confront him? All such thoughts were new and troublesome to Eric. He had never been in a situation anything like this.

CHAPTER 19

That night, back at the motel in his room, Eric turned his attention to the Legend document he had found that day. Although he had no idea whether it would help in his search for the 'key' to the language of the Code, he was intrigued by its content. He accepted his instincts that there may be much to be gained by working thru this Legend about the Soul. Thus, he put the photocopied page on the table in front of him, stared at it a few minutes and began to think about the words and circumstances of the inscription:

"The Place of the Cure of the Soul"

Why would the Soul need a Cure? Could that mean something was lacking within the Soul of humans at that time? Or, alternatively, could that mean an absence of something within the Soul now desired for metaphysical purposes? This might 'fit' with the placement of some type of Code in humans at some point. Who knows whether he was even talking about the same thing? Definitely off the chart thoughts. Was he just twisting things to fit his needs? Perhaps, on the other hand, maybe it was more about the Place than about the Soul. Could it have been a disguised conundrum intended to mysteriously add to the name and reputation of the Library at Alexandria. It would hardly seem so in that its renown, as far as Eric knew, was already reaching exceedingly high levels. Did it really need such an unusual type of distinction? He doubted it. And, what kind of person(s) could have committed such an act on the night of a monumental storm? This made no sense, whatsoever.

Moreover, having the word Cure follow the location, i. e. "the Place", obviously links and suggests that the Library is the remedy or relief needed for the Soul. But, is that so? The Library had already been there, as far as Eric knew, for several generations. And, its breadth and depth in terms of subject matter and language,

144

covered the known world at that time. So why does it all of a sudden have any relevance in connection with the Soul? If something had changed, or now come to prominence at the Library, it was going to be next to impossible for Eric to know, recognizing the Libraries subsequent destruction.

Therefore, as used in this carving (the inscription), which 'Words' (i.e. parts):

SOUL   **CURE**   **PLACE**

are the:

MEANS   **OBJECT**   **SOLUTION**

he should use and follow.

One could see, that these word relationships, could be viewed and argued in differing ways, similar to solving arithmetic equations. Eric supposed that it was intended to be that way. That's why the inscription was a riddle, a puzzle, to be solved. No doubt this was to be a guessing game. Maybe, as the Legend itself suggests, he would find the answer within the Words.

And further, had the passage of time exposed or brought about an answer? This he did not know, but he would check. He would go to the most major library here in Jerusalem tomorrow. If there was an answer it would be referenced in connection with the Library at Alexandria.

That's where he would start. Hopefully it would lead to the break through he was seeking.

In the morning, first thing, Eric talked to the motel manager. He determined that the most respected and major library in the area was at the Hebrew University of Jerusalem. Getting there and back presented a problem because it was located in the Palestinian Territory on the West Bank of Israel. This was somewhat north-east of Jerusalem, probably fifteen to twenty miles beyond his normal daily activities and travel. He would prepare differently today by wearing his new 'Israeli' clothes. And, to fit in even more, he purchased at the gift shop a black scull cap, the same as the Jewish people regularly wore.

And, being determined to give the 'slip' to anyone that may be watching the motel, he had the front desk call a cab for him. It was instructed to pull up to the front door, next to the canvas covered walkway to the curb. When it arrived, Eric quickly moved to the cab holding his head downward, minimizing the possibility of being recognized. As the cab traveled to the University, he often looked back over his shoulder and found no likely vehicles that seemed to be following. It was not long before he was there.

He had the cab weave around until he was in front of the Bloomfield Library building. He quickly entered and moved to the front desk. His focus was on what was still known about the ancient Library of Alexandria. He would use encyclopedias to begin, finding those written in English. This did not turn out to be hard, because their were many, many encyclopedias to choose from.

As the morning and then early afternoon moved on, he had found that the small articles in these volumes tended to repeat themselves. Because the destruction of the Library at Alexandria took place long ago and was universally viewed to be a tragedy for history and knowledge of that time period, there was just not that much to read. These articles made it clear how complete this destruction had been. Little of what was known to have been there actually survived. The grounds were total ruins. There would not be much point in thinking of a side trip to Alexandria.

Fortunately, one article recounted, in its brief description of the Library and its grounds, that a hallway beside the Great hall, had at a very high location, the famous inscription: *"The Place of the Cure of the Soul"*. But, that was all, nothing more except, in traditional literary style a numbered citation. Eric quickly wrote this down and set off for the stacks to find the book named.

Twenty minutes later, trailing after a clerk from the main desk, the book: "Errata From The Study Of The Historical Remnants' Of The Library Of Alexandria" was found, dusty and dirty, as written by an author from England, namely Archibald P. Cox., Esq.. The book was an 1896 edition, with barely 125 pages, of very small print. Sliding into a nearby cubicle, Eric delved into its pages. It went on and on about a laundry list of small incidental subjects still known and previously recorded from annals about the Library.

Eric, in his hast, had failed to note the exact page or pages he was looking for. Not without some difficulty, he finally found the subject of the 'inscription'. It was stated exactly as Eric knew the Words to be (now by heart). The book mostly centered upon the 'inscription' location, implying but not knowing for sure, that it was an unplanned item. It was described and thought of as an oddity, a curiosity. No mention was made of any Legend existing. It did not even venture a guess as to the date or purpose for its creation. At the end, it stated that one of the most surprising things about the 'inscription' was that it was written in the Coptic language. It went on that this was not the language of the times. That was the Demonic language, descended from the Hieratic, and formerly Hieroglyphic language.

By now, Eric was sensitive to any mention of language. This was what the Code was all about. At first he read on, making notes as he went. Moments later, the gravity of what he just read struck him. His hand instantly went to his back pocket and out came the photocopied Legend page he had found yesterday. With the intensity of a laser, his eyes focused on the words by Jacoby: *"I translate:"* **_The Place of the Cure of the Soul_**. Eric knew he had failed to see, nor pick up on this subtle but key point previously.

The Words for the carving were a translation. A translation-- with no language mentioned. How could I have missed that? Like everyone else, I thought only of the riddle. I must have had blinders on.

And, just as important, he now knew that Jacoby was smarter than might appear from the crude writing of the Legend. He was no doubt right:

*"me think it **Yahweh:** the night and carving; left mystery for all; me no know answer- me guess; answer inside words; within carving!"*

Eric realized that Jacoby had spent his whole life at the Library. He would have looked at the inscription everyday, most likely more than once, and had years to think about it in his mind. Because of the work he did for the head librarian, he was use to seeing scrolls from all over the world. Due to his prior contact and association with different languages, which probably included Coptic, he was not all that taken by seeing Coptic used in the carving. He just did what he was trained to do and read it. Like everyone else, he thought mainly about the words. When, after that failed for years and years, he instinctively knew, that the answer must be 'within' the words, but still could not figure out what they meant. He did the best he could, he made a record of the Legend so that it would live on and perhaps be solved. It appeared to Eric that instead, it had all been forgotten. Simply, left as a remnant of history.

Eric looked at his watch. It was now almost five o'clock P.M. and he should be getting back, the Library closing bell had rung. Furthermore, he thought, he did not know whether he had found something important or not. He just knew that the unique inscription had originally been written in the Coptic language, a language entirely unfamiliar to him. He would now look into it and see if there was anything that related to the strange Code he was pursuing.

With the help of the Library front desk, Eric caught a cab back to the motel and entered quickly. Still anxious about being followed, he went in the side dining room and looked out towards the front for the man he had focused on yesterday afternoon. He studied across the street, up and down, looking closely at the corners of store fronts and at doorways to other buildings on the street. He was about to give up when he spotted some slight movement by a figure a step back in the shadow of the doorway to an apartment building.

At first he thought it was nothing. The man, a small man, moved about a little in a way that appeared as if he was trying to shake off boredom and inactivity. Eric looked closer. And, there he was. The largely non-descript man but for the same Nike running shoes with the bright blue trim. Eric was sure it was him. Now, he knew for sure that he was being followed by this man. The question now became, what if anything, he would do about it? He had no idea, but he would come up with something.

An hour and a half later, in keeping with his usual habits, Eric left the motel and walked down the street to the internet cafe he had been using. Turning to business first, he checked his e-mail. A couple of short memo's from work, related to ongoing grant projects, were there and he easily answered them and then signed off. Next, he called Janice, longing to hear her voice again. They shared tender and loving moments and how much they missed each other. By the end, she wanted to know how much longer he thought he would be "over there". Eric said: "he didn't know; although, he had a promising lead and hoped that it would work out."

When the call ended Eric had tears in his eyes. He was so lonely. Walking over to the window, he looked out and once again he saw the man that was following him. This, being the third time he had seen him, now made the man much easier to find. Allowing for the frame of mind he was now feeling, he merely accepted it, left the cafe and walked a short distance down the street to the deli-diner place he had been having his evening meals. He would face all of these things again tomorrow. Tonight, he was plain tired and overwrought with this whole business. Enough, enough, for today.

CHAPTER 20

    This new day arrived with clear sky's, bright and sunny, and Eric was feeling good and walking as usual to the Shrine of the Book. For the moment, he was not thinking about being 'followed.' He intended to run to ground the lead he had from yesterday on the Legend page. It had been startling to find that the inscription: *The Place of the Cure of the Soul,* was in a language that was unusual for even those times. He didn't know if Coptic, now an ancient language, was the same as that used in the Code, but he intended to find out today. At the Shrine, he would be able to obtain the information on the Coptic language that he needed.

Upon approaching, he noticed a lack of activity compared to that usually present at the Shrine on his many prior visits. When he walked up, he found it was closed, -- - closed, for the Sabbath. He should have realized that it was Saturday. How could he be so stupid --- he should have known? He was just not thinking straight. Now he would have to figure out what to do. With that, he turned left and kept walking. He was chagrined, irked at himself, displeased with this mistake. Made even worse by his desire; no his need, to find if Coptic was the language he was after. It was a terrible mistake.

Feeling bad and angry with himself, he kept on walking, walking. He was moving somewhat northeast, not paying much attention. About an hour later, now calmed down and looking about, he was at Herzl Blvd.. Moments later, he found the complex that is the Holocaust Museum. And of all things, it was open on this Sabbath with people coming and going. Eric debated with himself whether he should or would take in any of this tourist site. Especially after the bad start this day had taken.

Hesitantly, he entered the separate Children's Memorial off to the side. Viewing this underground cavern became an incredibly unique experience for him.

Points of light would gradually appear and then recede into space. Names were heard, images came and went, all seemingly part of infinity, in the dark and somber space. This was a touching and tender time for him, sad and melancholy, yet an uplifting place of respect and praise for the memory of these lost children. All in all, a memory that would be with him for a long time.

Afterward, the walk continued in a rather aimless way. It wasn't the same as his usual 'Church of the Walking Feet'; this was an urban setting in a foreign country. Still, Eric enjoyed the walking. People watching could be as much fun as being in the park by the lake. Even with it being a Saturday, the people, cars and buses were all quite busy. There was hustle and bustle everywhere, all of this was increasing the further he moved down Rupin Street. He was coming back into the business district. Venders had small outside covered stands showing their wares 'bazaar' style. The Synagogues had finished services for the day and spirits were high.

At the intersection with Ramban Street, Eric paused, and looked across. Once again, the man following him was there, lurking inside the doorway of a shop, still wearing the Nike shoes with the bright Blue swoosh.. He didn't know for sure, not having looked, but guessed that he had been followed all morning. Eric was no longer surprised. He pretty much assumed that 'his shadow' would be were he went.

The greater question was: What to do about it? Confront him? Was it time to do that? No, what would that prove? Probably nothing; No, Eric wanted to know what was behind all this? Who and why? He would have his investigator try to get to the bottom of it. He would try for a picture of this man. See, if he could be identified. That might lead to who he was working for. That would help. Maybe.

Moving down Ramban Street, Eric suddenly, turned left onto King George Blvd.. And then, instantly he crossed to the other side, stepping deep into the doorway of a store. He judged, that from his prior practice, the man following him would be on that side shortly, positioning himself to continue following Eric. Quickly, Eric prepared his digital camera to take the mans picture. He was ready.

Moments later, happening as planned, the man was there, right in front of Eric. The man had stopped for some reason; he was very close and studying across the street where Eric should have been. Eric snapped one quick picture and knew immediately, that it was no good, the man had been looking away. Eric wanted a side shot at least.

Suddenly, who knows for what reason, the man turned his head around, looking directly at Eric. *A moment of truth--he was being revealed, exposed.*

By way of reflex, Eric snapped twice, taking two straight on pictures of the man. It ran through Eric's mind at that moment, that the man would turn and run. But this did not happen.

Instead, this man came straight at Eric; he lunged; grabbed the camera from Eric and pulled it toward him in a hard way; but, it slipped out of his hands, due to the attached strap around Eric's head.

Desperate fear was in the man's eyes; he became menacing, agitated, swearing incoherently at Eric; he struck Eric's face full on, with a right hand fist, knocking him to the floor of this store vestibule. He reached down to pull the camera strap from around Eric's head.

Before he could do that, out of nowhere, the hand of a large uniformed guard for this department store, grabbed the man's arm and shoved him back, away from Eric. The man appeared stunned to have been stopped before he could grab the camera.

People were now gathering about; the man sensed that it would be useless to attempt any further acts against Eric; he turned and ran away as quick as he could go; he didn't want to have to explain to anyone who he was or why he attacked Eric.

Eric got up, dusted himself off, rubbed his cheek, reached out and thanked the guard for stopping this man. He was quite shaken. He had never been attacked in such a sudden manner. He knew that he would have lost the camera and the pictures in the scuffle had the guard not intervened. Without delay, he used his handkerchief to wipe his jaw and then take the camera from his neck. He had enough presence of mind to place the camera in his pocket with the handkerchief around it.

By then, the crowd had disbursed, but a police officer had arrived summoned by the store guard. In turn, the officer decided to make out a report as he was required to do because of the physical assault in a public place. He filled out his form, asking questions and writing down the particulars for Eric as well as the guard. Both Eric and the guard received a copy. The process took about an hour and it was the end of the afternoon by the time it was all over. In the end, Eric took a cab back to the motel. He was 'done' with his walk for this day.

Later that evening, back at the table in his room, Eric prepared a letter and package to Justin Avery, the friend and investigator he had hired. He had promised himself after the break-in that he would update Justin about it. Eric described what had happened and his suspicion that someone was following him. He went on about spotting this man three times and how difficult it was to describe him because of his unremarkable appearance. He didn't mention the Nike shoes with the striking blue swoosh thinking this to be too small and petty an item to center upon.

Then Eric went on to today's encounter and the attack that took place. He described how it all happened and that he was enclosing the camera in the package. He indicated that he thought there would be two good pictures of the man on the memory card plus the man's fingerprints where he had grabbed the camera. It was stated that the camera was still wrapped in the handkerchief and that it had not been removed since the attack. At the same time, Eric included a set of his fingerprints, that he had made that evening with some ink and paper. He volunteered that they would be helpful for comparison purposes.

In closing, Eric asked that Justin use the pictures and fingerprints to try to identify this man and why he was following him. He was also anxious to have any follow-up on his earlier letter. Thanking Justin, he added that he would send more money if and when needed. Eric packaged it all up and took this to the front desk, arranging and paying for its mailing. It would go out the next morning.

Eric had thought about asking if Justin thought he might be in serious danger. However he dismissed actually doing this, not wanting to appear a whining wimp. And, at the same time, he decided not to tell Janice of the incident and assault. She had become worried enough as the result of the Dr. John Howard inquiry and there was no need to upset her further.

Had he known of all that was about to happen to him, he would have done more. He would have packed up and left.

CHAPTER 21

Today marked the beginning of a new week in Israel and Eric was hopeful that he was close to the break through on the 'key' to the Code he searched to find. He would go back to the Shrine of the Book. He was confident that their expertise in language could tell him if 'Coptic' was indeed the language of the letters on his list. His spirit was running high. His intuition told him that he was close --- that this might be it.

After what had happened yesterday, taking pictures of the little man following him and the subsequent rush and assault, he was not going to take further chances today by walking. He had the front desk call a cab as he had done previously. Wearing the 'local' clothes he had purchased, he moved promptly into the cab and departed for the Shrine. Within a few minutes, he walked inside ready to move ahead. Although planning to seek help, he would only show the list of letters (i.e. characters) to see if they were indeed 'Coptic'.

By this point, Eric had become a 'regular' at the Shrine, by researching there for a little over a month. The staff now recognized him to have a serious interest in some aspect of the Dead Sea Scrolls. Hence, when he walked up to the librarian, the welcome was friendly and cooperative. After these pleasantries', Eric said:

"I need to talk one of your translators familiar with the 'Coptic' language."

The man smiled, pleased to speak with Eric again, and said:

"I know just the man for you. His name is Yves Neiberg. Let me try his number; see if he is in today;"

He picked up the phone, dialed a number, and said:

"Yves, I have a fellow scholar up here that wants to talk to you;"

Eric, while knowing this librarian briefly was stunned at his exceptionally friendly and helpful attitude. Even more surprising, Eric was then told to come right down to see Yves.

He was placed on a restricted elevator and descended two floors.

When the door opened, a huge room came into view that contained many, many offices. Eric was immediately greeted by a man who introduced himself as Yves Neiberg. He was of medium height, rather portly, wearing glasses and from his manner and expressions, one could tell that he was quite jovial. Eric started to apologize for barging in on him in such an unexpected way, only to be told, not to worry about it, they seldom got visitors down there and that he was more than happy to talk with him. Clearly, being a translator was a lonely solitary type of work with third party interruptions being welcomed rather than avoided.

It also turned out that Yves was a department head within the Translation group; but it was not clear to Eric, how high he was in the organization. Eric gave him his card and his letter of introduction, disclosing his status at the Medical Research Center back home in the United States. Recognizing his institutional status, Yves made it clear that Eric was quite welcome in coming to see him. However, he was at a loss to understand how Dead Sea Scroll translations could be helpful to a geneticist such as Eric.

Eric explained that his inquiry was not "official", but at the same time not entirely "unofficial", in that the research at the Shrine came about as the result of a discontinued project.

With the introductions now being complete, Yves asked:

"How may I be of service Dr. Rhodes?"

Eric described having found an ancillary document in the Cave 4 fragments, even older than the Dead Sea Scrolls themselves. He went on that it pertained to a subject matter of interest to him, namely the Soul, written in Hebrew to the author's rabbi and for some reason had come into the possession of the Essenes. He stated the title as: *The Cure of the Soul: the Place & the Legend* Eric followed by indicating that he had subsequently learned that an important part of the story indicated the legend inscription was originally written in Coptic. He had some letters from the writing he was working upon and wanted to know if they were in fact 'Coptic'?

Yves smiled and answered:

" I wish I could tell you that I was familiar with the document to which you make
reference. However, there are so many, it is impossible to remember," lifting his hands as part of his expression.

"Remember, that here, we live at the cradle of civilization. This part of the world, as you know, goes way back into antiquity. Coptic, is a very old and ancient language, with roots going as far back as the Greeks and Phoenicians. It became especially prominent with the Egyptians in the new era after Christ, and lasted for hundreds of years. Coptic also has deep religious connotations, being a part of two orders that exist to this day.

That it would appear in some way within the Dead Sea Scrolls is not in itself remarkable. Most likely, the fragment you selected referred to some ancient event or thing;

Eric answered: "Yes, yes; that's exactly the case here."

With that, Eric showed him the letter list from his back pocket.

This was no trouble for Yves:

"Yes, yes; these are Coptic letters or script; However, I must tell you that they are Coded. In ancient times, just as in our time, there was often a need for secrecy. So it happened that a simple coding method was often followed. It was minimal but effective, in that few people then could read or write one language let alone multiple languages. They would simply take a letter of the language, turn it upside down and then flip it backwards; putting these steps together gives you a coded word. Very few people could make out the word let alone what was being said."

Hearing that, Eric's face beamed with a broad smile and he was almost overcome with joy; Yves, sensing Eric's delight, said:

"If it would help, you can have a copy of the Coptic alphabetic chart we use here at the center. It lists each character or letter of script, and the equivalent English letter for conversion or translation purposes. We have them here in six other languages but I doubt that would be of interest to you."

Eric: "Yes, yes, the English one would be very helpful – I would greatly appreciate having that chart; I do not need the same for other languages right now."

With that, Yves handed Eric a copy of the chart offered and said:

"Now, Eric, you know where I am, as do most employees here at the Shrine; do not hesitate in the least to come here and talk to me; heavens knows that everyone else does. I try to be of help to all."

And with that closing, a huge smile crossed Yves face, and for the briefest of moments, Eric thought he saw a twinkle in Yves eyes. Seldom had Eric met such a warm personality and for some reason he felt especially touched as he left.

Shortly after meeting with Yves, Eric left the Shrine at the Israel Museum, taking a cab back to the motel. Avoiding another encounter with the agent weighted heavily on Eric's mind. He didn't want that to happen; perhaps this man would try for the camera once again. Consequently, he clutched the Coptic conversion chart in his hand and rushed past the front desk to his room and to begin the translation work that lay ahead.

Meanwhile, outside across the street, lurking in another doorway, stood 'Charles' the operative for Dr. Alex. Internally, he was still seething with anger over having been photographed of all things by his target, Eric, a bumbling academic. And, if that were not bad enough, he guessed that he probably left 'prints' on the camera in his failed attempt to take it from him. For a secret 'spy' such as himself, always trying to be unnoticeable and nondescript, he was kicking himself for having failed so miserably.

How could he have done that? Already, he had decided that this was something he could never mention to his employer, Dr. Alex. And to top it off, his target was now taking precautions, using cabs to avoid being followed and further possible confrontations. Maybe his target was not as dumb as he thought. He wanted that camera back from Eric in the worst way and would act at the first opportunity to take it from him. More than ever now, he hoped to get the word 'barbeque' from his boss. This would be what he needed to 'right' the situation. He was ready.

CHAPTER 22

That afternoon-evening was to be one of the most inspirational and outstanding times of Eric's life. It didn't start out that way, and in fact it was simply a quiet and alone period. Eric began by spreading out both 'back' pocket pages on his work table in the motel room. Next, he got out the 'chart' Yves had given him, listing the Coptic alphabet characters in lower case letters and as capitalized. Right beside them, in proper juxtaposition, were the alphabet characters in English letters, the same alphabet he had learned as a child.

The challenge was straightforward: take the Coded letter(s) within the three words of the MRI line headings, convert them back to Coptic alphabet characters without the code changes (upside down and backwards), and then find the English equivalent and write it down. This would result in a word which should give much insight into the mysterious lab Discovery. Sounded easy to him, but how to get at it; there were various steps involved; he knew that he needed a 'method'.

With that, he remembered the KISS principle --- keep it simple, stupid. And, that's exactly what Eric did. He took a plain single piece of paper and marked, on both sides in the same position in the same way, the first character of the first word in the MRI line headings. Next, he simply turned the paper upside down. And then, he just turned the paper over, to its other side. With that exercise, he knew he had reversed the coding steps Yves had described that the ancients followed; and there before him was the Coptic alphabet character of the subject word. It was then simple to find it on the Coptic chart and look beside it to determine the appropriate English letter. In this case, the letter was 'm'. Eric had done it and he knew it. He had broken the strange Code and he would have the 'words' before the evening was finished.

Carefully, Eric then marked the letter sheet with notations that he could use at anytime to reference this page, including the letter found. He sat back and savored the moment, smiling, excited and overwhelmed with these simple acts. He couldn't wait to decipher all three words.

With that, Eric prepared separate pages for each and every letter that remained. This totaled twenty more Coptic characters. However, there were some duplications of characters that made the job easier. He just marked a character to be a duplicate when that happened and entered the letter and made the necessary reference notations. The whole process went smoothly and Eric had the translations finished for two of the words by eight-thirty P.M..

There, before his eyes, were two of the three words, consistently found in the MRI readings for the 'live' samples for patients tested. These words and the underlying strange Code had become Eric's obsession. And now, he had most of the answer, the two words were:

morals and intellect. He would have the third word soon. But he was very excited.

Afterward, he knew he would have to face the issue of whether he had been right in theorizing that these Code regions could summarize the Human Spirit (the Soul) of an individual. Eric knew from the Code layout within the sample's, that these words likely represented broad categorizations for the rest of the content, but could they alone be complete enough to set forth something so central and meaningful for every human being? That was something he would have to think about and ponder as time went by and he completed this final word and translated the lengthy Code samples at home.

For right now, it was good enough, to say 'yes'; and he just was so excited that he could not contain himself. Without thinking about the intrigue going on, he telephoned Janice, his lovee that he missed so much. Her phone at the office rang and rang, but there was no pick up. He realized that she was likely deeply involved with a patient or some Hospital matter. Next, he called her at home, but no one answered there and he got her message machine. Eric distinctly disliked talking to these recorders so he kept his message short:

" Janice, I found it, I found it --- I have broken the Code --- it's simple --- we are right on track with our theory --- will be back soon --- I love you, I love you, bye for now. Eric."

Eric was shaking when he was done. He was beside himself. He knew he wanted to get out of

Jerusalem and back home. Back home. Back in the arms of Janice --- the rest would have to work out.

Knowing that he was too keyed up to try to sleep, Eric started to take steps toward going home. He bundled up all of the papers he had worked with that night, wrote a quick loving note to Janice, telling her to keep these pages safe and confidential, and that he would go over them with her when he got home.

With that, Eric hurried down to the front desk and made the arrangements for DHL Express to transport the large envelope he had just prepared for Janice. He put the cost of this package on his bill for the motel room. Also, at that time, he gave notice that he would be leaving within a few days; actually, just as soon as he could make the arrangements to return home. The manager at the front desk took care of the DHL Express package, and noted that Eric would be leaving soon.

Having a guest that had been burglarized was embarrassing to their management and security and it would be nice to end this matter as soon as possible. The manager smiled with relief as Eric left to return to his room.

Upon return, Eric was intent on finishing the last of the three region Code words before turning in for the night. He went back to work feeling jubilant with the progress he had made. Following the same practice as before, the next letter turned out to be a 'v'. And the next was an 'a'.

And, as he reached out to mark it down, the focus of his eyes evaporated to 'spots', his mind 'disconnected,' he lost all strength and his head dropped downward making a thud on the table. He passed out! He totally lost consciousness! His head and body were slumped on the table, inert. He was to remain that way the rest of the night.

Meanwhile, back in the United States, Dr. Alex Howard intercepted and heard the latest telephone message from Eric to Janice almost immediately. Certainly, it was before even Janice would have listened to the message herself. She had not arrived home yet due to some emergency surgery at the hospital.

After listening to it twice, Dr Alex almost dropped off his chair. It was the message he had hoped never to hear. The very thing he feared most. He wanted Eric to fail at finding an answer to the strange words for the Code found in the MRI listings.

And just as much, that he would have been successful by now in obtaining a copy of these MRI images, before having to make anymore 'big' decisions. But all of that, it was clear, had now failed. It was too late.

Eric was coming back and he conceded that it would be extremely difficult to stop him from making his project public. If only he was sure of what had truly been Discovered, he could more fully judge the potential impact it would have on him, his life's work and especially his publishing enterprise.

However, he reasoned that he knew enough, and that Eric must be stopped or he would face a coming disaster. So, Dr. Alex decided to act now rather than bear the future consequences. After all, he had a man in place and even though it would be expensive, he would do it to be 'safe'.

Dr. Alex knew that it was the middle of the night in Israel but called 'Charles' anyway. This had become an emergency and he was paying plenty for this privilege. He had prepared for this type of moment by purchasing a prepaid disposable cell phone.

There way no way it could be traced because there was no registered owner.

"Hello 'Charles', sorry to disturb you at this hour." Dr. Alex said.

Charles: "OH, HUH, I'm glad you called anyway."

Dr. Alex: "OH, why is that?"

"Think I was spotted today, when he left the 'pit'. Probably suspicious following my earlier visit, you know." Charles said.

Dr. Alex: "Well, that doesn't matter much now; overall conditions changed greatly this evening. Anyway, I was calling you with an invitation. You must come to my 'barbeque', soon, real soon. Bye for now. I must go."

In case Charles was secretly taping it, he would be ambiguous. Dr. Alex thought he had done well.

Charles smiled, as he removed the recorder from the phone, quite pleased with this brief conversation.

He knew Eric's daily habits in detail. As with most of his 'subjects', Eric followed the same steps and practices each day. He had already figured out Eric's most vulnerable points and times. In the morning, he would settle on how to deliver the final touch to Eric's life. After, of course, confirming with his Swiss Bank, the arrival of the one million dollar payment. Then, he would discreetly cross over the border into Egypt and be on his way back to America, the land of opportunity and 'sudden wealth,' especially for him.

CHAPTER 23

The next day, about 10:00 am., the maid for the motel let herself into Eric's room, after knocking in the usual manner. The window blinds were still drawn and it was dark, unlike the way she normally found the room for this ongoing guest. Coming around the corner, past the bathroom, she found Eric slumped over at the table. A few papers were all about him, making it clear that he had been working and not gone to bed that night.

At first, she was greatly startled, immediately thinking that he might be sleeping despite the unusual and uncomfortable position. She looked at his face, turning on a light to see better. Even though he was breathing lightly, his skin was almost white and he was not becoming aroused or showing any signs of coming awake. With that, she became alarmed and quickly called the front desk for the manager to come, "something is wrong with Dr. Rhodes!"

Moments later, this manager entered the room; an emergency call was placed to the local version of the American 911; and a paramedic team promptly arrived. They examined Eric right away and decided to take him to the hospital on Mount Scopus, their home base, near the Hebrew University. The motel manager went along

174

knowing that some personal follow-up would be needed. He gathered together the personal information he had on Eric. He made sure he had Eric's wallet, trusting that hospital cards would be there and the name of whomever he should call for medical purposes.

Outside, a small group of people had been attracted by the van carrying the paramedic team. They could see the patient being carried from the motel and placed in the van for transport to the Hospital. Off to the side, 'Charles' was intently watching all the commotion. When he saw the patient being carried out, he was greatly surprised that it was Eric. 'Charles' knew for sure that he had not taken one step last night to harm Eric despite having been told to take action.

And, before coming to the motel, indeed, he had checked and found the one million dollar bank transfer had been made to him. Immediately, he made the transfer of this money to his account in Baltimore, Maryland. It was time to go. He didn't want to be around should the police discover in Eric's room the camera with his picture and 'prints'. Not wasting any time, and knowing that he had left nothing that could identify him in his prepaid hotel room, 'Charles' drove to the airport, turned in his rental car, paying cash, and left. This was made easy by 'borrowing' a car from long term parking area and driving south to a town just over the border north of Egypt. There he hired a 'jitney', paying plenty, taking him to the airport in Cairo. The rest was easy.

Upon arrival at the Hospital, the team quickly moved Eric into a room in the Emergency Department, where the first of a number of doctors took a look at him. He confirmed all the vital signs that the paramedics had found, opened his eyelids and looked deep into each one, had nurses take blood samples, placed him on an assisted breathing machine, added intervenes feeding of glucose and tried to arouse him in a gentle way. Nothing happened – Eric was there (alive) but not responding to any stimulation. The doctor then told the paramedics to leave; he was admitting Eric to the Hospital as a patient. Then, the doctor, summoned other colleagues to have a look at him. Three hours went by before a Doctor Jaffer, came out to talk to the motel manager.

Dr, Jaffer: "Sorry to keep you waiting so long, but your Mr. Rhodes has kept us busy working on his condition."

Motel Manager: "How is he? What has happened to him?"

Dr. Jaffer: "Well, he is in a 'coma.' But, right now, we don't know how or why. Its all rather strange. We have checked his stomach contents and found little there, his body fluids, i.e. blood, urine, etc. even waste, and there is nothing unusual. We have decided to stabilize him as best as we can and hope he snaps out of it. Or, he may die, we just don't know for sure."

Motel Manager: "Should I notify the police, his room was burglarized a few days ago. Was there any signs of foul play?"

Dr. Jaffer: "That is something I didn't know. However, there were no signs to indicate an attempt to take his life, such as poison, or any physical injuries or needle marks. If there was any foul play, the means and method are not apparent."

Motel Manager: "Thank you, Doctor. I'll notify his folks back home; do not be surprised if you receive a call in that connection. We will stay in touch --- call if his condition changes --- we will see that your payment department gets the medical insurance info that it needs."

Once back to the motel, the Manager did two things to follow up on his time at the hospital and the situation with Eric. He immediately placed a call to the lead detective investigating the burglary to Eric's room. Within Israel, it is not a good idea to keep things such as had happened to Eric from the police. The officer was pleased to have received this prompt report and said he would be following up with him soon. He was first going to the hospital to talk to the doctor(s).

Next, the manager reviewed Eric's sign in and room file information page to determine who to notify in America of these sudden happenings. From this search, he found Eric's most frequent contact telephone number. Eric had not bothered to mark his registration card with any 'next-of-kin' designation. Picking up the telephone, the manager dialed this recurring number, calling the U.S.A., and immediately hearing "Dr. Westphal speaking." The manager, after introducing himself, asked if he was speaking to a relative or the wife of Dr. Eric Rhodes? Slowly, Janice answered that she was his finance and asked why he was calling?

The manager nervously answered: "Maam, I am very sorry to be calling to tell you that something has happened to him and that he is in our local Hospital, unconscious, and in a coma ....
.....................................!!.

CHAPTER 24

After getting over the sudden shock of learning that Eric was in the Hospital in Israel, Janice's mind raced into overdrive. She immediately called Dr. Jaffer in Israel to try to understand Eric's condition and prospects. After several long hours, Dr. Jeffer called back and they talked.

Janice explained her relationship to Eric, that she was an experienced neurosurgeon, her position at the Hospital's Department of Neurology, and that she was ready and willing to do all things necessary on Eric's behalf. At that point, it was clear that she was medically well beyond the training, depth and experience of Dr. Jaffer. Rather than go on, he made arrangements with for her to talk to their head of neurology who would call her back and go beyond the questions he did not feel comfortable in answering.

After another hour, a Dr. Sibowitz called introducing himself as the head of the Hebrew University Hospital Department of Neurology. He and Janice talked at length about Eric's condition. He went over the tests that had already been run and those that were planned in the next couple of days. The whole matter was an unusual case, something not ordinarily seen and he was perplexed that a more objective diagnosis was not available. Nonetheless, Eric was stable, his vital signs steady, no trauma's were found and there were no signs of any injections or medications within his body. Eric was in a *coma!* There was no prognosis available because the nature and cause of the *coma* could not be determined at the moment.

Janice asked him if it would help if she would come over there or if their was any thing that he felt she should do? Dr. Sibowitz paused a little and then reacted with the comment that:

"Its hard to be sure of anything in such a case, but it is possible that seeing a loved one, especially his fiancée, might snap him out of it. It's hard to tell; and it

180

may do no good at all. But, in the end, someone from his family, is going to have to deal with this situation."

"Alright, alright, that can only be me; he has no one else. And, I want to come anyway. I will call you back tomorrow and let you know how I am doing on making the necessary arrangements."

And Janice ended the call and started on preparing to leave. From working in the hospital so long, she was vaguely aware that there was a way that patients were able to be transported, even internationally, if the person was in a stable condition. With a few phone calls she found the person in the Human Resource Department that knew how to arrange such special treatment. They met, talked at length, and settled on beginning preparations to make a transfer of Eric. It helped that Eric was so well known within the hospital as well as an employee of the Medical Research Center. And, financially, there was even some in-house financial coverage for him, but it would still cost Janice a large sum personally, if it came to actually making this move. She then called Eric's boss, Dr. Johnston and brought him up to date on Eric's condition and the points she knew about such things. He was thankful for her call and promised to keep the in house knowledge of this to a minimum.

At the same time, Janice was pushing her travel agent hard to make airline reservations and obtain a visa for a quick trip to Israel. It helped immensely that she was a Doctor, that the purpose of the trip was a medical emergency, and that the Doctors in Israel could and did confirm all of this.

When Janice arrived home that evening, tired and overwrought with the news and events of the day, she routinely pressed the message button on her telephone recorder. Needless to say, she was amazed to hear the voice of Eric, at the end of his day in Israel, telling her of his *break through* in translating the Code. She listened to the message at least five times and then sat there wondering, in her mind, if this had in any way caused or contributed to the fact that he was now in a *coma*. She could not believe this to be possible, but there was no way to be sure one way or another. The human mind has been known to react in strange and mysterious ways.

With that she took a long hot bath and went to bed exhausted. Janice slept soundly until about three-thirty or four a.m., when she awakened thinking of the Eric's circumstances and her preparations to leave. After that she only slept fitfully the rest of the night, even oversleeping in the morning. She was awakened suddenly at eight-thirty a.m. by a delivery from DHS, the international express carrier. An unexpected package from Eric had arrived.

In her less than clear state, wearing only her nightgown, she signed for it, and sat at the breakfast table drinking a stale cup of coffee, opening the envelope. Reading Eric's brief note, she realized what she had in her hands --- the translation of the two Coded words, always alike, from the head of the regions for each MRI listing for the live patient test samples. She then went through each page trying to understand what Eric had done to arrive at a single letter and his referenced notations. This was confusing, although when finished, she found the last page and the two words:

morals and intellect;

And with that, she knew right away what Eric meant when he said that:

"we are right on track with our theory."

It was true, then --- the Code did carry content from the Human Spirit (the Soul) --- a Discovery of immense importance and meaning. Reading Eric's note again, she settled on his request that she keep this info confidential. She would do that right away --- she would place it in her safe deposit box on the way to the Hospital. And, she did just that, proud of her lover and the threshold they were upon.

Back in her office, she received word from the travel agent that she would be leaving mid-afternoon the next day. She would fly to New York and then on to Israel and Jerusalem. Everything was greatly accelerated by the medical nature and emergency of the trip. The hospital in Jerusalem had certified to the Israeli government all the particulars and Janice was approved to go. Meanwhile, she had been working through hospitals channels and had received an approved leave. As if there would be any question when it concerned one of their own being in jeopardy. The word had spread like wildfire that Dr. Eric Rhodes, Project Director at the MRC, was in a *coma* at a hospital in Israel.

In his office at the MRC, Dr. John Howard made sure, right away, that his father, Dr. Alex, knew of this development. Smiling, upon learning of this news, Dr. Alex, immediately sent an e-mail to 'Charles':

"Nice Work, and so Quick!".

Janice left the following day to *save* Eric!

Would she be in time? Would she be able to bring him back 'physically' from Israel?

And more importantly, would he ever *come back* from the *coma* alive? Or alternatively, would he return in a coffin?

PART 3

THE HEAVENS

CHAPTER 25

Around and about, everything was moving. Eric's spirit was moving; moving through the ether's sphere, the Heavens, at an incredible rate of speed. His spirit felt raw, new, reborn, trying to sense what was happening. It was all so strange, indeed, but nonetheless, somewhat reassuring and comforting, in an unknown way and for no reason at all.

There was no sense of time, all seemed endless. There were no separate days, nor any sense of direction, or for that matter, any sense of purpose. And, one's human senses, namely sight, smell, hearing, touch and taste were all gone, they did not exist in this reality, if in fact, it was a reality. However, it did not matter, nothing was as it had been, and all things that related to his physical life were entirely vague and fuzzy.

Then, the more his spirit moved on, he began to feel that *he was not alone;* that someone or something was around and about him, and seemed close for some reason. This presence was entirely white, flowing and translucent. It totally enveloped his spirit! Although, he knew not why, the sense of this presence made his spirit feel better. There was even a sense of relief and wonder about what it all meant? Would there be a communication? But how?

About what? With who? Say what? There were no answers.

Now, all of a sudden, it felt like he was being held in one place. All movement was suspended. It did not seem that they had arrived at any destination. It was all so ethereal, so celestial, so other worldly.

Now, for the first time, his spirit felt a communication. It just arrived.

It was a *welcome*, filled with warmth and goodness. It did not use words or expressions; it was just a communication, made clear simply by its arrival. Eric's spirit knew what was being communicated. And, there was no indication as to the source of the communication. It just happened, and that was all. Even so, it did not make him feel anxious. Something was happening, but his spirit could not sense what that might be?

Before long, *information, data and numbers were flowing out of his spirit at a speed beyond anything that was human*, faster and faster. It was simply amazing. As this happened, his entire life flashed bye so quickly that it was almost unrecognizable, even to his own spirit. When it ended, that was it, there was nothing but silence. Absolute silence. Silence. Silence. Dead silence.

Eric's spirit was at a loss as to what had happened. What was the purpose of this? Had something been taken from him? Would his spirit be extinguished? What was to happen next? And, Why?

Sometime later, no telling when, since time did not exist within this ethereal setting; all that had flowed out was transmitted back by way of visions, dreams and instant reflections, returning at super speed. There was a change, however, in the way it was all returned. This time, it all came back in a different order, with all good and positive deeds, actions, experiences, thoughts and words coming first, followed immediately by the opposite, with all the bad, evil, negative deeds, omissions, experiences, thoughts and words of his lifetime coming last. And, then nothing. Eric's spirit was left with a feeling of bewilderment.

Not long afterward, another communication was received.

"You have been summoned at this moment because of your recent actions and Discovery during earthly life. Here, in Heaven, we always knew that it was inevitable, that the strange earthly Code implanted within the Human make up, would eventually be seen. You have found it; Congratulations!

However, know that, you have not found the Human Spirit (the Soul), itself;

You have, however, found 'indicia' of the Human Spirit (the Soul). This tracks the Human Spirit (the Soul) as it develops and grows during the life of each and every person. This happens within the body, separately. Know that you correctly translated the headings for the Morals and Intellect 'regions'. And, had you not been interrupted by my action, you would have translated the third 'region' to be Values. The Code records and accumulates the major substantive points in these core 'regions' as they take place or occur during ones physical lifetime.

The Code does not, however, provide the basis for the final *judgment* for acceptance into Eternal Life and Heaven. This happens separately. Let me emphasize this again; final *judgment* takes place separate and apart before Eternal life and Heaven.

Turning back to the Code, let me add, that it does record personality or character traits. While these are a fundamental part within the essence of ones Soul; experience has shown that these traits are mostly found in combination with the three major elements (i.e. regions) of the Soul. In other words, they compliment, supplement, support and facilitate the core regions of the Soul. Therefore, they are not forgotten; simply, not recorded. Even so, these traits are thought of and recognized as being indelibly integrated within the Human Spirit (the Soul). In Heaven, they are accepted and celebrated in combination with a Spirits: Morals, Intellect and Values.

Moving on, the purpose of this interruption to your earthly life is to show and teach you the meaning and significance of what you have found, so that you may continue on this path during the *remainder of your earthly life*. Despite thinking of yourself as just a scientist, your future role will expand so that you may 'teach' one and all. Eric, I bless you!

You will now go on a journey that will give you much insight into the nature of ones Spirit (Soul) while taking part in Eternal life within the Heavens, including the use and importance of the Code you have found. You will be accompanied on this journey by my able assistant; you will travel throughout the Heavens and see the Spirit life firsthand.

"You may now ask your questions."

Eric's spirit formed a thought and it was presented:

"With whom am I communicating?"

"I am not the Creator, our LORD GOD; nor am I our LORD and savior, JESUS CHRIST; I am the HOLY SPIRIT, and I attend to all Spirit (Soul) matters in Heaven and on Earth."

Eric's spirit again: "Will my spirit be returned to Earth to carry out my remaining life."

From the Holy Spirit:

"YES, Yes, As I have said: You will return!!! You will be returned for what is to come."

"This will all be good and serve God.

CHAPTER 26

Eric's spirit felt reassured by this last communication and he waited for what was to happen next. His spirit now sensed being moved away, separated and somehow relocated. The how, why and where was unclear. Then again, this was followed by the inevitable wait. Wait. Wait. And Wait.

And then, without warning, a presence was beside his spirit. It seemed bigger than his spirit, moving about freely, somehow reflecting a superior position within the existing order.

And moreover, he learned that now his spirit would be privileged to communicate with this superior. His channel had been opened, somehow? It was made clear that communication would happen simply by "presenting" a thought and that this pattern would continue while together.

The Superior began:

"I am the assistant to our Holy Spirit; I will be your guide and resource."

"Before embarking on our journey, you are to know more about the Human Spirit (the Soul) and what you have really Discovered before coming here; and you will learn about a Spirits Eternal Life here in Heaven."

"Let me begin by telling you that this is an unusual event; seldom, if ever, does a Spirit come here for a short visit; to be followed by a return to an earthly life. This is unique; and this will likely bear on all mankind on Earth; and, also on the future of all those Spirits yet to be accepted in Heaven. Having said that, I do not know all that will change or grow out of finding the Code of the Human Spirit (the Soul); only that it is likely that new things may take place."

Eric's spirit: "Before leaving, can you tell where we are now?"

Superior: " Yes; We are in-between. At an ethereal holding point where Spirits (Souls) accepted for Heaven bask in the Glory of our Creator and Lord. After acceptance, this goes on until ones Soul is prepared and ready for eternal life and service in and about the Heavens. This is a very special place and experience for those Souls accepted. To bask in the Glory of our Creator and Lord presents to those Spirits an aura and character that sets the stage for what comes in Heaven and Eternal Life. They become attuned with the magnificence of Nature in its many forms and ways, plus learn of their ability as a Spirit to 'settle' within Natures actions and events. But, I am getting ahead on this. Your Spirit will see what is meant by soon enough."

Eric's Spirit: Do I guess correctly that, notwithstanding the content of one's Code, being 'accepted' means that one's Soul has already been 'judged' in the biblical sense?

The Superior: " Yes, that is a matter that is easy and hard, at the same time, to answer. "*Judgment,* is the sole province of our Lord, JESUS CHRIST; there are no known details about this; only that the answer resides within the 'true nature' of the supplicant and only our Lord can see that deeply; looking at the Code tells much, but it does not tell 'all'. One's Soul must be worthy to be accepted."

Eric's Spirit: "I'm confused; if the Code is just a part of the Human Spirit (the Soul); why then is finding the Code of particular importance?"

Superior: "This comes back to the fundamental nature of Human Beings. You know, surely, that human beings are endowed with free will. Exercise of free will during one's lifetime, not only determines what happens to them on Earth; it also brings about the growth and development of his or her Soul, preserving the highest levels of human achievement; in other words the essence of their Human Spirit (Soul). This is part of God's plan and ongoing creative purpose."

Eric: " I accept that, but what then gives the Code its importance?"

The Superior: " The Human Spirit (Soul) is more than what transcends from a human on Earth to the portals of Heaven. It embodies the most highly evolved aspects of that persons free will during their lifetime as a physical being.

The Code simply holds these core elements: morals, intellect and values, in a form to be of service throughout ones Eternal Life here in Heaven. The gift of this *legacy* happens by way of one's Spirit acting, interacting and reacting with other Spirits as well as other beings and life forms throughout Heaven. This is all very different than what you have known in your earthly life. You shall see the meaning of what I have described as we travel about."

Eric: "Wow, that's a quantum leap; on Earth, ones legacy is usually thought of as being remembered for some lifetime event or action, or for giving money to someone, something or some cause."

Superior: Yes, and there is some element of similarly here in Heaven; only the giving part is indirect and is part of a Soul's Eternal life; You will see this firsthand, but in order to do that, we will have to do some travel in and about the planets, galaxies and universes. By the time we are finished, this will answer your question and explain much about the interconnection of the Code, with Heaven and the Eternal Life of one's Soul."

Eric's Spirit: "Before we go, please tell me about the nature of being a Spirit?"

Superior: "Yes; I should have mentioned this already; a Spirit is not physical in anyway and can never regain physical status; it has no needs; it does not eat, sleep, go to the bathroom, have sex, reproduce, or take up space in human ways and it lacks human senses. Yet, it see's, hears, communicates, travels on light, and lives on and on. In addition, it is able to 'settle' on or in all manner of natures wonders and life forms taking on the size and shape needed at the time. What's more, a Spirit is active, interested, challenged, creative, knowledgeable, sensitive, and satisfied serving God in a host of ways throughout Heaven. But, I am getting ahead of myself again. You will see and get a feel for this as we go. I hope that helped."

There was nothing Eric's spirit could present at this point, it was all so surreal; it was in a place beyond any dream or understanding one could imagine. It would have to wait and see what was to come.

CHAPTER 27

The Superior and Eric's spirit were now traveling on a beam of light in the Heavens. They curved around a galaxy, banking their way along, making use of gravity. It was a ride that would surely make a human being dizzy. It was easy to recognize the planet that came into view.

Eric's spirit: "Ah, I see we are back at Earth. What am I to see?"

The Superior: " You are right, we are looking at Earth; here, I will show you the most common type of association that brings happiness to one's Soul during Eternal Life. This is the ability to make *linkages with kindred spirits* with whom there has been a connection in ones past. Take that one, for example;" as the Superior focused and directed Eric's spirit below.

Surprisingly, it could see the Spirits of his mother and father in a setting in the countryside, around and about a church, where an earthly Pastor was conducting a service; whereupon he presented to the Superior:

"I see that Mom and Dad's Spirits have come together; guess they were truly happy as husband and wife before passing away?"

The Superior: "Not only that, look a little more closely."

Eric's Spirit did: "Now, there seems to be more Spirits; what is that?"

The Superior: "Well; that's more *linkages*, going back a few generations, dominated by your father's ancestors; Spirits with commonality in some way or form, choosing to be linked together for their mutual happiness or for some other purpose."

The Superior went on; "Keep in mind that such *linkages* can be and are fluid and dynamic, ever changing to please the associated Spirits. Much of this is driven by the nature and content of their Spirit; this can be creative to a degree or, on the other hand disruptive, although we do not let things get out of control. The content of their Spirit is revealed by the Code, both directly and indirectly.

Linkages can be broken easily and reassignments happen all the time; And, if and when Spirits grow weary of filial *linkages* or simply seek new *linkages* or a challenging placement within Heaven, other associations will be made. You will see this more as we move on."

Eric's spirit: "Ok, I now see that, but what are Mother and Father and my ancestors Spirits doing? The

Pastor is earthly and is not paying any attention to them whatsoever."

The Superior: "Patience, Patience; You will learn the answer to this at our next stop. But, first, there is something else you must view before we leave. This will particularly interest you given your lifetime pursuit of Nature in all its forms and variations. Watch what happens. "

With that, the Soul (Spirit) for both Eric and the Superior became 'settled' and widely spread across the leading edge of a violent storm cloud sweeping on, over and above the Rocky mountain area of planet Earth. As seen and experienced from this position, the magnitude and power of the lightning, thunder, bursts of rain and the inner action of fast moving cloud formations were nothing short of stupendous. Even more amazing, their Souls were able to observe the inner workings and hydromechanics as this storm took place.

Eric's Spirit: "How is that possible? Apart from the wonder of it all, it could be possible to interpret this and theorize the scientific aspects for this. Somehow, its sequence seemed to have been 'slowed' to allow our understanding of what was happening."

Superior: Yes; you have just received a brief but clear view of what it means when a Soul 'settles' on something it finds in its travels about the Heavens. Note again, that when a Soul 'settles' it is able to assume whatever shape and size may be needed and appropriate for what it is doing or where it is going. Let me show you this again from a different prospective."

Whereupon, they descended down, down, and down to the surface of an open water tank in a field on Earth. There, together, they 'settled' on a small spot of water at just the moment that a big longhorn steer gulped this spot 'up' within its mouth.

Eric's spirit thought about this and then relaxed, awed and overwhelmed with it all.

In the same manner as if they were in a movie theater, together their Spirits moved with and witnessed the flow of this liquid inside the mouth of the steer, on down its throat, inside the stomach, passing through the internal organs and finally being voided as it was urinated. The Spirits then returned to their 'hover' position in the Heavens.

Superior: "While that was not as interesting as the storm we witnessed, your Spirit now knows more about the insides of a steer than it likely ever wanted to know. Aside from that not being especially important, think about what it would mean for a geneticist like yourself to 'settle' on a particular gene to observe its lifespan and its effects and interactions on the life of a human being. Would that not help the knowledge and understanding of human beings and what medical science could do for improving their lives? I think so."

Eric's Spirit: "I can hardly believe it. Of course, advancements of medical science could be studied and quickly derived in this way. Being able to 'settle' to a miniscule size and go through the body and survive would yield incredible knowledge to serve mankind. Beyond being a means of gaining knowledge, it there still a further purpose?"

Superior: " Yes, an important one. It arises by virtue of the essence of God; and that is Creation. The more that is revealed about the many aspects of Nature, the more that follows from this ongoing process. By and through 'settling', Spirits know the glory of God's Creation, bask in its multifaceted Nature, and gain a deep and abiding appreciation that they carry on in their regular activities."

Eric's Spirit: "Yes, but what is that? I don't get it from what we have seen so far."

Superior; " Ok, patience, this will be the main reason for our next stop. Are you ready?"

CHAPTER 28

And then, without warning, and with a rush of movement, they traveled on, moving together again on a beam of light, faster and faster. On and on they went, his Spirit knew not where or why. Finally, they arrived at a planet on the fringe of a universe, far, far beyond the universe that included Earth.

Together, Eric's spirit and the Superior observed this planet from afar. This planet had sufficiently evolved to house some life forms: including animals and early humans. They were tribal in nature and likely nomadic, observing the minimal structures they used. The animals and humans did not bear any resemblance to those Eric's spirit knew on Earth. And, the landscape consisted of high plateau's, deep valleys with a liquid but not necessarily water, because it appeared red in color. This thought was presented.

The Superior responded,

"Do not be surprised by this; this will be the case throughout the Heavens. These things are not the important point here; please observe more closely."

And so Eric's Spirit did. At first it was pointless. And then there was some movement. And then, all around and about there was more movement --- but what was it? What was happening? His spirit presented these thoughts.

The Superior answered: "You are now viewing more Spirits participating in Eternal Life in Heaven .

They are among and about the animals and human life forms; but they cannot be seen or touched by them. The animals and life forms do not even grasp, sense or know of their presence. They go on and act in accordance with their instincts and free will, whatever they decide. Even though you do not recognize any of these Spirits, as you did on our earthly visit, these Spirits are doing essentially the same thing."

Eric's spirit: "What then is it that the Spirits are doing? What purpose do they serve? Why are they here?"

"Well, *Spirits always work indirectly.* They communicate, influence and bear upon the decisions, acts, omissions and overall lives of these beings. They always do this *indirectly.* The Spirits can and do present thoughts and have the beings question their own thinking. Essentially, they act as a 'conscience', to use an Earthly word. However, the cardinal rule is that they can *never interfere with the beings exercise of free will.* The being must make its own decisions; act in the way it chooses; thereby molding and forming its own Human Spirit (Soul), for better or worse."

Eric's spirit: "I don't understand --- what good does that do?"

The Superior: "Think of it this way, consider this from our point of view. We are in Heaven, so in this situation, it's all about the Spirits, not the life forms. The Spirits are here taking part in their Eternal Life. You see, they can and do move about on assignment or freely accepted placement; they 'settle' on what may interest them; they are happy and without concern or worry. They are not temporal. And, as already described , they have no particular needs, physical or otherwise. Furthermore, with time being non-existent, they have no such constraints; they do not have to be at any particular place at a specified moment."

Eric's spirit: "Do they always stay here? Don't they get tired of this poorly evolved planet?"

"Eric, you are still looking at this as a human. The Spirits are happy; and they are able to visit other planets in this Universe as approved via a light transfer. They carry on endless communication with each other and they can link together in various ways, as you witnessed earlier. And, it does not bother them that the planet is poorly evolved; they have no physical needs; and, the beauty here is in the eye of the beholder, for it can be seen and found in ways that make little sense to human thinking."

Eric's spirit: "As I have seen, preservation of free will is at the heart of human development; it facilitates the growth of the Human Spirit (the Soul); nonetheless, it has always been wondered, whether predestination fits in this grand plan anywhere?"

The Superior: "One's fate, or destiny, is not predetermined. Otherwise, free will would be a nullity. The force within each person to 'aspire to' and reach their own best level, via their successes and failures, would be compromised. The development of their Human Spirit

(Soul) would be stunted; their struggle with morality, good and evil, would not be entirely their own. God's work would be flawed; a hollow exercise. One would not ever achieve 'acceptability' here in Heaven or have an Eternal Life worth enduring.

There is however, a small caveat to what I have just said. And, that relates to ones physical body. All humans die sooner or later. One cannot and does not physically live on forever. You know more about this than most due to your expertise on genetic matters. Hence, in the physical sense, it can be said that the death of the body is predestined. Surely, that is not a surprise."

Eric's spirit: Yes; I agree.

Following which, in a blink of an eye, they were off traveling again.

CHAPTER 29

As the Superior and Eric's spirit traveled, they continued to communicate.

Eric's spirit: "Tell me, are the Spirits we witnessed at the last planet numerous within Heaven?"

Superior: "Yes, you will be amazed with the answer. You know by now, that when a Spirit has been judged and admitted to Heaven, it goes on to Eternal Life. In fact, it goes on until it chooses to be extinguished. Consequently, to use an Earth term, that can be 'forever' in 'time'."

"Now, think back in the history of Earth to early man, and how far removed that may be; next, consider the names of the civilizations that have existed throughout that history, and the wars, famines, diseases and empires of history and so on. And with that, try to imagine the number of humans that have lived during such times."

Eric's spirit: "I can't even begin to guess at the number, but certainly billions and billions."

Superior: "Yes, yes, that is right; many of whom have been accepted and admitted to Heaven and the Heavens. And, as you may no doubt have guessed by now, many still continue as Spirits. Therefore, you must conclude and see that the Spirits throughout the Heavens include the Eternal Life 'survivors' from all Earth 'time'."

Eric's Spirit: "But, that could be a number beyond anything ever known to mankind."

Superior: Yes, precisely. That is correct. And, I tell you truthfully and without exaggeration, that Earth is not alone in producing and providing Spirits that are granted Eternal Life in the Heavens. There are many more Planets in the Heavens that give rise to Spirits having Eternal Life."

Eric's Spirit: "That's beyond belief for any human being. It is a concept so large that it is hard to believe that you are even saying it."

Superior: "Yes, I know, and from your perspective, I agree; but you are still missing the key point when looking at it from this level. That being, the scope and dimensions of Heaven. Actually, and more accurately, the Heavens that we are traveling within and about. It is really all interchangeable, because our Heavens are incredible; they are immense beyond any size considerations or descriptions humans could ever imagine. And, beyond that, the Heavens are and have been continually expanding. This, I believe, is known on Earth to physicists and astronomers; but it is still not known and understood well enough to envision what I have just been presented to you."

Eric's Spirit: "Do you mean that the Heavens are so great in size, that there is more than enough room for the many, many, many Spirits, especially given that they do not have a physical size."

Superior: "Yes, now you have it; there is room enough for all, including the never ending coming and going of these Spirits."

Eric's Spirit: "I can understand that the Eternal Life of a Spirit can be fully occupied by way of being made a part of the Heavens; but I sense, and anticipate that there is still more involved?"

Superior: "Yes, much more; indeed, you are perceptive; your insight is striking. I am about to show you more on this at our next stop. There you will see that GOD, our Creator and Lord, continues his grand 'design'; continuing creation even through Spirits Eternal Life within Heaven, in yet another way. I will show you an example of this very special type of connection at our next stop."

CHAPTER 30

After swooshing thru space again at the speed of light, Eric's spirit and that of the Superior arrived at a different Universe and beheld before them a beautiful planet, lush and desirable in all ways. Eric's spirit was impressed and it started to think again, wondering what would be different here versus the planets they had already visited?

The Superior read his thoughts: "You want to know how ones Spirit comes to be here, instead of being placed at our other stops? Let me tell you, that it's not all that complicated and should be of particular interest to you, considering your earthly pursuits. Because, in large measure, it is comes once again from the content of the Code for the Spirits (Souls) that have been gathered here.

Eric's spirit listened carefully, a little perplexed, within his thought pattern? With this, the Superior went on:

"I am sure you recall that before I came for you, you felt the transfer of info and data from your spirit, and then its return, but this time, in a different format and order.

Eric's Spirit: "Yes, you 're right. I remember."

"The stop at that portal was to 'assess' the state of one's Spirit (i.e. Soul). And, of course, this assessment comes from the Code within ones body. It is read not only for its quantitative history, but also for its qualitative content. This reading bears upon that Spirit's subsequent activities and travels in and about the Heavens, including placement, associations, projects, scope of communication, linkages, and other connections, direct and indirect. I think I communicated this before."

Eric's spirit: "I think I understand about a Spirits placement in the Heavens, but how and why are these other things taken into consideration?"

The Superior: Do not think of placement as if the Heavens were a resort for ones Spirit to be forever on vacation. Because one's Eternal Life goes on until extinguished, Spirits seek to be of value and have a

211

meaningful purpose while in Heaven. While all Spirits can choose to have the same or similar activities and happiness, they can also choose to engage in different ways to give them a *challenge, purpose and value*. Much of this flows from the nature of their Soul, as disclosed by the content of their Code as well as the Spirits 'one of a kind' character.

Eric's Spirit: "What do you mean? How can that work to benefit one's Eternal Life?"

The Superior: "Its more than that; it's a bit complicated, but it comes down once again to being with ones like kind; in other words, as demonstrated before, this is an association of kindred Spirits but in a different way. In this case it is an association for more than the happiness of these kindred Spirits; here, they have, the additional purpose and challenge of supplementing God's creative work.

Kindred here, is not based on past relationships; 'kindred' can arise in many ways; in this case, it means Spirits with like 'intellects,' being especially knowledge they gained during their physical lifetimes in various ways. This is important, because when such Spirits come together, and are given access to storehouses of knowledge held by kindred Spirits, who have come together with 'pasts' from over many centuries'; guess what happens?"

Eric's spirit: "I am guessing; breakthroughs and discoveries on difficult subjects in special ways."

The Superior: "Yes, yes, you're right --- but here and everywhere else, this is known as *Creation*, in fact, sometimes *Devine Creation*. It comes from the synergy that flows from the gathered Spirits who burst with excitement as it all takes place; it is a quite remarkable experience. Some might even say, Earth shaking; actually, in this case, it becomes World or Universe shaking.

Eric's spirit, excited: "And, if I am following correctly, someone or some institution, would be given recognition for such discoveries, lets say on Earth, as a new generation scientist or technology."

Superior: Yes, you have got it, mostly, but not entirely. And, this reaction by you is still quite human; however, you should know that earthly credit means nothing in Heaven in that what was found and by whom matters little. No Spirit gets credit or acclaim, because such things take place everyday and are common events in Heaven. This sort of thing is just not important here. Adulation has no meaning here; it is replaced by the satisfaction of working with one's historical peers and being useful and constructive and of value in ones Eternal Life. "

Eric's spirit thinking further: " Well by implication, do you mean, then, that I really did not discover the strange Code within the human body?"

Superior: "No, that's not right, either. Don't try to apply what has just been described to your situation. *Inspiration and discovery* is not just a simple extension from those indirect Spirits surrounding you. It still takes the creative input and intelligence of the author, flowing from the accumulated content within the authors Spirit; it's just that it all comes together at a specific moment, from all the synergy that is surrounding and active at the moment of the break through."

Eric's spirit: "Would it then follow, that this can be happening around and about the Heavens, either at the same time or one after another?"

Superior: "Yes; now you can see why this is complex; for us the challenge is to make the 'right' associations at the 'right' moment or, failing that, to redistribute these associations forward, in order to bring about the continued advancement of *Creation* in whatever form and way, wherever the conditions are just right."

Eric's Spirit: "Therefore, we are witnessing the Spirits of famous innovators from history (in certain fields) and they are trying to influence the life form they are with to realize a step forward or advancement on a particular subject or science."

Superior: "Yes, that's right; this influence may help or it may not; the life form may have a better 'take' of this innovation or it may be frustrated in its efforts. The Spirits indirect influence does not control the life forms decisions ---but they may help or they may not. The free will of the life form makes the final choice(s) and the results are determined, as happens on Earth."

Eric's Spirit: "That's awesome. In the final analysis, it's the content within the life forms Human Spirit (Soul) that counts. No wonder, the interest in understanding what's there."

Superior: "I can tell that you grasp much of the essence and purpose in having a Code for the Human Spirit (the Soul). Let me add that the example we have just covered is only one of many, many ways that the content of the Code may be helpful in Eternal Life; its not simply about creation; its importance lie's in the endless possibilities for meaningful connections."

Eric's Spirit: "Before we go, there is one more thing. And that's about Angels; you have not mentioned them at all?"

The Superior: "Yes, thank you for asking Eric. Yes, there are Angels. However, they are not Souls that have been promoted because of exemplary conduct. Angels are special creations of God, our Lord. They do God's bidding, often as messengers or helpers on specific missions, coming and going as instructed. They are quite powerful if need be. I have no idea of how many there may be and would judge that the number varies depending on what is needed at the moment. That's all I know about Angels – it's beyond my duties and responsibilities. Does that help?"

Eric's spirit: "Yes, I think so. Thank You, your comments are helpful."

Superior: "Meanwhile, I have received a command for you to be returned to our starting point, the portal to Heaven. Still though, on the way back, we have the opportunity to make one more short stop. I want you to watch another Spirit that is taking part in its Heavenly life? This Spirits physical life was about one thousand earth years ago, even though he comes from a different planet."

Eric's spirit: "Sounds fine to me, I 'm always anxious to learn. It is hard to get use to the idea that one could meet and communicate with a Spirit that may have existed way back in time. I bet that this could lead to some very unusual communications."

" That's for sure."   And with that, they were off.

CHAPTER 31

While returning, the Superior and Eric's spirit communicated further.

Superior: "While we move along, I am going to share with you the Code of the Spirit we will visit. Although, in this instance, it will be more about the unrecorded part of its Soul than what would be found by a literal translation of the Code. Please recall that this duality was explained earlier by our leader, the Holy Spirit."

Eric's spirit: "I'm still a little confused; does the Code include the character traits even though they may be unwritten or are these traits separate and apart?"

Superior: "Yes, this may be a little strange; how can something that is unwritten be part of a written Code? That is a conundrum. Let me say that on Earth this would be impossible; nonetheless, we are in the Heavens and such things happen here. Please take this to be simply a matter of *powers* held by those with duties and responsibilities pertaining to the Souls in Heaven. I have been granted such a power. I do not know how many others hold the same *power*. Does this answer satisfy you?"

Eric's spirit: "Yes, of course; however, it does give rise to a problem for me upon return. Especially, for Code translations; only the recorded part will be available for translation."

Superior: "Yes, that right; depending on what lies ahead for you, this may or may not be a problem; I shall pass this on."

Superior: "Back to our journey and the Spirit you are about to meet. Before I tell you about this Spirit, you must promise not to disclose in the Spirits presence any of the Code matters. Between us, this may seem minimal and simplistic; but to a Spirit, this is never discussed; their Eternal Life and happiness flows and occurs spontaneously."

Eric's spirit: Ok. I promise; I gather this arrangement is to avoid troubling Spirits with prospects and plans?"

Superior: "Yes, that's about it; now, since we are getting close; this Spirit is an outstanding example of one whose *character trait* rises above and overshadows all aspects of its recorded Morals, Intellect and Values.

In this case, this has been accomplished by virtue of the *force* of the Spirits personality. It has given rise to great *leadership,* and this has been used for the benefit of the culture it represented during physical life. Moreover, this has happened in a nonviolent manner. On the other hand, in looking at its recorded Code, the Values associated with this Spirit, center on honesty, integrity and reason, all aiding and supporting the Spirits dominate leadership trait. But, it must be stressed, that *leadership* is the key driving force. All in all, this has been quite remarkable."

Shortly after the Superior made this comment, they arrived at another planet. From the planets appearance, it had evolved over many eon's and included oceans and land masses, largely resembling open plains with occasional plateaus in the northern areas. And, in what would be the equator belt on Earth, similarly, the planet was ringed , for hundreds of miles, with what seemed to be deep tropical jungle.

Looking down, the Superior focused their attention narrowly, upon a certain Spirit hovering above and around a population guessed to be about two to three hundred. These life forms were well founded when Eric's spirit mentally compared them to others he had observed on his travel in the Heavens with the Superior.

Soon, a tall life form arrived on what seemed to be a machine much like an earthly motorcycle, except that it had no wheels. It appeared to use the movement of circular whirling air, propelled by a cyclonic device never seen before.

This tall figure strode before this population to a stage like platform. Some life forms cheered and others remained passive. It became clear that the tall figure was there to urge the group to join with it in some way or some form of action. Physically, various life forms within the group, were reacting in both positive and negative ways.

It was at this point, that the hovering Spirit moved and pulsated in a way visible solely to the Superior and Eric's spirit.

Superior: Let me interpret for you Eric. The hovering Spirit is urging in its strongest way, to influence the tall figure, to bring forth the *force* of its person as a *leader*. Its indirectly telling the tall figure to persuasively lead this populace with honesty, integrity and reason. It is urging restraint, nonviolence and meeting with a delegation from the opposition to arrive at a solution. This Spirit is acting to influence the tall figure be a leader in the same way it acted when it had great success in its physical life."

Eric's spirit: "When I first arrived, my question would have been: Will it work? But now, because of our travels and visitations and what you have shown me, I realize that this is not the point. That lies separately, in that the tall figure and the population group shall choose to act in whatever way by their own volition. And, equally important, would be that the Soul, acting here as the hovering Spirit, is participating in Eternal Life in a way that makes sense for its happiness and possibly for the benefit of these people. Furthermore, the role of the hovering Spirit is in keeping with its Code, both written and unwritten. In other words, this is yet another version of the Code and its useful purpose in Heaven."

Superior: "My, my Eric, you have come a long way; we could go on and on but we are to end now. We must leave now for we are wanted back at the portal to Heaven. And off they went.

CHAPTER 32

Upon arrival, back at the portal where Eric's spirit first arrived, the Superior left and returned to its regular duties; communicating upon leaving, that it had been a pleasure to meet his Spirit, and that they will be together again upon its later return, but please do not make that "to soon."

In keeping with the first visit here, the wait that followed seemed interminable. And then as before, Eric's Spirit was gradually surrounded and enveloped by the white, flowing, translucent and ethereal aura.

Once again it was made clear that Eric's spirit was in the presence of the HOLY SPIRIT.

"Welcome back, you have seen and learned much on your journey. Before moving on, there are a few remaining things for you to know before you return to Earth. I shall make them clear:

First, you will not directly remember this visit or your journey.

You will, however, 'know' all that happened and you 'witnessed' on this visit.

This knowledge and insight will simply 'come' to you as you go on with your life and are asked questions by others. You are not to hesitate with your answers; you will just 'know' of what you speak. You will be confident but not understand why.

This is to 'aid' in your work on the Code of the Human Spirit (the Soul). It will also 'aid' as you will 'know' about Heaven and Eternal Life. *God wants every being to know of the afterlife that awaits those whose Soul is 'worthy.'*

You have correctly 'identified' two regions of the Human Spirit (the Soul), as *morals and intellect.* The third is *values* as mentioned before. This simply awaits your return to consciousness and continued translation.

You are to 'go on' with the translation of the sub-parts for each region. They will be different for each person but be in keeping with the meaning(s) of the applicable region.

The 'slashes' following each sub-part reflect each important (major) instance pertaining to that subpart. They can be and are 'called up' in the review of the Code here in Heaven. Forward 'slashes' are positive and back 'slashes' are negative. The 'sashes' are read and interrupted at the portal to Heaven. They present images that are replayed about what happened at the time. Perhaps, someday Earth technology will also be able to read these slashes.

One further point in connection with the unwritten part of the Code you learned about from the Superior. I am referring to *character traits* of course. I am granting to you alone the *power* to see, translate and understand them within the Code. This is a special grant. Use it wisely.

223

Goodbye. Eric Rhodes, I bless you and what is about to happen to you during the balance of your Earthly life. Know that your continuing true purpose shall be to serve God. He loves you!"

With that, their was a 'caress' or 'touch' if you will, in the most delicate of ways; so light, effusive and ethereal as to make one wonder if this really happened. Moreover, whether it did or did not, who was to know in the absence of the presence of anyone or anything else?

Eric's spirit did not receive any moment or opportunity to communicate. It was over, that quickly. It was instantly returned to Earth for all that was to follow.

This would, no doubt, be a special journey throughout the remaining years of his life.

PART 4

RETURN, RENEWAL &

CONSPIRACY

CHAPTER 33

Eric opened his eyes slowly, dazed and bewildered, barely able to process what he was seeing. His instant reaction was that he must be in Heaven, for he was seeing an angel. Only this angel had a huge smile across her face, a smile that radiated all the warmth and love that he had only known with Janice. And, in fact, it was Janice, looking down upon him with the greatest of pleasure. Truly, it was her, she was there, right there, before his eyes, reaching out and tenderly touching his face.

"Your back!"   She said, as she planted a light little kiss on his lips. "How do you feel?"

Eric struggled to form an answer: "What happened? Where am I?"

"Eric, I'm so happy you woke up. You have been out, in a coma. We did not know if you would ever wake up."

"A coma, a coma?" Eric said, rolling his eyes in a strange way.

Janice: "To this day, we still don't know the cause, --- but you have been plain 'out' this whole time, more than a month."

Eric: "A month, two months?"

Looking about he could see that he was at Janice's place, lying on a hospital style bed, in a small room.

Eric, again struggling with his thought process:

"My last memory was being in Israel and I think I went to bed at where I was staying?"

"Eric, I want you to go slow, don't try to quickly recall all that happened; let your memory regain itself at its own speed. For some reason, you have had a substantial shock to your body and mind. I want you to listen to your "Doc" and rest easy for now. Know that you are at my place, safe and secure; that I brought you back from Israel and have protected all your work. Lay back, close your eyes, and rest. When you wake up tomorrow, we will be able to talk."

With that reassurance, Eric did as he was told, and fell deeply asleep within fifteen minutes.

At his home, Dr. Alex Howard, was informed daily by his son John on any developments concerning his boss, Dr. Eric Rhodes. The Medical Research Center had put out a memo to all staff that Eric was now on a Medical leave following his return from a Sabbatical with an unknown illness. The date of his return was still pending. Alex knew all of this and it made him uneasy in that there was little or no additional information about Eric's condition.

Would he or would he not recover? After all, he had paid for him not to recover. He was definitely chagrined about that. What went wrong? Since his middle of the night call, he had had no contact with his 'operative', who now had his million dollars. What was he going to do if Eric came out of his coma? He doubted if he could get his money back. And, he questioned whether his 'operative' would redo the 'job'. And furthermore, whether that would be necessary, depending on the state of the mind that Eric would be left with, if and when he recovered?

What a messy situation this had all become ---- and he still was not entirely clear in his mind if it had all been needed in the first place or if he had jumped the gun in assessing a danger from Eric's Discovery?

So many questions with so few clear answers. It all made him angry, very, very angry.

Justin Avery, the hometown detective Eric had engaged, was a rugged looking guy, of medium height, with glasses; and he was a most contentious professional. His training and work years in the F.B.I. had prepared him well for his new roll as a private sleuth. Usually he worked for the many attorneys' in the area digging up information helpful for divorce matters, searching for and interviewing potential witnesses for all types of cases and generally making enough to keep his bills paid. This allowed him to keep his early retirement pay and benefits and build a fund for that time when he could retire without further working days.

When he received Eric's first letter from Israel, he was more than happy to undertake this assignment for his longtime friend. It was a bit unusual in that the stated purpose was limited to obtaining information that would bear upon someone's motive for pursuing info his client wanted to remain confidential. Furthermore, his client was absent for now, unable to explain it all in more detail and there seemed to be only a few starting points.

Justin had met Dr. Janice Wesphal once at a hospital function and thought that he would start by interviewing her, his sole authorized contact. Within a week of receiving Eric's note and retainer, he met with Janice at the hospital. At first, she was reluctant to talk with him; but she soon became satisfied as to his 'bona fides' by reading Eric's note, looking at his check and knowing that Eric had revealed to him the request for MRI records by Dr. John Howard. Actually, in retrospect, when she thought about it, she was pleased to have this help and promised to keep his involvement confidential per Eric's request.

Janice and Justin talked at length. In broad strokes she painted a verbal picture of the project they had worked upon and that the MRI data requested was to be held secret and this was the entire reason Eric was in Israel doing a particular kind of research. Justin had asked about the computer that she used when she e-mailed Eric that Dr. John Howard inquired and requested copies of the MRI listings. Upon learning that it was her home computer, he said he would need to see it ASAP. At the same time, he learned that Eric had his own place and computer; he also requested to see that one.

Two days later, after Janice had finished surgery for the day, she and Justin went first to her place and he went over her computer while she busied herself with lunch and a quick change of clothes. After that, Justin went right to the telephone, took it partially apart, made a few notes on a pad, and asked to go right away to Eric's condo. On the way, he told Janice that he had found a hidden 'tracking' piece of software on the computer and a 'bug' on the phone, and that they were in each case, very sophisticated, intercepting both incoming and outgoing messages. She was shocked and more than a little displeased that someone would do such a thing. Once at Eric's place, Justin did the same steps on both the computer and telephone. While returning, he reported finding the same set up on Eric's computer and telephone, using the same type and style equipment.

On the way back, Justin and Janice talked about these findings. He cautioned against taking any 'removal' action right away, until he had time to get to the 'bottom' of what was going on. Additionally, he thought that perhaps, somehow this connection to 'whomever,' might be useful at a later time in prosecuting this illegal surveillance. He needed more time.

Next, Justin went to his only other lead, Dr. John Howard, Eric's colleague at the MRC. Obtaining his curriculum vitae was straight forward via readily available information on the academic qualifications of their key staff members. This pointed back to his New England roots and the University he had attended. In turn, while looking into this education, Justin discovered that Dr. John Howards father had been prominent there at the same time as a professor, not all that unusual by itself. And then, while searching for more info about this father, he came upon a vague newspaper article on his early retirement for "family reasons," a sure indicator that something went sour with Dr. Alex Howard that led to his departure.

Thereafter, more searching disclosed Dr. Alex Howard's subsequent activities; namely, his specialized publishing business on 'evolution science,' the founding of a related association, and his most noticeable, outspoken, passionate participation, and 'no-holds-barred', 'take-no-prisoners', attitude, advocacy and actions in support of 'evolution science.' This was accompanied by numerous published articles calling for the defeat and destruction of support for 'intelligent design and/or creationism.'

Justin quickly realized, that his research established, the strong probability, that Dr. Alex Howard was an extremist in this 'academic' area. And, at the same time, a D & B report showed that this 'specialized' publishing business was a huge financial success.

Could this be what he was looking for? Was this a motive to move against two unsuspecting professionals?

Was it possible that Dr. Alex Howards livelihood and activist purpose would be threatened by his clients work. Justin was not entirely sure, but he was going to keep working on this possibility. He needed to talk to Eric and Janice in more depth.

CHAPTER 34

Friday, the next day, Eric was sleeping again and Janice was at her Hospital office. She was still all smiles and breathing much easier, now that her 'lovee' was 'back', from his coma, starting to talk and eat. Sipping a second cup of coffee and slowly eating an English muffin from the cafeteria, dressed in smart business suit instead of scrubs, she was startled by a phone call. It was Justin; they had not talked since the day he visited her and Eric's place, finding the hidden software and 'bugs' in their computers and telephones.

So much had happened since then; her trip to Israel, Eric's ongoing coma, moving him back to the Hospital and immediately to her home; it was all a blur; it had happened so fast. She simply had not got around to calling him and giving an update; she was feeling a little guilty about that.

Janice answered and listened carefully as Justin talked:

"Janice, something's have happened; I'm calling to see if you knew of them and to see if you can tell me when Eric will be back?"

"Justin, You don't know the half of it; I have a lot to fill you in on. But, you go first, since you called."

"Ok; about two weeks ago, I got an envelope from Eric. Did you know that there had been a break-in at his motel room? And, Eric had found someone following him in the days after the break-in. He even sent me a camera he used to take pictures of this person. In his note, he insisted that I handle the camera carefully to obtain fingerprints of this man. I have the pictures but have not been able to identify him so far. I am still working on the 'prints.'"

"Wow: I had no idea of any of that happening; I need to tell you a lot more, but think that this should be in person. Can you come over to my office a little later?"

Justin: "Sure; how about eleven this morning?"

"Ok; see you then." And she hung up, and went about her usual Departmental duties.

Later, when Justin arrived, she greeted him warmly, and they went to the adjoining conference room. Janice then briefed him on Eric having been in a coma for over a month, her 'rescue' trip to Israel, and the frustration of not being able to find a medical cause for his coma. She also mentioned in passing that just before all this happened, Eric had made the break through he had been searching for in Israel. Then she disclosed to him that Eric was now coming out of this coma and was lying in her side room at home sleeping.

Justin and Janice started comparing dates for when these things were taking place, including postal marks and telephone calls. Their sequence and immediacy became clear and they concluded out loud, "that this could not have all been 'coincidence'; and that definitely, Eric was a target."

Justin wanted to know if anyone else was aware that Eric was 'back' from his coma?

Janice: "No, it was only yesterday this happened and even today, I can see that he is coming along quickly."

Justin: "I recommend that we keep it that way; with all that's happened, someone is definitely after him; and I think I know who it is."

Justin then revealed what he had learned by looking into Dr. John Howard and how it had led to his father, Dr. Alex Howard, a volatile and motivated extremist. Since then, Justin had also tailed Dr. John Howard, on both a week day and a weekend. He had found him to be rather boring; apparently dedicated to his work and having only one side hobby: bicycling. It did not appear the he participated in any unusual activities or organizations, even his fathers association.

That left the father, and Justin was working on connecting him to the man that had been following Eric. He went on to outline the nature of Dr. Alex Howard's activities, and how important 'evolution science' was to his financial well being, a major motive in itself.

In closing they agreed that all of this would be kept confidential between them; that they would brief Eric on what they had learned and reviewed as soon as Janice thought his condition was up to it; and that Janice would quietly switch the day nurse she had for Eric and put in her place a body guard to protect him while she was at work. She would see that this guard would wear clothing appropriate for a male nurse while on duty. Justin would dig in with his sources to identify the man in the pictures and 'prints' and continue to find info on Dr. Alex Howard, who definitely appeared to be the likely source of the conspiracy against Eric and his work.

Around this same time, 'Charles' the operative, having returned from Israel, was touring the eastern shore of Maryland, casually looking into buying a small property on the waters of Chesapeake Bay. With his recent financial windfall and what he had previously saved, he was ready to step up in the world and live a more sedate lifestyle.

Personally, he was not troubled by knowing that he had not delivered the 'barbeque' requested by his client. It was hard to feel 'guilty' about not killing someone. Even his client did not know for sure if it was necessary to kill Dr. Eric Rhodes. Furthermore, his client had no idea that 'Charles' had not touched or done anything to Eric. Dr. Alex simply assumed that somehow 'Charles' had worked his magic and put him in a coma. In his view, "Dr. Alex Howard was a fool and he deserved to lose his money."

And personally, 'Charles' only knew that by the time he was in place to do the 'job', the target was on his way to the Hospital and beyond his reach. With all those doctors and nurses hovering around, it would have been too risky to attempt anything at that location. And besides, why bother; most comas never end well anyway? He would and did accept credit for a job well done, collected his money, and returned to the good old U.S.A. and was now moving on.

In the unlikely event that the target did recover, he would make it clear to his client that it was not his fault. He had done enough on this case and he did not want to go any further. His client would have to move on without him! It was not going to be his problem any longer.

CHAPTER 35

The next few days were finally good ones for Eric and Janice. Gradually, his awake and alert time increased and he caught up with Janice on how she managed to get him back from Israel. When he first looked at himself in the mirror, he was quite taken aback by the ghastly appearance of his face and the white look of his skin. This improved, however, on a daily basis with the 'scrubbings' he gave himself and actively moving around her apartment. By then, he would have gone out for his longtime favorite 'church of the walking feet' exercise except that Janice had absolutely prohibited this activity. From her windows, the sky's were a cobalt blue and filled with fluffy clouds, all of which beckoned unto him. Really, they must talk about this soon.

Not only that, he had to contend with the day nurse (the bodyguard). He kept after Eric like a 'mother hen' making sure that he stayed in and seeing that he was well feed. Another strange thing, Eric finally realized, was that the telephones and her computer had been removed so that he could not reach out and talk with anyone. He was anxious to be in touch with the Medical Research Center and his job responsibilities. They were also due to talk about this soon. It was almost like he was being held prisoner.

By Wednesday evening, Janice felt that it was time to have that 'talk' she had promised. It began:

"Eric, do you remember what happened to you; how you came to be in a coma?"

"No, not really; I had been working in the evening and was trying to translate a word."

"Do you recall why you were in Israel?"

"Yes, of course, I was searching for the key to the Code found on the MRI listings for our Project."

"Ok; what is your last memory on finding that key?"

And that did it; Janice thought she could see a bright light actually come on in Eric's head; he seemed to swell up with excitement:

"I did it; I did it; I remember now. Eric exclaimed.

"You did what, Eric, spell it out for me; tell me?' Janice said:

Eric paused a moment, thinking back, remembering that evening;

"Yes, yes; I broke the Code --- Its Coptic, but with ancient encryption. I used a simple means of translating; flipping sheets of paper over and then upside down. I remember now.

"All right Eric, what did you do with the sheets, do you remember?"

He paused a moment at that point, clearing his mind and thinking back:

"Sure, you know of course; I bundled them up and sent them to you from the motel front desk before going to bed, isn't that right?"

"Yes, Eric, that's right and I have them for you in my safe deposit box. You told me in your short note that 'we were right on track with our theory', I want you to tell me why?"

"Ok; that's easy, I think; because of the three words; actually the three region words;

"I think I remember translating two of them, ...to be, 'morals and intellect; isn't that right?"

"I don't know; you didn't send those with your note" Janice said; "and what happened then?

"I think, ... I think, I, I, I went back, back, to the table, and, an, started again and, ... Its all a blank, a blank; how can that be?" said Eric;

"I don't know Eric, ... as near as we can tell, that's when the coma started.

The Doctors in Israel and I still can't tell what happened. You became unconscious; stayed that way all night, and were taken to the Hospital the next day. You were stabilized. Medical tests were run, all of which I have reviewed; no particular medical conditions were found to have caused your coma. There is no definitive diagnosis for what happened to you."

"But, for the moment, lets not go into that discussion, there is more we need to go over, now that I can see that you are up to it." And, Janice went on:

"While you were in the coma, I met several times with Justin Avery, the detective you hired. You remember this, don't you?"

"Oh yes, I remember writing to him I think, at about the same time I sent you the 'break through' papers.

"Do you remember what you sent him with your short letter?"

Eric frowned:

"Its coming back; I sent a camera with pictures, I believe, of the man that had been following me and then attacked me after I took his picture. And, in my note, maybe notes, I told Justin of the break-in at my motel room, and the attack after the pictures by the following man and I think, perhaps 'fingerprints' on the camera."

"That's right; you didn't even tell me of the break-in; I would have just worried anyway; and this attack all happened so fast, apparently the day before the day you entered the coma." Janice said;

"I'm sorry; but I couldn't help it at the time; it was all so very fast for me."

"There's more Eric; Justin and I discovered 'bugs' on the telephones and hidden software installed on the computers that we use at our places; no wonder 'they' know so much about our Project and related activities. No doubt, this explains why you're Dr. Howard, asked

the Hospital for the secret MRI listings. This was in our e-mails." Janice said;

"How does he fit into all of this --- he always seemed so uninterested in things other than what he was working upon?"

"Justin will have to explain this; he thinks there is involvement by Dr. Howard's father, Alex; we feel that your life is in 'jeopardy', probably from the stranger you photographed; and consequently, and this is the hard part, that you should stay here at my place, pretending to remain in your coma."

"Wow, I have a hard time understanding and believing that our Discovery could be so important; and I want to meet with Justin to hear what he has to say. And, I need to think about all you have told me. So, for now, I will cooperate, and stay in. But, I do want to meet with Justin soon."

"Good." Janice said: "Now that you're in such good shape, I need, very much need, to examine you thoroughly --- so take off those clothes ASAP."

And then, as Eric disrobed, Janice moved toward him, and slipped out of her robe and lingerie, sliding into his bed as naked as the day she was born..............

CHAPTER 36

Several days later, in the late afternoon, Janice and Eric met with Justin at her place. Eric was now looking and feeling much better. Color had returned to his face and skin. And importantly, he was becoming more energetic each day. He was ready to get moving and was 'antsy' about continuing the charade of still being in a coma.

Their meeting started with catching up on the points Janice had covered Wednesday evening. Still, Eric wanted to hear first hand from Justin about Dr. Alex Howard. Justin spelled out the various info and things he had uncovered so far in his investigation. In doing so, he went over what Janice had described adding more details as he talked. He confirmed all the things she had said.

Upon hearing this, Eric found it hard to believe that someone that he had never met could want to kill him. After all, they were both men of science, academics and had no grudges, professional or personal, that could be so huge. Eric had had nothing to do scientifically with 'evolution science' in his view. He had paid little or no attention to this supposed science, thinking of evolution as basically a process within Nature much like the many others, such as weather, plant life and so on. His field, genetics, could show mechanisms related to evolution, but it did not dwell on the historical evolution of human development in particular.

These overviews lead Justin to get to the heart of the issue before
them:

"Eric, I have to ask, does your Discovery have anything to do with the fundamental principles underlying 'evolution science'? I am only asking to have some idea of whether there could be a strong connection within what you are working on that might be contrary to the interests of a hard core evolutionist . This could give rise to a motive for his actions against you."

"Maybe, I'm not sure; I never gave this much thought before." Eric said;

"When you think about it from that direction, the most striking thing that jumps out is the lack of DNA in a small piece of tissue from the human body." Janice said. That, in itself, is off the charts. It leads to unknown territory and thinking on the origin of man."

"I guess that, when you add the finding of a strange Code within this small piece from the human body, it amounts to something that obviously did not come by way of evolution. When, you couple this with learning that this piece collects ongoing information during the life of the person, you strike at the core of

evolution as the primary basis for human development."
Eric stated;

Justin: "Wow; if that is what you're up to with this Discovery, you are going to shake the roots of not only evolutionists; the world's religions will also be impacted. How much of this can you document scientifically?"

"Justin, as you know, Janice and I are highly trained scientists and Doctors. We can back up all of what I just described; and finally, this includes the translation of the Code words; technically, that's about where the 'science' ends; beyond that, one must interpret and speculate on the meaning of these findings; anyone and everyone can and will likely do that. We do not plan to hold ourselves out as authorities on that part."

"We just don't want to do that. This is for others to do that are more qualified than Janice and I." Eric said.

Justin: "Have you written and documented your Discovery yet?"

Eric: No, that's next."

Justin: "Well, being your friend as well as investigator, let me propose a plan on how to proceed. Before I ask for your authorization you may need to think about it."

" On your end, while you're still under the cover of the coma, the two of you would prepare and document this Discovery. This will help keep you safe; being out of circulation makes you less of a target and easier to protect. At the same time, I will get busy with the leads I have and need to move forward upon; once I run them down, I'll be back and review them with you. At that point, with your approval, I will go to the authorities to move this to an official investigation and then a prosecution. It will have to be Federal because of being so geographically wide spread. How does that sound?"

Eric turned to Janice: "What do you think?"

Janice: "Justin, do you really think you can get the goods on whoever is targeting Eric?"

Justin: "Janice, this is the kind of thing I have done my whole working life; I can and will do it; you can count on that; you and Eric need to go on as you have been doing; just keep the bodyguard in place. Keeping what we are doing hidden and secret is the best thing we can do under the circumstances. "

Janice: "Eric, I don't see that we can do much else; I agree with Justin; lets see this through to its conclusion; its what we have been working toward."

Eric: "Ok, Justin, I am ready to do it; where do we start --- I bet I need to get my checkbook."

Justin: "You're right on that point, Eric; the same amount you sent me before will be fine for now; meanwhile, I need to remove the telephone bug -- this will help me convince a certain 'someone' to bring in the 'Calvary'.

Justin knew from examining the telephone 'bug' that it was a very sophisticated device and not something you picked up at the local "spy' store. And, he could tell that it had been used by a 'pro'; most likely some one that had been with the U.S. Government. From his years with the FBI, he knew that it was not one of theirs; it did not come from their source. That left some other agency, for example, the Nat'l Security Agency; or, the more he thought about it, the likely connection would be the CIA supplier.

This in turn, led him to contact a past 'friend' at the CIA that still owed him a favor. Their situation had come about while he was still at the FBI. Their paths had crossed when Justin was doing an investigation in Maryland on foreign non-profits activities in the U.S... After interviewing this 'friend' and running him through the FBI database, he discovered him to be a CIA agent, all of which he later admitted. He was a secret 'plant' from the CIA and more importantly, involved in an 'illegal' operation that the CIA was not supposed to be doing in the U.S.A.. Justin endeared himself by obtaining a 'pass' on this matter from his supervisor and letting the whole issue drop.

Afterward, they had talked at length, kept in touch and settled into a mutual aid relationship. From that association, Justin had learned that the CIA took a very dim view of former agents that hired out to do 'black' bag jobs and other clandestine work for third parties. Being 'off the farm' so to speak, engaging in nefarious operations in the manner they had been trained, was highly frowned upon. Given the purpose of the CIA, who could know whether one was still employed or not. A misinterpretation was a distinct possibility, especially in a foreign country, and that would be bad.

When they met, Justin showed him the 'bug' and the pictures Eric had taken in Israel. He also mentioned that the camera had the 'prints' of the unknown man. He painted a broad outline of what was going on and asked for his help. His friend looked at the 'bug' first, studied it under a magnifying glass, and then confirmed that it was from their supplier. He was not happy about that. Next, he looked at the pictures. Justin then described the attack that followed taking the pictures. The 'friend' really reacted to that and the poor judgment it displayed. And, he was largely outraged that it had happened in Israel of all countries.

Justin then told him that the second night after the pictures were taken, his client went into a very serious coma, and although he did not die, he was out of commission for over a month. This made his 'friend' even more unhappy with the thought --- that the coma had been a botched an attempt on a persons life in a foreign country. Justin said he only wanted a name and address from him if he was a 'rogue' former agent. His friend said he would see what he could do.

In parting, this man made it clear that, "if this guy had been one of theirs, he would be more than happy to identify him, especially if this would take him out of circulation."

Justin assured him that this was his goal, although he wanted to do it legally and above board.

CHAPTER 37

That evening Janice and Eric talked some more. They realized that it made perfect sense to use this interim coma period to write the paper documenting the Discovery of the Code. Janice gave Eric all the papers, reports and print outs that he had given her for safe keeping while in Israel. She had even retrieved the translation papers post mailed to her by Eric early the evening the coma began. So, there at her place, he had all that he needed to get busy writing the paper. That was it, he would do it. "I will start tomorrow." he said;

"Janice," Eric asked: "To what extent do you want to be a co-author, participant, and partner in this Discovery. There could be pluses and minuses and risks to being identified with this revelation to the scientific world; and don't forget that other areas may well be impacted, i.e. religious, evolution science and who knows what else. Are you in or out? I would sure like you to be my partner in whatever happens; it was your decision to test the snippet that started it all?"

Janice replied:

"Eric, don't you doubt me for a second." Smiling, she went on: "I didn't bring you back from Israel just for the company, if you woke up; or, for the sex, when you did recover; Eric, I do love you, deeply, and we are a team; when you get one of us, it also comes with the other one; and besides, I now have a big investment in you ---

251

and we are going to do this together, all the way; one way or the other."

Eric: "Wow Janice, even if we were married, I couldn't have asked for or received more support and encouragement.

And then, he just blurted out: "Janice, I want you to be my wife; I have had enough or our 'separate but committed' arrangement; lets do it as soon as we can. OK?"

Janice: "Yes, I agree, I accept, that's the best proposal I have had in a long time. I'm also tired of our 'separate but committed' life. Having you here with me full time makes me very happy and I don't want this to change to the way we were before. But, what are we going to do? I think we have to get thru this situation first. I don't want to be a bride one day and a widow the next. This cloud we are under has to go away, or we won't be able to live together peacefully."

Eric: "Ok; I agree; I'll start writing first thing. Let me cover a few points first, and make sure you agree. This is why I asked if you were willing to join in taking this Discovery public. Ok."

And, Janice nodded her approval.

Eric: "Two decisions; I think we should divide the paper into two parts. The first part, being the most authoritative and well documented narrative we can prepare on the Discovery of the Code, with examples from

252

the related snippets, the recurring regional words, followed by a translation of each 'live' snippet, and a history with supporting points about the underlying patient. The goal would be to make this part absolutely credible within the scientific community because we will no doubt be assailed without mercy or end, if we don't get this right.

The second part, would be our interpretation of part one; I believe we should start with an extensive caveat, to express a sense of humility about what we think has been found. We would make the point with great emphasis, that this interpretation is solely ours, that it arises from our personal logic and instincts after having worked with the words of the regions, the sub-areas and slashes so long; and further, that this second part is not meant as the bottom line conclusion on what one could or should perceive from the Discovery of the Code. To this, we would add that everyone present, as well as outside interested parties, are invited to join in and do the same thing we have done by way of interpretation. And perhaps, even suggest that if enough of this debate takes place, a consensus may sooner or later arrive at an agreed upon conclusion. What do you think?"

Janice: "Sounds like you have been thinking a lot about it. And, I agree with making it a two part paper; that would be a much safer way for a pair of scientists like us to proceed. Who knows what others may think of the second part; maybe it will keep them from confusing the first part with the interpretation found within the second part. On the other hand, I don't think you need to go quite as far on the second part as you described; it make's you seem to have a lack of confidence on the interpretation you offered.

Otherwise, and beyond that, I may want to separate myself from the second part. Let me think about it and read what you come up with. Can we leave it that way for now?"

Eric: " Sure; of course; I will start part one tomorrow morning."

It didn't take Justin's CIA 'friend' long to get back to him. He received a very brief call from him three days later. It was not a telephone recorded message --- just the statement:

"The name you're looking for is: Jeff Sullivan, with an apartment address of: 3421Poplar St., Apt. 3, Arlington, Virginia. I have the 'prints' if you need them." And, that was it.

After that, Justin wasted no time in packing his overnight bag; he then dressed as inconspicuously as he could and he drove off to Arlington, Virginia, a suburb of

Washington, D.C.. It took him four hours to get there. He parked in a location and watched for a while to try to get a 'feel' for the neighborhood. It was very quiet with not much happening and only one woman left the apartment building the whole time. So, he casually walked into the building and past Apartment Three. He was surprised to see a 'FOR RENT' sign on the door. At first, his instincts were to leave and call his 'friend' that had provided the address.

On second thought, however, he reverted to something he used to do when he was with the FBI. But in this case and without his badge, he opted for the use of a little deceptiveness. He found the 'super' for the building, guessing that he probably lived there for free in exchange for his in-house work. After introducing himself with some fake I.D., he asked:

"Say, would you happen to know where my friend 'Jeff Sullivan' moved?"

The 'super' stammered a little and said: "I don't like to give out that info --- its kinda private."

Justin had seen this reaction many times and knew exactly what to do --- he took out a fifty dollar bill and asked if this would help him remember?

The 'super' allowed as how he guessed it would be all right since he was talking with a 'friend' any way, and went and got the new address he had for forwarding mail and expected packages.

With this in his hand, Justin wrote down the address in his little memo book; and handed the 'super' the fifty and said he would be back if it didn't check out. With that Justin left; disappointed, but knowing this kind of thing was just a part of the job. The address he received was:

4700 Marine Drive,
Rock Hall, Maryland

From many trips over the years, Justin knew that Rock Hall was a quiet little waterfront community on the eastern shore of Maryland, known to tourists for its boating facilities, fishing delicious blue 'spiced' crabs. This would definitely extend his trip.

Before long, Justin was back on the D. C. Beltway, exiting on Route 50, proceeding east past Annapolis, Maryland, over the stunning Chesapeake Bay Bridge, past scenic Kent Island, and turning left on Route 213, going thru farming country, north to Chestertown. He decided to stay there overnight since it was the end of the day and he was tired. And, he had a hunch that he would check out the next day.

Arising at 7:00 am, dressing quickly, and after having a crab omelet for breakfast at the Inn where he stayed, he went over to the Courthouse for Kent County, Maryland; he knew from his maps that Rock Hall was located in Kent County, and just guessing, he would check to see if Jeff Sullivan had recently purchased a property. It might save him a trip thru the farming countryside.

The lady at the Recorder of Deeds office was very helpful. They first checked the current Deed Book index and found nothing, but that was not surprising if the recording was at all recent; then, they went to the ongoing temporary Deed Book, and there it was: a purchase within the last two weeks of a substantial property; it included five acres, a two-story house and a boat house with a dock; it was on the water because the land metes and bounds referenced the shoreline; and, the stated consideration was $950,000. Eric had the lady make him a copy of the Deed. Next, he had her check if a Mortgage had been recorded concurrently with the Deed? The answer was No; there had been no Mortgage to finance the property. Justin knew that was a lot of money to explain -- - was this a smoking gun? It could be important, so he decided to follow up.

His next step was to visit the Sales Agent for the Seller. He decided to take a chance and stop in at a nearby office and simply ask, thinking that a transaction that large would likely be known in the real estate community for a small town and a rural county. The head man in the first office didn't know but he had better luck at the next office. The answer was:

"Oh yes, that was a prize property and we all wanted the listing. The property was in foreclosure and the bank listed it with its usual agent in Rock Hall; that would be Molly Bentford of the Bentford Agency; she's quite active up there. Can't miss her, she's located on Main Street.

As he drove to Rock Hall, Justin observed farm after farm, and cornfield after cornfield. It would have been boring if his mind was not concentrating so much on the Jeff Sullivan lead. The drive took Justin about two hours. Arriving there about 11:30 am, he decided to try 'dropping' in at the Bentford office with no advance phone call. This would not be unusual in a small town like this one. He knew that formality was not needed in these country towns. His luck held and Molly was in by herself, things not being all that busy that morning. She was attractive, around 35 years old, a little short but bubbling with personality to go with her bright blue eyes. And, from the lack of a wedding ring on her hand, it would seem that she was unmarried.

Ever polite, Justin asked if they could talk a little while about one of her recent sales. Quickly looking him over, her answer was a very friendly:

"Of course, come with me, we'll do lunch."

At a nearby seafood grill, they talked and got acquainted for almost
fifteen minutes before they went on to the subject of the property sale to 'Jeff Sullivan.'

Molly was very forthcoming; she went on about what a great property it was; what a shame the prior owners couldn't afford it; and finally she wanted to know why Justin so interested? He explained that he was an investigator and was curious that there was no Mortgage --- he had checked. He explained that he could not disclose why or for whom he was investigating, although he could say that it was not all that important. She indicated that "yes" the buyer had just paid 'cash' and that it was a check to her client's bank --- she volunteered that there was a copy of it and would have this in her file. After a little more friendly chatter and asking her to keep his interest confidential, Justin paid the check for lunch and they both went down the street to her office.

Once there, she gave him a copy of her copy of the buyers check. She also gave him the name of the man she worked with at the bank office in Annapolis, commenting that money did not seem to be a problem for this Buyer. Then, Justin showed her one of the pictures from those Eric had taken of the man following him and asked if this was the Buyer? And bingo, it was him, no doubt about it. Justin thanked her for her most kind help and cooperation. And, as he left, in that he was a bachelor, Justin asked if Molly would be open to a date should he come back this way. Her answer: "Yes; Yes I would; I am looking forward to it" and they parted with big smiles.

Before leaving town that day, there was one last item. Justin drove past the property in question. It was quite a nice estate situated right on Chesapeake Bay. With his Nikon camera, he took a number of shots

using a long distance zoom lens. One picture focused on the dock and boat house accessing an arm of the Bay. Justin would have liked to take a peek in there but choose not to try for fear that he might be discovered. He noted that the main dwelling appeared to be an updated farmhouse with several sloping side roofs but no outside stairways. The land surrounding the house was a well cared for lawn although it was adjoined by the rest of the acreage. This property would provide a nice quiet setting for someone seeking minimal contact with the world. Actually, a good place to hide. Maybe, that was the point???????

Justin drove back home that day. He was pleased with his trip. Now, as a next step, he would see if he could enlist the help of the authorities on behalf of Eric and Janice. He thought that now he had enough to interest the Assistant Attorney General. That would be his next stop.

CHAPTER 38

The next day, Janice went to work as usual and Eric went to work in her side room. Now that they were sleeping together every night, they had converted the small room where Eric had recovered into a work room where he could concentrate and write. The bodyguard arrived as usual, looked bored, and sat in the living room right in front of the entry.

Meticulous as ever, Eric began by reorganizing and reviewing all papers and materials accumulated so far in pursuing the Code project. This went rather fast because these papers had been put in good order by Eric himself before he left for Israel. Next, he turned to the papers he sent via DHS packet to Janice the evening he entered the coma.

In retrospect they were the most interesting and he was drawn to trying to remember the sequence used in making the word translations. This helped him recall his trip to the Hebrew University of Jerusalem library to look in depth for more on the Legend document related to the Library at Alexandria.

In turn, this jogged his memory, about finding the footnoted document indicating the mystery inscription to be written in 'Coptic.' Then, his mind flashed upon his conversation with Yves Neiberg, a translator at the Shrine of the Book, confirming the Code letters to be ancient Coptic characters. He had it. Then, he remembered being shown how the letters had been encrypted via manipulation, upside down and backwards. By the end, Yves supplied a character chart, Coptic to English, to aid the final step of this process. It was all flooding back, quickly.

He remembered that for each of the two translated words, he had reversed the process letter by letter, arriving at the Coptic letter first and then the English alphabet letter next, resulting in the words: namely, Morals and Intellect. With that, he took the pages he stapled together that night and placed them in a stack in the right order. Now, he would finish the third 'regional' word.

Immediately, using four of the stapled pages, he had the letters: _ AL _ ES; then, writing the two other characters on the front and back of a blank page, he turned each upside down and backwards (over), and compared the result to the Coptic chart. The missing letters were V and U, respectively. Hence the word: 'VALUES.' The regional words, that had been consistent within each 'live' sample were: Morals, Intellect and Values.

He could not help at this moment to once again to ponder the words significance. Do these words confirm my epiphany? Was this leap of faith and understanding right? Intuitively, now more than ever, he was confident of his conclusion: these words and the other Code subparts and slashes are a part, at least, of the Human Spirit (the Soul). Of this he was sure. And yet, something in the back of his mind, told him there was still more. Try as he might, he could not put his finger on it. This would just have to come to him.

With this introduction finished, it was clear that this would now be his main pursuit for a while. It made no sense to start writing part one of the paper until he had translated the words for the four 'live' samples with MRI results. These translations, in turn, would provide a statement of what had been important enough to track during the patients life on his or her Human Spirit (Soul).

Eric's next move was to gather together by patient the print out's of the MRI magnifications (5000x). He would start with the one for Barney, the patient from whom the first snippet was taken. In his mind, Eric knew, of course, that all he would get would be words, just words, followed by slash and backslash marks. That would not tell much in and of itself; therefore, for this listing to make any kind of sense, there would have to be follow up with either the surviving patient or, if deceased, with past or surviving family members. Being that he was 'technically' still in a coma; he couldn't do this personally; he would ask Janice to take on this task. If his Human Spirit (Soul) theory was correct, their should be a strong correlation between the history of the 'real life' person and the decoded words disclosed by the MRI. This would be a clear and detailed test of what had really been found. If this was a failure, there would be little need for the paper and all their efforts would have been a wild goose chase.

In making this translation, Eric used the same simple steps he had followed to get the three 'region' words that evening in his motel room in Israel and today. Carefully he went through this process. He started by listing the 'regional' words, namely: Morals, Intellect and Values (the MIV's). After that, it took him the rest of the morning to decode the following:

Barney, age 60, Patient 1:
        Morals: religious \; adultery \; stealing \;
        Intellect: school /; trade \; skill \;
      Values: dishonest \; respectful /; intemperate \; nonviolent/;

     Eric had never met Barney; and did not know him in any way; however, if he were to take what this listing at face value, it was fine with him that they had never been introduced.

     Nonetheless, something still bothered him. It was like trying to grasp something that was always beyond ones reach. It was in the back of his mind and he struggled to find a way to know what was there. He looked to the translation he had just completed, and said to himself: "that's awful short; its bare bones; surely there must be more to this mans Spirit than this?"

     He went on to remember his 'pals' and the 'professor' with whom he had been close. "What is the personality of this man? What is his character like? Where is the unique stuff that makes him memorable to those that knew him? Why is this absent?"

     Thinking that perhaps he missed something, Eric started to shuffle through his papers. He went quickly, recognizing all the forms, information, tests and so on. Not long afterwords, he picked up the MRI Code listing as magnified in the lab. Intensely, he looked and studied it and set it down in front of him. Absently, while thinking, he placed his hand on this printout. Leaning back in his chair he closed his eyes; somehow images flashed in his mind with amazing speed, of a man, his words, acts, qualities, attitudes, and behavior.

Seized by the moment, Eric immediately wrote of Barney's qualities and nature:

+'s: quiet; cooperative; non-confronting; sociable;

-'s: sneaky; deceitful; deceptive; alcoholic; thieving;
untrustworthy;

Afterward, Eric wondered why he did that? On what basis did he write this down; he allowed that it definitely was not 'scientific.' Still, he would keep it there, pending what Janice thought. It all seemed mysterious to him.

That evening Eric showed Janice this translation for Patient 1: Barney.

She had met him in the course of preparing for his surgery. She didn't know much about his personal life so she begged off on making any comments in reaction to the translation listing. On the other hand, she greatly agreed with Eric that a follow up inquiry would be needed to see how the MIV's would match up with his life history. She agreed to take on this responsibility, and she would promptly fit it in. A Patients family's always appreciated having a follow up discussion with their Doctor. It would not be difficult to do this.

On the other hand, after reading Eric's add-on for Barney's nature and qualities, and learning how he came to write this, she couldn't help but wonder about him. It wasn't like Eric to think and act in a way that didn't have a quantitative or objective basis. Maybe she had missed something. Perhaps, Israel somehow changed him in some quiet way. She would have to keep an eye out for more signs of this, whatever it was?

At about the same time as Eric started working, Justin, his investigator, was sitting down with the Assistant Attorney General (AAG) for the Eastern District of North Carolina, at his office in Raleigh, N.C.. Being able to meet with such a U.S. official on short notice was one of the side benefits of employing someone with the FBI experience that Justin possessed. During his twenty-five year career, Justin had often worked hand in hand with this office of the Attorney General and in particular, with the man who was now the AAG. At that time, he was a new young lawyer and Justin had only been with the FBI for two years. Being about the same age they worked hard on various cases and became well acquainted. You could not say they were close friends, but they had been close in their work; they had gained many convictions together and mutually respected each other. His name was Jared Turner; he was about 6' 2" inches tall, easily two hundred pounds, with dark wavy hair and a booming voice.

Jared said, after a pleasant greeting:

"All right Justin, to what do I owe this honor; I thought you retired years ago."

"You're right on that point Jared and I am glad of it. On the other hand, I have run into something I can't handle alone and it would not fit with what the local authorities can do. It's a case that I am asking you and your office to take a look at for prosecution under both State and/or Federal law."

"As if I did not have enough to worry about." Jared replied.

"Now, now, let me see if I can offer enough to gain your interest; this is not your every day run of the mill District matter; its tentacles run to several other states and even to Israel; and it involves my client and friend, a prominent geneticist at the renowned Medical Research Center (MRC) in the Research Triangle."

Jared's ears perked up a little: "I'm listening; I hear you; tell me more?"

Justin launched into his description;

"This scientist has Discovered and is on the verge of announcing to the Medical world, what amounts to a phenomenon within the human body; even though he is first and foremost a scientist, this Discovery will have religious and many other implications; somehow, and I think I know how, his security has been breached by a MRC co-employee; due to this breach, a related 'zealot' with a lot to lose financially, has attempted to kill my client to prevent the Discovery from ever becoming public; and, if that were not bad enough, he has a former CIA operative working for him, who went to Israel, burglarized my clients room and somehow caused my client to suffer a coma from which he is now quietly recovering; meanwhile this ex-CIA operative has purchased for cash a million dollar property on the Eastern shore of Chesapeake Bay. How's that for complicated?"

Jared: "Whoa, whoa; slow down; if I heard a story like that from most people, I would dismiss it; but I know you from our years of working together; now, tell me what you already have in the way of 'proof', and just as important, what do you need Federal muscle to obtain?"

Justin: "Let me start with what I have; beginning with complete cooperation from my client and his partner;" and then he listed:

1. Telephone taps have been placed on my clients home phones; with the kind of device used by the CIA, probably via their supplier;
2. Hidden software used to duplicate my clients home computer files;

3. Actions arising from info that could only
   have come from being able to hack into
   my clients e-mail.
4. Israel motel and police officials able to
   confirm the break-in to my clients room;
   searching for something related to a
   secret Code that is part of the Discovery.
5. My client's photo's of the ex-CIA
   operative following him the day
   after the burglary; he was attacked after
   taking the man's photo's. My client
   got his 'prints' on the camera.
6. The identity and real name of this former
   CIA operative.
7. The location of this former CIA operative at a
   sizeable new property he recently purchased on
   Maryland's Eastern shore. This
   includes a copy of the payment check drawn on
   his bank in, I believe, in Baltimore.
8. My clients coma as documented by records
   from both Israel and the University
   Hospital associated with the MRC; the
   timing of the coma was the night of the next
   day after my client took the daytime photos
   already mentioned.

Sitting back, Jared said: "Lets say that your list is
solid and that it would hold up in court or lead to further
evidence; what do you see that we could bring to the
case(s); I gather it would come from our ability to marshal
evidence across state lines, obtain search warrants and
seize items needed to verify evidence; and then, of course,

making the arrests at the appropriate moment, followed by interrogation and prosecution(s);"

Justin: "Yes, that's exactly the kind of help we need; I have a little list that may help in getting started on that part:

1. The phone records and computers for both the ex-CIA operative and the target 'zealot'; I know that FBI technicians can recover items from hard drives that these men likely deleted from their files. We would be after hard proof of their connection.

2. Bank records in the real name of the ex-CIA operative; especially, any transfers from a European bank associated with his return, or shortly thereafter, ultimately used to purchase the million dollar property on the Eastern Shore.

3. Cooperation and a records request with the local officials in Israel on the motel break-in; I am guessing there may be surveillance camera video that would include the ex-CIA operative, that they can't identify.

4. Visa and entry/exit info on this ex CIA operative related to the timing of events happening to my client and his ensuing coma.

Justin went on; "And that's only for openers; you know better than I how much more Federal investigators would likely turn up if they tried; I can supply the real name of this ex-CIA operative if your office chooses to go further; let me add before I leave, that when my client and his partner 'go public' with their Discovery, I believe it will be a 'sensation' all over the news; any actions your office would take in connection with the conspiracy and attempted murder of this scientist would be well received by the public and the media, that will be all over these stories."

Jared smiled (he had been taking notes as Justin went through his items):

" All of us at the Justice Department and the Administration, deplore and dislike hearing of the kind of activities and behavior you have described by one of our former Agency employee's; that alone, though, does not add up to a decision to prosecute them; however, that coupled with illegal acts against citizens within our District, such as your client, does get our attention and I thank you for telling me of what's been happening; with that said, I am not committing to you that we will take action on this case; I will however take it up with our District Attorney General; I will get back to you if and when we decide to go ahead; we would need to go into all the details you have given and interview your client and his partner."

With that the meeting ended and Jared walked Justin out. As he walked away and Justin looked back, he saw that Jared gave him a big smile and a 'wink.'

He hoped and thought this to be a good omen of what would come from their meeting; Jared would do the right thing.

CHAPTER 39

Over the next few days, Eric concentrated on the translations for the remaining three patients that had 'live' samples with MRI results listing the Code. He was most anxious to get thru this part. Once he had these listings, he could give them to Janice for follow up interviews, move on to writing the narrative of the paper, document it with exhibits, and then prepare their explanation. The better he felt, the more anxious he was to escape his solitary existence hidden away at her place. He appreciated that it was for his own safety, but he still wanted too get back to the outside world.

Taking the patients in the order of his earlier summary, Patient 2 was Ralph, age 65, married, and a retired professor. Working diligently, he did the translation smoothly, determining the MIV to be:

Ralph, age 65, Patient 2:
   Morals: God /; religious ///; Sabbath /;
      ethical///;
   Intellect: school //; degrees ///; pragmatic/;
      books /;
   Values: honest //; truthful //;

On the face of it, Eric estimated that he would have gotten along well with this gentleman. He would give this info to Janice that night.

Inspired by what had happened at this point while working on Patient 1, Barney, Eric decided to try once again: 'reading what was not readily apparent.' He searched for and removed the magnified Code listing for Ralph. He placed it on the table and put his hand on it. For the second time, images flashed before his mind, this time showing a man, disclosing his words, seeing his acts, his qualities, attitudes, and behavior; undeniably his earthly Spirit.

Eric immediately wrote what he saw:

+'s: genuine; resourceful; through; talented; smart; thoughtful;wise

-'s: demanding; choleric; anxious; fretful;

He smiled, although wondering why? Accepting this for the moment, he went on with the work he was doing. He had a lot to finish.

Next, Eric turned to Patient 3, Loretta, age 53, married, a hair dresser by occupation; and also Patient 5, John, age 63, married and an aircraft engineer about to retire. Their translations were;

Loretta, age 53, Patient 3:
      Morals: God/; religious /; parents /; adultery \; justice /;
     Intellect: school /; trade /; skilled /;
     Values: frankness /; lustful \\; human /;

John, age 63, Patient 5:
      Morals: God /; religious /; family ///; faithful /;
     Intellect: school //; degrees ////; engineer /; inventor /;pragmatic /;
     Values: integrity //; reassuring /; self starter /; circumspect //;

At this point, acquiescing to the means of finding more on the patients Spirit by way of the magnified Code listings, he located the listings for Loretta and John.

Putting his hand on the printout for Loretta, he saw 'images, words, etc., etc.; for her and wrote down:

Loretta, Patient 3:

+'s: loyal; helpful; active; straight forward; blunt;
easy going; friendly;
-'s: naughty; adventurous; secretive; deceitful;

Eric went on, touching the Code listing; seeing this Spirit as before;

John, Patient 5;

+'s: smart; ingenious; independent;
commonsense; loving;devoted;

-'s: restless; over focused; calculating; doubtful;

By this time, Eric had stopped trying to 'size up' these pluses and minuses on the patients underlying Spirits. They were there, and for the moment that was good enough for him. He did not know what to tell Janice about this. He would wait for her to read these Code results. Perhaps, he thought, her independent follow-up and investigation would show his Spirit interpretation to be off base. He would wait and see.

Later that evening, Janice told him that she could now describe the results of the interview(s) on Patient 1, Barney. She would have it in writing for him the next evening. Her description of Barney went like this:

"After talking with his ex-wife and his brother, and the warehouse manager where he worked, it turns out that he was not a very laudable fellow. He did not go to church during his life except to get married. He was a drinker, and pilfered things at work. He outwardly did what his boss directed him to do, but took advantage of any opportunity to undermine these directions. He did serve his parents and elders and stayed away from physical confrontations. He cheated on his wife and that led to their divorce. He had minimal schooling and worked for years in customer service, not having the ability to do much else."

Eric's reaction was that he would have to think how well this matched up with the Code and whether the Code was an accurate insight to his Human Spirit (Soul). How did it fit? What did it all mean? There would always be speculation.

In the interim, sitting in his office at home, Dr. Alex Howard was feeling more at ease about the whole threat he had perceived related to Eric, his Project and the unidentified Code. The longer things went on without hearing of any change in Eric's coma, the more he concluded that this status might never end. And, even if it did, its result would more than likely be devastating for Eric. He was satisfied that he had his son on full alert to let him know of any news, should it happen, about his boss's condition. The MRC would be the first to know and he would be the second, if and when there was something new.

Also, Dr. Alex had tried several times to get his operative 'Charles' to call him to discuss the situation. So far, there was no call back and this made him feel somewhat troubled. He 'got' the message that 'Charles' no doubt intended; that it was over as far as he was concerned. Not knowing his real identity and not having any other way to get in touch with him, left Dr. Alex 'out' of his million dollars with no way to get it back should Eric suddenly recover. Dr. Alex knew that this was his 'pay back' for engaging in such nefarious activities. This could become untenable for him and he knew it.

Suddenly, it was what Justin had been hoping for. Jared, the AAG had called, initially to verify a couple questions he had from their prior meeting. Then, within an hour afterwards, Jared called back again and said it was a 'go'; his boss had authorized taking on the case and now they would have to get to work. He had assigned an attorney in the office to take the lead on the day to day preparation of the matter and its later prosecution. Justin would have to spend the next few days helping him get up to speed and working out a strategy. Justin called Eric and Janice right away with the good news and said he would brief them following the days he would have to spend at the District office for the United States Attorney. Planning and timing would be crucial in gaining the proper evidence and arresting the defendants. This was really 'big' news for them. The tension was definitely building.

Justin spent the next three day's in the office of the Assistant Attorney General(AAG) for the United States for the Eastern District of North Carolina. The assigned attorney was Andy Cardwell, a likeable, hard working attorney five years out of law school. He was young, of normal height, preppy looking having had an Ivy League education, with bright piercing eyes. He was a rising star in the Office and one could tell from his enthusiasm he wouldn't mind the press coverage if and when it got to that point.

They went over, at least twice, everything Justin had talked about with Jared, the AAG. Curious, Andy wanted to know more about the Discovery and the mystery Code than Justin could answer. They finally agreed that these questions would have to wait until the interview with Janice and Eric. By the afternoon of the third day, it was time to get down to strategy. Andy did not see this to be at all difficult. The Office policy was to go after the leader, the top person, the villain who was hiding behind the scene but calling all the shots. And, in order to do that, their practice, typical to criminal prosecutions, was to use an intermediary to testify against the person(s) he or she was working for. This approach had worked many times before.

In this case, that would make the ex-CIA operative, that had been photographed in Israel and Justin later identified, the intermediary they would concentrate upon. This step would have to be done carefully because they did not want him to run. Andy would first be in touch with the police in Jerusalem that did the follow up on the motel burglary. He would send the photo of the man Eric had caught following him. This could lead to either a match with the motel's video surveillance, or jolt a motel employee's memory and recollection. Next, they would see if they could locate the passport used and/or visa's issued for this trip and would start with the 'real name' Justin had provided, being "Jeff Sullivan.' Andy correctly judged that Justin's source would not be willing to 'out' himself within the Agency. However, he would get the camera back and try to lift the 'prints' if present there. Justin passed on the 'prints' for Eric that were included when the camera arrived. This would help sort out the 'prints' of the attacker.

At the same time, Andy would follow the financial trail himself, contacting the bank official the realtor, Molly Bentford, had named to see what he could obtain from this bank. The warrants and the rest of the home based items would have to wait. Andy took the position, and rightly so in Justin's view, that their would not be a case worth acting upon if the 'operative's' actions in Jerusalem could not be established. For him to make a case for Conspiracy and/or Attempted Murder, they would need solid proof as to the acts taken at that time. Andy's goal was to have his case against the ex-CIA operative 'in place' before arresting him and seizing his records, if any, related to the telephone taps, the computer hacking, and anything else that might link him to Dr. Alex Howard.

Experience had taught Andy well, that a person like the ex-CIA operative, would not take the 'fall' alone if he were truly caught in carrying out illegal actions on behalf of a client. Agents like him, worked in a way, where they could come up with indicting and compromising materials, if need be, in order that they could work a 'deal' for themselves, if needed; and let the person for whom they were working take the 'big' hit. There was no honor among these people. It was every man for himself.

Consequently, many things were now in 'play' on Eric's behalf, although entirely unknown to the co-conspirators, 'Charles' and Dr. Alex. Nonetheless, Eric was single-minded on completing his work and proving the body's physical connection to the Human Spirit (the Soul). Could it be done?

CHAPTER 40

It was a fresh new day and Eric was hard at it, digging in and writing the first part, being the scientific facts, of the Paper on the Discovery. This was rather easy and straight forward, the kind of thing he had done before in preparing reports on projects. He had all the pieces in place, and they were described in narrative form, making use of listings and charts, to show the results of the lab work. He documented all the items with copies of the original findings in a very careful and detailed way. Many references were incorporated as Exhibits in support of the narrative.

He knew that several points would be most prominent, in terms of believability, among his colleagues. He would address these head on and challenge them to conclude otherwise after studying the supporting documentation. The first would be finding a part of the body, namely the 'snippets', to be 'blank,' totally lacking in DNA. Next, of course, would be finding within that same 'snippet(s)' a strange Code, via the MRI image subjected to high magnification. And finally, determining and showing the Code to be a human language that dates back, to well before the modern era, known and recognized as Coptic.

Scientifically, these points would pose 'new' questions for years to come. Eric wasn't offering any answers on these issues; that would be left for others in the future. All in all, Part One of the paper came together rather quickly, and it was essentially completed in short order; all that remained would be the addition of the write-ups Janice was preparing for Patients 2, 3, and 5; the write-up for Patient 1, Barney was already included.

That evening, after dinner, Janice presented the story for Ralph, Patient 2. The sources included Ralph, himself, family members and colleagues from the university:

Several things stood out right away in his history. He had always been very active in his faith and church. Within his family, he made a strong point of observing Sunday, the Sabbath, and not permitting contrary activities such as 'work'. Educationally, he had been successful at all levels of schooling, achieving a doctorate and teaching. This was accompanied by a practical, everyday manner with his students. He was known to be honest, truthful, loyal and ready to help others as their need became apparent. He had led a good life and was still going.

Eric took this information, and commented: 'Seems the translated Code pretty well captured the essence of Ralph. Doesn't that make you wonder how this is possible?" How can the make up of a person know, track and record a life's substantive content?

Janice: "I agree; how does the brain know and judge these qualitative aspects that happen during the period of ones life; let alone record them in encoded Coptic and place this in summary form in a tiny 'snippet' of the human body. Incredible, just incredible."

Eric: "I know, I know; I can hardly believe it; that's likely to be the reaction when the Paper is announced and understood. And, even more striking, will likely be the reaction to Part Two; despite our Caveat that it represents solely the author's interpretation and opinion. I suspect that we will be assailed and criticized endlessly. I hope not; we will have to bear with it, whatever happens."

At about the same time, Jeff Sullivan, alias 'Charles' the operative, was feeling pleased with himself. He was sitting 'pretty' on the Eastern Shore, at his new property and house. It was just the kind of 'country' place he had always imagined he would own. In addition, he had also purchased a new high powered speed boat and could travel throughout Chesapeake Bay at anytime he desired. He now considered himself 'respectable' and no longer worried about his past catching up with him.

As far as he was concerned, he had carefully covered his trail and did not plan to ever talk with Dr. Alex Howard again. And, if by chance, something went wrong with his prior services on Dr. Alex's behalf, he had his secret file that could clearly shift the blame. And further, even though he had been on the scene in Jerusalem and been paid a handsome sum, he knew that he 'actually' never did a thing to Eric that would put him in a coma. He had no idea how it happened, but he knew for sure that he did not do it. Period. Period. He was safe, he smugly reassured himself.

After contacting and sending pictures via overnight mail to the police officials in Jerusalem, Israel, that had investigated the burglary at Eric's motel room, Andy Cardwell turned his attention to the money trail. He had assigned the passport/visa search effort to other Office members so that he could concentrate on following the money. His first step had been to obtain a warrant that he could and did present to the bank official in Annapolis the realtor had named. This part went smoothly and the recipient bank quickly produced a copy of the complete closing file, including a copy of the check used for payment. It was the same as the one Justin provided.

Andy then had the warrant expanded to include any and all other account activity by or for Jeff Sullivan during the preceding six months. This worked well and Andy had these records in short order. The cashier's check issued for the purchase of the Eastern Shore property was in order. What drew his attention though was the credit for a transfer of one million dollars from a Swiss bank account, the day after Eric went into the Hospital with his coma.

He obtained a copy of the remittance advice from the Swiss bank and the Maryland banks notification of the transfer to their account holder. This was a 'smoking gun';

the type of circumstantial evidence that could add up to a conviction. Now, he would expand the search warrant once again, to have the Swiss bank named, and see if he could have this bank disclose the name of the holder of the account and put a date upon when this money (the one million) arrived in the account. Over the years, statutes and arrangements had been made with Swiss government officials obligating their banking industry to cooperate in bringing an end to facilitating transfers of money related to criminal activities. The Swiss banking industry's need to do business within the U.S.A. outweighed there secrecy practices where a criminal offence was involved. This was distinctly different than broadly 'fishing' for U.S. citizen accounts that might be involved in questionable tax activities. It might take a bit of time, but the information Andy wanted would be forthcoming. Not everyone was familiar with what was now possible. This may well break the case if and when it was received.

While working on the financial part of the case, Andy had scheduled a late afternoon meeting with those working on the passport and visa records for the ex-CIA operative's trip to Israel. This part was easy for properly authorized personnel of the Justice Department. Because of the thoroughness of the Israeli visa practices, the 'operative' had to use his real identity, being Jeff Sullivan; therefore, they now had the info on his leaving the U.S. and arriving in Israel and then on to Jerusalem, including where he stayed.

Finding out when and where he left Israel was however, more difficult. After searching quite a bit, they discovered passport and flight records showing that he returned via Cairo, Egypt. Tracing this back, with Egyptian immigration cooperation, they determined that he had left Israel at the southern crossover to Egypt. But what stuck out the most, was the timing of his movements. Leaving, including the travel to and over the border, all took place on the day following the night Eric's coma began. Clearly, someone was in a hurry to leave and was not taking any chances of being detained in Israel. That would take a terrific explanation. The circumstantial evidence was piling up.

Andy was pleased with their work and how quickly it had been done! He told them so and took them all out for a modest thank you dinner.

Once they arrest this Jeff Sullivan, Andy would see how long he would hold out before seeking a deal in exchange for evidence and testimony to convict Dr. Alex Howard. Andy's confidence was growing.

CHAPTER 41

Eric began the new day full of enthusiasm. Pleased, because he had part one of the Paper completed except for any changes his partner, Janice, might want to make. Now, he could concentrate on what would be the hardest and most challenging part; being, part two, the interpretation and opinion of the meaning of what the Code contains and represents; and, as translated, the words recorded for the four patients tested; compared with the description of their lives from those interviewed. He intended to keep this part short and not go too far 'out on the limb' with the unknown. In fact, he would approach this by staying as close to the 'known' as he could.

He planned to build to a final conclusion for part two. In other words, he would draw as close as he could, upon the *translation(s)* of the Code; and then asking:

What is it that we 'know' from the facts found and stated in part one?

Furthermore, what do we think we 'know', notwithstanding the findings of part one; taking notice, however, of 'generally recognized universal thinking' pertaining to mankind; and then,

What can be 'drawn' from the answers to these questions, through *reasoning and extension*, as a conclusion?

Noting, that this must be done, setting aside our normal inclination to prejudge what the conclusion should be from one's individual perspective. If we are going to speculate, let's try to do it without substituting our pre-existing bias.

The answers to these questions would be a tall order, but nevertheless, that would be the way Eric would approach the discussion within part two. When he started writing, he stated this to be the analytic method he would apply within the ensuing narrative:

He began with the three key 'region' words found within the Code for each person. He observed and stressed this repetition to be of great importance, because it established a uniform pattern for all the 'live' tested humans. Because of the limited sample, he speculated that 'others' would no doubt find the same thing in the years to come via further operations.

Then he turned to the words themselves: Morals, Intellect and Values (MIV).

He refused to get fancy at this point and stayed away from any deep philosophical views or meanings for these words. Instead, he simply accepted their straight forward definitions, as appropriate, from within the dictionary. He also observed that if one were looking to ascribe an overall meaning to them (the MIV's), it could be as simple as thinking of a ones 'character;' each persons special and unique human character. Taken together, these words go to the heart of each person and their human traits.

Using that as an opening, he went on to the subparts and slashes that followed each 'regional' word (the MIV's) for the decoded snippets. He observed and declared the decoded subpart words to be easily within the broader meaning of the preceding MIV word(s). Again the dictionary definitions were sufficient for determining their meaning as part of the 'regional' words.

Setting aside the slashes for the moment, he made comparisons of the MIV translations with the written descriptions that had been prepared by Janice from the interviews of the Patient and/or others that knew of the life of the Patient (i.e. family, friends and colleagues). This analysis became more lengthy than Eric wanted, so he made separate exhibits for each Patient. Then he summarized the exhibits and made a bottom line finding that there was a strong correlation between the persons Code translation and what had been the Patients actual life history. He supported this correlation with examples from the exhibits for the Patients.

More troubling and difficult, however, was making an interpretation of the slashes, especially the varying number of them; Eric clearly recognized this to be a challenge. Even so, he did make a finding that the slashes seemed to be in keeping with a trend or a time period for that attribute of the Patient. And, he openly speculated that the forward leaning slashes were positive actions and the backward leaning slashes might be negative events or consequences. Even though he didn't say it, in his mind he wondered whether some day new technology might make it possible to 'read' these slashes for their substantive content. With this finished, it allowed him to move further with part two.

Moreover, in order to be careful, choosing to limit part two as much as he could to objective points, he left out what he had written beyond the Code itself. He had no answer for the how or why he saw what he did after touching the Code listings. This would have to be 'out there' for further thinking and study.

Then, he turned back to his analytic methodology and what it is 'we think we know.' For this next observation, he made clear that what he was about to say was not from part one, nor was this conclusion in any way 'scientific'; nonetheless, this follows from what is considered to be generally recognized 'universal' thought or dogma, by various religions, religious scholars and philosophers. And that; he was thinking of it here as being relevant to this situation, inasmuch and because, he could think or find no other explanation that made sense.

Furthermore, for those reading what he was about to say, he invited one and all to agree or disagree with its relevance at this point. However, in doing so, intellectually he challenged that this disagreement, should be designed to suggest a meaningful alternative. That, it was not enough to just disagree, unless something could be offered that provided a better explanation.

Thus, he was giving 'notice' that his next observation was fundamental to the importance to this paper. This being:

"That mankind, clerics and philosophers, and the bible, over the centuries of human civilization, have recognized and held that we all have a Soul. Furthermore, that our Soul is one and the same with our Human Spirit, because it is a part of our nature as a human beings. And moreover, equally as important, that our Soul (Human Spirit) upon death, leaves the human body, and upon rising, is 'judged' whether it is accepted for Eternal Life in Heaven."

Eric emphasized: "that he could not state this 'universal dogma' more simply than that."

And that, upon accepting this 'premise', it clearly follows from logic and reason, and by extending one's mind, the *conclusion* must be that the body part found (being the snippet) is in some way a 'window' into the Human Spirit (Soul). That such *conclusion* is further supported by the fact that the snippet is only a ' blank container' that accumulates an ongoing record of the underlying person's life history. And equally important, the snippet performs no other 'function' within one's body, as do other areas of our body.

Continuing, Eric did not claim the Code to be a complete statement of the Human Spirit (Soul); he viewed that to be clearly impossible for something that is entirely transcendental and effusive as the Soul. He was only claiming that they have demonstrated a *connection* to the Human Spirit (the Soul), that gives great incite into the person. That's all. That' was it.

Beyond that Eric refused to assert what, if anything, this meant to the Worlds religions. Neither would he take a position on any effect that this Discovery may or may not have in other fields, whether it be science or otherwise. He would leave that kind of analysis and argument to others in a better position to come to such conclusions. He would stick to being the scientist-geneticist. That was enough for him and he stated this once again in the Paper.

Having now completed part two, Eric settled on a title for the Paper:

"A BRAIN DISCOVERY: The finding of a human language Code within a physical part of the Human Brain." By Dr. Eric Rhodes and Dr. Janice Westphal, and the Medical Research Center and Hospital.

Later, Janice was back from work and she eagerly gave Eric her latest write-up, in this case, for Patient 3, Loretta. The cooperation received had been excellent and the woman was easy to know. At the same time as Eric read this narrative, he had Janice read part two of the Paper, the result of his efforts that day. Eric would add the write up for Loretta to her exhibit tomorrow.

Loretta's history was a varied mix. She believed in God, attended church but not always on a regular basis, taking part in some things and passing on the rest. She had a heart of gold, full of concern for her friends; while at the same time, speaking her mind as she saw fit. She had committed adultery, now and again, but even so, her husband had remained faithful to their marriage. She had minimal schooling, but learned through beauty school and work to become a sought after hair dresser. Her translated

294

Code fairly well summarized Loretta's life. It seemed to be on target. How did it do that?

By the time Eric finished reading about Loretta, Janice was done reading part two of the Paper. Her reaction was that she thought Eric had done a good job in presenting the logic and his conclusion; he had definitely been careful, perhaps even a little too careful.

However, even beforehand, she had decided not to sign on to this part of the Paper. She felt that her education and life experiences had not prepared her to venture an opinion as to where the facts from the Discovery should led as a conclusion. She was more than happy to leave this to Eric; after all, it was Eric that had the 'epiphany' that Sunday evening, when he suddenly realized the connection to the Human Spirit (the Soul). That was good enough for her. She would leave it at that.

Meanwhile, turning back to Andy at the Attorney Generals Office for the Eastern District for North Carolina, his case was moving along better than expected.

Momentarily, he had finished a telephone call with the head detective reviewing the burglary in Eric's room at the motel. This detective confirmed that the lobby video surveillance camera did indeed pick-up the person in the photo sent to him, both coming and going. And, of equal importance, a secreted camera in the hallway to Eric's room, had a little video of the same man walking toward the room about the time the burglary occurred. He would now take the pictures of this man to the store Guard and witnesses to the attack when the pictures were taken. He had the report for this incident right in front of him.

He also disclosed having a fingerprint from the outside door knob to Eric's room. They couldn't be sure of its date, because finding the print was delayed to the morning after the coma had begun. Disappointing, however, was the absence of similar video on the night that Eric slipped into the coma. This policeman would send all of this info over to Andy's office ASAP. Andy thanked him for the quick and professional follow-up and said that he would let him know if he was needed to testify.

Andy sat back in his chair and concluded that it was time for an arrest warrant for Jeff Sullivan as well as a warrant to seize any and all records, computers, telephone gear, and such other materials, that may be found on the premises in furtherance of the Conspiracy and/or Attempted Murder of Dr. Eric Rhodes.

Andy did love this part and would go along to see if Jeff Sullivan would try to make a break for it, or be in a hurry to turn the blame on to someone else. He and Justin knew who this person would likely be. On the other hand, they wanted it to come from Jeff Sullivan first. Establishing this connection with admissible evidence was now the key break needed in their case.

How long would it take for Jeff Sullivan to start to talk in exchange for a deal.? This part was always the most interesting.

CHAPTER 42

The next day, Eric spent the entire time putting the finishing touches on the Paper and its attached exhibits. There was nothing complicated about this work, although it turned out to be a bit time consuming. He had to make sure the terminology and captions were consistent throughout the paper. At the same time, he was somewhat distracted thinking about what their next step should be. He would talk it over with Janice that night. And, Janice promised to have the last life history description ready for Patient 4. He would add this narrative to this patients exhibit to the Paper, already having satisfied himself as to the general correlation with the translated Code.

Thereafter, later, as Eric and Janice talked, he started by noting that his sabbatical leave and medical leave had now gone on for more than three months. And, that only he and she knew that his coma had ended almost a month ago. Furthermore, during this entire period, he had had no direct contact with the MRC, or his boss, Mr. Richard Johnston. All of this made him feel 'guilty' of deception for his own personal benefit, and he wasn't comfortable with that position.

Janice then pointed out that they had talked about this earlier; they could tell that the direction the Discovery was taking may be well beyond the type of 'project' the MRC would be willing to support.

Even so, Eric wanted to try to be loyal to the MRC if he could. And, he knew that if they backed this public disclosure of the Discovery, it would be significant for him as well as the MRC. With that in mind, he asked Janice to go along with him on having a private and secret meeting with Mr. Johnston to determine if the MRC wanted to take part in going public with the Paper. He then went over with Janice how he wanted to approach setting up this meeting. They planned that she would invite him to her place; that Mr. Johnston would not even know Eric was out of the coma nor have any suspicion of the Discovery or the preparation of the Paper.

As they finished, Janice gave him the write-up on the life history for Patent 5, John:

"John had been an exemplary student his entire life, finishing public school with top grades, graduating

298

from college and graduate school with Honors, and going on to become an inventor of labor saving everyday items. He was active in his church and made his family the center of his world, especially being faithful to his wife. He was respected within his community, known for his honesty, skill, reasoning and ability to get things done on his own. One and all felt sorry for his Essential Tremor affliction, concluding that it could not have happened to a nicer guy."

Eric would add this to John's exhibits. They were now all completed and that felt good.

In the pre-dawn hours of the coming day, Justin met Andy Cardwell and his SWAT team at a gasoline station on Kent Island, a few miles east of the Chesapeake Bay Bridge. Andy had asked Justin to go along with his group on the arrest Jeff Sullivan, the ex-CIA operative, and to assist in the search of the premises for whatever they could find to connect Jeff Sullivan with the attempt on Eric's life and Dr. Alex Howard. Andy had gone so far as to have had Justin deputized in order for him to join in this search and seizure operation. Being an ex-FBI agent, this was just like old times for Justin; he had done this many times before.

As they wound their way through the fields and pastures of Kent County, Maryland, on the way to Rock Hall, Andy was busy with the SWAT team on exactly how he wanted to conduct this raid. He had some idea's that might be helpful in furthering the case they were building. Furthermore, he was happy to have Justin along, because he could take them directly to the home and property where they expected to find Jeff Sullivan. This was the 'big' day, and it was important that it all be conducted well. This was not the time for any screw-ups.

They paused outside the entry to the property; quickly going over once again, who was to do the talking to the suspect, who was to do the seizure of the computer(s) and memory disks, and who would do the other search assignments for records and documents. Then, at around 7:30 am, their three big black government Tahoe SUV's, quickly moved down the lane to the front entry of the sizeable house. As the group fanned out, the SWAT team leader, named Rex, an African American, big and tall in physique, walked straight to the front door, pressed the door bell and pounded on the door at the same time.

Upstairs, bleary eyed and still in bed from the previous late night, Jeff Sullivan stumbled out of bed, put on a robe, and went down the steps to the front door. Upon opening the door, he received the biggest surprise and shock of his life. Thrust directly into his hands, before Jeff could even speak, were the Warrants for his arrest as well as the search and seizure of the various named items. Rex then directed him to step aside so that they could move ahead with their business. Jeff then pleaded:

"Can't I at least go back up (stairs) and put on some clothes, all I have on is my robe?"

Rex answered: "Yes, but don't try anything – you are not permitted to go any where." And, he signaled another member of the group to follow him and 'watch. ' Going up the stairs, and while gathering his jeans and clothes together, Jeff's mind was going a 'mile a minute.' He was desperate; he decided to do what he had only casually planned a while back in case of such an emergency. He guessed that he had about a fifty-fifty chance of getting away. He signaled to the watching Agent, that he was going into the bathroom to shower, clean up and dress. He'd be a few minutes. That was Ok.

He went in the bathroom, swing the door around, and quickly dressed, throwing on whatever. Then, he turned on the shower. Moving to the side, he quietly slid open the bathroom window and stepped out on a slanting side roof at the backend of the house that covered a large pantry. He eased himself to the edge of that roof and leaped down to the ground, falling and rolling a short distance. Quickly recovering his footing, he silently moved along the border of small grove of pear trees down the yard.

Looking around, making sure that no one was watching, he made the short dash to the boat house. Freedom was just beyond its door. His hot new speedboat could and would take him anywhere he wanted to go on Chesapeake Bay and the bordering states. Quickly, he threw open the door to the right, moved to the left, grabbed his get-away bag hanging by its strap from the wall and jumped into the boat. Just as he reached to untie the lines securing his 'water rocket' he heard from behind:

"I wouldn't try that if I were you." This came from Andy Cardwell, standing behind the entry door and against the boat house back wall. He was there with Justin and they both had their handguns drawn and pointed directly at him. Jeff was facing two thirty-eight revolvers and he knew it was now the moment of truth. Should he choose to die or should he put his hands up and surrender?

His mind made this calculation instantly, and he surrendered. He would, in the end, never take the 'fall' for a client, especially one like Dr. Alex Howard. He would revert back to taking the position that he had done 'nothing' and/or that they couldn't prove that he had done anything illegal. He wanted a lawyer and would now refuse to say anything. That would be it, all he would say for today.

As Jeff was being handcuffed, Andy smiled and said:

"Your attempted escape will be valuable additional evidence of your guilt on a number of crimes. With what we have on you, I doubt that any jury could find you to be innocent."

At that same time, Justin was looking thru the bag Jeff grabbed from the boat house wall as he attempted to flee. At first, it appeared to be only some hand tools; but then upon looking further, he found some cash, some modest bank accounts and a few new credit cards with fake ID's. And, when he lifted the back flap, there was an inch thick manila envelope with the name Dr. Alex Howard written on the front. Justin handed it to Andy, who paused to open the envelope; there he found copies of various e-mail communications between Jeff and Dr. Alex, dating back to notes he had taken when he first started working for Dr. Alex. Andy quickly browsed through this material, and then made sure his agents secured it in the chain of evidence found at the search site, and said to Jeff as they took him away:

"It isn't going to matter much what you have to say in your defense; this envelope 'crosses all the T's and dot's the 'I 's' on what happened and when it took place. I will see you and your attorney later."

And that ended a most successful operation. Andy congratulated the team on a job well done. They packed their vans with all the seized items, materials, files and computers and drove away with Jeff Sullivan in handcuffs and his arms secured to the side of the van.

Now it was time to focus upon Dr. Alex Howard and the evidence that would send him to jail in disgrace for at least 10 to 15 years. Andy smiled thinking, "crime is not going to pay for him" if I have anything to do with it.

And that was the end of a good day. A very good day.

PART 5

THE CONFERENCE

&

THE ARREST

CHAPTER 43

Today, Janice and Eric were to meet with Mr. Richard Johnston, Chief Administrator for the MRC. Janice had arranged for this meeting at her apartment via a telephone call from the hospital. It was ostensibly for the purpose of an update on Eric's condition. As far as Mr. Johnston knew Eric was still in a coma. Finding him back to normal would be a pleasant surprise.

When Janice showed Mr. Johnston into her dining room, Eric was sitting there with a big smile on his face. The two of them greeted each other warmly, exchanging a small embrace. Eric was looking good, hale and hearty, with a skin color to match. He had on fresh clothes that Janice had retrieved from his condo. And, Janice was also nicely dressed wearing an upscale casual outfit that complimented her natural good looks and figure.

Mr. Johnston: "Well, what a terrific surprise. Eric, I am so glad to see you up and about. How are you feeling?"

Eric: "Much better now, thanks to the special care and help from this lady, right here!" beaming at Janice.

Mr. Johnston: "You look terrific; I can't wait to get you back to work; your scientists and projects are driving me crazy."

Eric: "Well; that's why we called you; there are some things I need to tell you about and explain about what's been going on."

Eric then talked for quite a while; explaining that he had actually gone to Israel as an extension of a Project that he had closed out at the MRC beforehand. He told of the Discovery during that Project; the finding of 'blank' DNA results followed by the Discovery of the strange Code through the MRI scans and their dilemma on what to do following his epiphany . He told of his concern for the MRC's connection with the non science implications and the need to be certain of what the Code actually stated.

He described the suspect things that happened to him in Israel; the burglary, the attack and the attempt he believed to have happened on his life. Eric also advised of the 'bugs' on their telephones and the hidden software on their personal computers. He went on, talking about the need for personal safety as the reason for keeping his recovery secret; and that he had used this time period to complete a major Paper on the Discovery and that it was now ready for presentation. He summed up by describing the dilemma of whether this was something the MRC would or would not want to be a part of because it goes well beyond pure science in its scope.

At that point, excited, Mr. Johnston had to speak:

"You mean that someone actually tried to kill you because of this Project.?"

"Yes; Yes; I do; it is all being investigated and will be prosecuted in the not to distant future, I believe."

Mr. Johnston: "Do I know this person: Is there a connection to the MRC?"

"Yes, we believe so." Eric replied.

Mr. Johnston: "What do you want me to do; we want you to be safe and able to return."

Eric: "That's what I am getting at. First and foremost, let me say that I want to return. However, I believe that the MRC needs to decide if they want me back; I need to announce this major Paper written about the Discovery, the Code and its meaning. Once this is done, this should end any further attempts on my life. Even so, I still want to do the right thing for my relationship with the MRC. This matter is potentially so controversial that the MRC may not want to be a part of it."

Mr. Johnston: "How am I to decide that? What can I tell my board?"

Eric handed Mr. Johnston the finished Paper and asked him to read it, which he immediately started to do. You could tell by his reactions, that he was overtaken by the magnitude of what was described. As he worked his way through Part 2, one could tell by the way he smiled, that he was enjoying what was being said. Upon finishing, he chuckled and said to Eric and Janice:

"Now, I see what you mean; I would be concerned whether or not the MRC would join with you. On the other hand, it is an amazing piece of work and I congratulate you both. I will take it up right away with my board; my vote will be 'yes, wholeheartedly 'yes'; how's that?"

"That's about as much as I could hope for. Please keep this Paper confidential. I must stress that it needs to be 'safe.' Having it 'get out' could be very troublesome, and this is a worry I don't need right now." Eric replied;

"Don't worry, Eric; I will be back to you with an answer real soon; you have my word. Thank you for confiding in me; I have a feeling that the MRC will not let you down after all that you have been through."

Mr. Johnston finished, after touching on a few other points, and shook hands with them as he left.

The meeting had gone well.

Not long after Mr. Johnson left, Justin Avery called and asked if it would be convenient for him to stop by. He had some good news. Janice and Eric approved and he came right over. They were happy to hear from him.

When Justin arrived, he had a big smile on his face.

"We got him; he's in jail right now. I was in on the arrest; he tried to run but didn't get away with it. We were waiting for this and forced him to surrender."   Justin said;

Then, Justin took his time and explained all that had happened, since he had told them that the Raleigh, N.C. office of the Attorney General agreed to pursue the case. He described some of the evidence found at the scene of the ex-CIA agent's arrest. He also mentioned some of the evidence that had been obtained via separate warrants served upon other parties. He surprised them with the news that one million dollars had been paid for the 'barbeque' of Eric.

Eric allowed as how he did not know that he was worth that much dead, or for that matter, alive. He openly wondered what he would have done if that amount had been offered to him to just forget it (the Code). Probably, nothing different, but one would have to wonder?

Eric then told Justin that he was now finished with the PAPER and it was ready to be announced and published. This wasn't to congratulate himself; instead it was to ask:

"Am I now free to leave Janice's place, to go to work and move about the area?"

Justin allowed: "I suppose so; I doubt that our chief conspirator (bad guy) will try it again."

Eric and Janice then filled him in on their earlier meeting with Mr. Johnston. They would let him know what the MRC decides on Eric making the announcement and presentation of the Paper as a spokesman on the behalf of the MRC. They told Justin why this was a 'jump ball' type of issue; because the Paper and its conclusion 'pushed' the

envelope beyond science toward religion. This took some explanation, but Justin pretty well understood by the time he left. He would tell Andy, who would most likely want to interview them at some point. This would all be important for trial preparation and to establish the motive for the attempt on his life.

With all these 'balls' in the air, the pace was picking up and becoming exciting for Janice and Eric.

What would be next? How would it work out?

CHAPTER 44

Andy Cardwell was ready for this day. In fact, he had been ready since the day of the arrest of Jeff Sullivan. He was about to have to the first question and answer session with him. Jeff had obtained a lawyer for his defense and was starting to press for a hearing on bail. It was time to put the pressure on him; time to make him sweat and worry on whether he might ever be free again.

Shortly beforehand, while still in his office, Andy received the response from the Swiss bank in connection with their transfer of one million dollars to the account of Jeff Sullivan in the Arlington, Virginia area of the U.S.. There help was no surprise to Andy, he had done this before; on the other hand, he supposed that it may well be a huge surprise to Jeff Sullivan and his lawyer. Few in the United States had paid any real attention to the changes that had become common place on cooperation with foreign banks as a result of needing access to U.S. banking transfers and locations.

Andy reviewed the letter and the supplied account records right away. They showed an account that had been open for some time with a small balance and very little activity. And then, a sudden deposit of one million U.S. dollars, followed by the transfer to Jeff's U.S. account the next day. The deposit was made the night Eric's coma began and the withdrawal/transfer was following day. This day also matched with the day Jeff Sullivan crossed the border from Israel to Egypt, returning via Cairo to the U.S.. It was all in the nature of a pay-off; Andy had seen this type of exchange before and knew full well what it signaled. This meeting should be interesting. Andy didn't expect much; this session was to put some cards on the table to give them some idea what they were facing.

Andy walked into the conference room with his assistant and after opening pleasantries, started right away:

He put the photos before Jeff Sullivan and his lawyer and said:

"Why were you following Dr. Eric Rhodes in Israel this day?"

"I don't know what your talking about, that isn't me and I wasn't in Israel;" Jeff answered;

So Andy picked up the photo's, sorted thru his file, then set in front of them copies of Jeff's visa, passport and airlines ticket, and said:

"Well, if that's the case, what do you make of this travel info during this time period?"

Jeff and his attorney looked at this documentation closely and the attorney nodded his head to Jeff;

"I have nothing to say on this info."

"I thought so;" Andy said;

Andy then moved to the video photos for the lobby and hallway at Eric's motel for the day of the burglary, presenting them across the table, and asked:

"What were you looking for when you broke into his room? We are sure that is you at that time."

Jeff and his lawyer huddled and Jeff answered:

"I have no idea what you are talking about."

Andy, smiled and went on:

"Maybe this will refresh your memory on why you attempted to murder Dr. Eric Rhodes at this time, putting him in a disastrous coma?"

Andy slid the U.S. bank records across the table for their inspection.

They didn't know at this point whether Eric had recovered; Jeff's attorney answered:

"That doesn't mean anything; it doesn't show any connection to your Israel allegations."

Andy: "Nice try; but have a look at these. They tie into what I just showed you." and he slid copies of the just received Swiss bank documents across the table for their review:

They looked at them and wondered out loud:

"How did you get that; that's supposed to be a protected account under Swiss law."

Andy answered:

"You will have to get with the times. Things have changed.

Andy went on:

" There's more of course, but I won't bother you with that right now; although, I do want to thank you for getting together a nice file of the e-mails and computer hack/theft files obtained from when you broke into the residences of Drs. Eric Rhodes and Janice Westphal: and, if that were not enough, we were also pleased with your notes on meetings and phone call's with your employer;"

And with that, Andy passed over copies of some of the items found in the envelope at the boat house and verified by files on Jeff's computer.

Jeff and his attorney paged through this info and struggled to say:

"You have nothing; that search was illegal; this would never be admitted into evidence."

Andy replied: "Oh, sure; and I guess these warrants didn't exist." and he passed them across the table.'

With that, Jeff's lawyer smirked and said:

"No matter what you say or have; if, and I meant a big 'if', my client did any of this, which we strongly deny, it took place in Israel not the United States. I don't see them here after Jeff and its unlikely you could prosecute him here for something that purportedly took place in Israel."

Andy responded: "If you think I forgot about such things. You're wrong. Dr. Eric Rhodes is a citizen of North Carolina, U.S.A. and as such, criminal acts against him can be prosecuted here in this District; that's why you are talking to federal attorneys, not local officials. Furthermore, I can tell you from my conversations with Israeli officials, they take a dim view of people like Jeff, a former CIA operative, coming to their country to kill someone, anyone, within their country. They are more than ready to move this case to Jerusalem, and try Jeff there under their laws. How would you like that Jeff?"

With this, Jeff looked a little dumbfounded; he turned to his attorney, whispered in his ear and the attorney then said;

"My client and I need to talk; I will get back to you soon."

And that ended the meeting. They walked out looking rather solemn. Andy was not troubled by what had happened. He knew he had a solid case; but, to make this complete he needed the chief villain; and he wanted him with the testimony of Jeff Sullivan. It was not a real 'win' without seeing Dr. Alex Howard twist and turn in

316

his courtroom seat as his devious and torturous plan was made public for all to see and hear.

That would be a great day.

CHAPTER 45

Mr. Richard Johnston, Chief Administrator for the MRC, went to the office of their Chairman, to discuss the latest development with Eric. The Chairman was the head of a large private foundation that supported many charities in the area, and was a frequent and generous grant maker to the MRC. He was an older, friendly and jovial man, always happy to see and talk to Mr. Johnston. Furthermore, he was well acquainted with Dr. Eric Rhodes, having been solicited by him for funding for specific projects over the years. Altogether, they had developed a warm collegial relationship.

The Chairman, upon learning their meeting was about Eric, wanted to know what he was up to now; he knew that Eric had been on a sabbatical leave that was followed by medical leave. Mr. Johnston briefed him thoroughly, describing in detail what he had been told by Janice and Eric at their meeting. He talked about Eric's dilemma on doing the right thing in consideration of the MRC and handed over a copy of the Paper to be announced and given; and spelled out the decision the MRC faced in making this public.

Mr. Johnston, outlined the Paper, emphasizing that Part 1 was entirely factual, with all the testing having been done at the MRC, followed by the MRI tests being completed at the Hospital. He indicated that the Code translations were partially made by Eric while on his sabbatical leave in Israel before entering a coma. He noted that the rest of the translations had followed Eric's recovery back home. He advised about the break-in to Eric's motel room, the attack by the man tailing him and the purported attempt on Eric's life. That, Eric has now recovered and is ready to come back to work if the MRC still wants him. That, the reason for this question in Eric's mind, arises from the nature of his findings and comments in Part 2 of the Paper. And, at this point, it was now important for the Chairman to read Part 2, to judge if the MRC wants to go along with this conclusion coming under their banner.

The Chairman leaned back in his deep chair and moved through the document in a deliberate way. Meanwhile, allowing time to pass, Mr. Johnston excused himself to visit the rest room. With his return, he chatted with the Chairman's secretary in the waiting area. This didn't take very long. The Chairman buzzed for Mr. Johnston to come back in. He had a big smile on his face.

318

"Well; well; the Chairman said with a flash of his eye; I think Eric is to be congratulated for his initiative and special insight. This Project, his findings and the story of all that has happened to get to this point are incredible; as long as Eric presents Part 2 at the announcement and presentation in the way he describes, you have a hardy 'Yes' from me. I propose that the MRC do all it can to make sure this Paper becomes well known in the scientific and academic communities. Beyond that, as Eric says, others more qualified can, and will no doubt, settle on the meaning(s) of all that has been discovered. This is a blockbuster."

"I agree; I agree; your reaction was the same as mine at the time he went over this with me."

"I will have him come back to work ASAP, and move ahead with MRC plans to make this announcement a big deal. Even if public reaction is somewhat controversial, it will be beneficial for the MRC to be at the forefront of something of this magnitude."

"I agree." the chairman said and added; "At the end of the year, its time for a big raise for Eric and perhaps a promotion; after all, he is still our 'star'."

Days later, Mr. Johnston met with the three other members of the MRC Board. This included two men and one woman, all prominent in and about the community, having been successful after graduating from the University. They all knew Eric, some going back as far as their youth together and in at least one instance, having attended the Church where Eric's father was the pastor. As they came to know and understand the circumstances, especially Part 2 of the Paper, they whole heartedly approved and agreed with what the Chairman concluded. Of course the MRC wanted Eric back and if it was his finding that the Code was a 'Window' into the Human Spirit (the Soul), that was good enough for them.

Promptly, Mr. Johnston, called Eric and told him of the Boards wholehearted support and wanted to know how soon he could be back to work. Elated, Eric promised to be back to work beginning Monday morning, having the weekend to prepare. Mr. Johnston made it clear that Eric should move ahead right away with planning the meeting at which he would make the announcement and presentation of the Paper. As Eric and Janice discussed this development that night they grew more and more excited. That which they had only dreamed about was now going to happen.

A few days after Andy Cardwell's meeting with Jeff Sullivan and his attorney, this attorney called and wanted to talk with him. Always amenable to such sessions Andy agreed to sit down and meet about the case and what may be done 'in the name of justice.'

The next day, Andy and his assistant sat together with this attorney:

Andy started: "Well, here we are, we acknowledge that everything we have to say today is off the record; what do you have in mind?"

"Jeff and I were talking, and we guess and believe that you would rather have the man that he was working for; Jeff is nothing more than a pawn under the circumstances? Is that right?"

Andy: "Yes and no; there has to be some level of penalty; Jeff cannot walk away without bearing some degree of responsibility; however we are open to a deal if your client can present testimony that will advance our prosecution?"

The attorney: "Yes, of course, you will have a much better case against this man with Jeff's testimony; no one cares about poor Jeff. He wouldn't even make the evening news."

Andy: "Well, you're right on that; but there is the matter of Jeff breaking a number of statutes on behalf of this man and enriching himself to the tune of one million dollars. There has to be some level of justice coming back upon him. Besides, former CIA agents just can't go around practicing their tradecraft without repercussions. The Agency frowns on such things especially in foreign countries. And, of all countries, Israel."

"Yes; yes; we know – I told him as much; that would be a part of the deal we work out. How's that?" The attorney said;

Andy: "Ok, now you're talking. I'm listening."

" Jeff can and will corroborate all of what you have said and provide all he knows that has not been mentioned so far. He will surrender and accept placement in jail without bail pending trial; he will testify as you need him, for both the indictment and trial. He will give back one-half of the one million upon sale of the Maryland property he bought and he will plead to a lesser charge(s) on the condition that the time he serves up to that point is sufficient and acceptable to the Justice department and the Judge. This must also include any charges that he may be responsible for under government law and regulations as an ex-employee."

The attorney then stated; "But, there is one point of exception because a key part of your scenario is incorrect and not true at all."

Andy: "And what would that be?"

"Jeff did not do anything; meaning that he did not commit any act, that actually gave rise to the coma Dr. Eric Rhodes suffered. Sure, he received the message to 'barbeque' Dr. Rhodes, and upon checking his Swiss account the next morning, the money was there. He even agreed to do it; he admits to the conspiracy. Notwithstanding all of that, he absolutely insists that he did not take any action the night the coma started.

Jeff specifically described to me what happened the next day when he went to Dr. Rhodes motel; As he arrived, there was an ambulance out front and a small crowd of onlookers. He blended in and watched for a few minutes; the ambulance crew carried a person out on a stretcher and put him in the ambulance. Peering over the crowd, Jeff saw that it was Dr. Rhodes, the very man he was there to 'barbeque'. After asking around, he learned that this man had suffered an unknown medical event and was now in a coma. Having already planned to leave town anyway, he just drove away and came home. He knows that being there makes him looks guilty of causing the coma. But he knows for sure, that he did nothing before or after the 'barbeque' message to Dr. Rhodes to induce the coma. He's maintains that even those who treated him medically cannot identify a specific cause for the coma. If you don't believe him, go ahead and check on what 'caused' the coma?"

Andy listened closely:

"That's a pretty tall tale. If that's true however, it should and will make a difference in the sum total of what the Government will want as a penalty from Jeff. Let's do this: we will list two versions of the deal you propose, pretty much along the lines we have gone over. If it should be found to be true, that no 'outside' cause was found for the coma, then we will agree to the points you stated, including the one-half million dollars. If, on the other hand, it should be found that a medical cause was determined and that it was man made, not self induced, then Jeff will plead to a felony and forfeit the entire one million dollars.

And further, either way, the penalty he will pay will be whatever applies to breaking the employment law applicable to our Agency ex-employees. Additionally, there is one more thing that is fundamental: and that is a confession that will be incorporated into and made a part of the record at the time Jeff pleads guilty. We will start drafting the confession and the 'deal' discussed today, but delay its signing until I have had time to meet with Dr. Eric Rhodes and make the right inquiries with those medical personnel that treated him. I want to get to the bottom of this."

"Ok, that's fine; write this up for our review? I am confident that we can agree to what you have stated. I will bring my client up to date on the addition of the confession as well as the employment law penalties." The attorney said;

Andy looked over to his assistant and said:

"Do you have all that?; let me have a first draft by the end of tomorrow; I will go meet with Drs. Rhodes and Westphal, as soon as they can see me."

Their meeting ended; each side walking away thinking about how well they had served their clients, Jeff and the Government, and additionally, the innocent and 'injured' Dr. Eric Rhodes?

On second thought, however, one could not help but wonder:

"If Jeff Sullivan did not cause Eric's coma, then how in Heaven, did it take place?"

It came as no surprise afterward, that no one could ever be sure of the answer to that question. This would always be one of the great and enduring mysteries about the life and times of Dr. Eric Rhodes?

CHAPTER 46

Andy Cardwell wasted no time following up on his meeting with the attorney for Jeff Sullivan, the ex-CIA agent. He knew that when the other side wants to make a deal, shape it to your advantage and make it happen. And, take the initiative and write the agreement yourself. He wanted Jeff's testimony against the main 'villain', being Dr. Alex Howard and he intended to get it. He did however, have to get to the bottom of the allegation that the coma Dr. Eric Rhodes suffered was not 'caused' by Jeff Sullivan, even though all the circumstantial elements were in place.

Immediately after that meeting ended, he was on the phone with Justin, the investigator, and set up a meeting with Eric and Janice. Even with the next day being a Saturday, Justin and Andy went first thing to Janice's place to talk. Justin had explained the relationship between Eric and Janice, and most importantly, that Janice was a highly skilled and experienced neurosurgeon. If there were an overt cause for the coma, she would know about it. She had even been to the hospital in Israel, met with the doctor's that first saw and treated Eric, and reviewed their records on his treatment. She would know of the results from the tests run at that time. They could trust her knowledge and judgment on what, if any, was the 'cause' of the coma.

As they sat down in the living room, Andy was struck by this couple and he could tell right away that they would make credible witnesses. Although it was their first meeting, the flow of conversation was easy and relaxed. They couldn't wait to tell Andy and Justin that the MRC was going to back up Eric completely and that he was returning to work on Monday. It was readily accepted that it was now safe to take this step.

Before coming to the heart of the purpose of Andy's visit, he asked to be brought up to date on the status of their Discovery and the results of Eric's visit to Israel. Proudly, they indicated that the Paper was now done and they would give him a copy on a strictly confidential basis. They intended to keep its content secret until the time it was presented at the announcement Conference that Eric would now plan on behalf of the MRC.

Before leaving that topic, Andy wanted their view on what was so earth shaking that someone would want to commit murder to keep it from becoming public knowledge.

He wanted to hear it from them this time; he had heard enough on this point from Justin. That request led to Eric, taking his time, telling the whole story in summary form, going back to patient Barney on through the night that his coma had started after finally decoding two of the three key region words: Morals, Intellect and now the third, Values.

The implications of that break through were now in writing, stated as far as Eric was willing to interpret them; and they were presented in Part 2 of the Paper, now in Andy's hands. The bottom line for all this, Eric explained, was that the factual side (per Part 1) can only be understood, by the finding and conclusion, that a physical 'Window' had been found into the Human Spirit (the Soul) of man (Part 2). This was his 'take' on the subject.

He then stressed that this was as far as he was willing to go; however, he noted that others would no doubt pick up on this and take positions 'visa vie' their point of view and agenda. That this may vary widely when religions, evolutionists, creationists and other's think about its meaning for them. Justin chimed in at this point, noting that the chief suspect had a huge financial and personal position on what the impact might be on 'evolution science.' Because of his son, working at the MRC under Eric's direction and control, the father had received advance knowledge of what had been Discovered and had acted on this basis to keep it from becoming known to the World.

After a few questions, Andy allowed that he understood better what was at stake and that he would read their Paper carefully.

Then, Andy turned to the chief purpose for his visit at this time. He explained that the man Eric had photographed and they had arrested was after a deal in exchange for his testimony against his client, the man that had set it all in motion. Andy added that he wanted this testimony in order to assure a conviction against the chief 'villain.' He went on, that the ex-agent would still have to pay a price in both money and jail time, but that the degree of this penalty would depend on his level of culpability. All of this would fall right in place, except that this man (Jeff) did not and would not admit to actually 'causing' the onset of Eric's coma. What did they know about the actual cause of the coma?

With that, Andy looked directly at Janice, who answered:

"I was afraid someone might get around to that point sometime."

"When I was contacted by the Hospital in Israel, I talked to them right away. A Dr. Jaffer and Dr. Sibowitz, I believe. They told me what they could over the phone. I went as quickly as I could to see for myself Eric's condition and meet with them. They apologized profusely about failing to have a clear answer about Eric's

329

condition. They shared with me the toxicology and other tests that had been run. They had even inspected every part of his body for a sign of an injection or topical patch of some kind. It was not there; no physical signs were there. I'm sorry, It was just not there. To this day, neither I, nor them, can give you an answer on what really caused the coma. We just stabilized him, took good care of him, brought him home, and he finally came around, thank goodness."

"Do you think it is possible that this ex-agent is telling the truth?" Andy asked;

"Yes, perhaps; I have been a doctor of neurology and a surgeon for almost twenty years now, and I can tell you with certainty that not all things that affect a person's brain or neurological system can be identified with an objective 'cause'. There are still huge area's of uncertainty for which the medical profession lacks substantive answers. Therefore, this may be true; as doctors can't tell for sure." Janice replied;

Andy said that he would take this to be his answer and report it to his boss the way Janice had described it. And further, that he would go on and make the deal with Jeff, and prepare to seek a 'sealed' indictment against Dr Alex Howard from a closed Grand Jury, in that he is the principal Jeff is prepared to name; and the person the recovered e-mails, notes and taped telephone call's, identify as the culprit. This would all go very fast according to Andy, and he would take care of it.

Andy then noted, as he had been told at the beginning of their meeting, that Eric was going back to work on Monday. Following that observation, Andy shared some thoughts and idea's he had on how Eric could use this return to work to their advantage.

He went on and described what he wanted Eric to do………??

CHAPTER 47

When Eric returned to work on Monday he was all smiles, greeting fellow MRC employees, technicians and colleagues with enthusiasm and warm expressions. Everyone could tell he was happy to be back. One and all remarked on how good Eric looked after having recovered from a coma. His skin color was good, his eyes were bright and he moved about in a way that showed no ill effects. Even so, he chose not to say much about the coma feeling somewhat embarrassed although not knowing why.

When Dr. John Howard arrived he was stunned to learn that his boss was back, fit and healthy, sitting in his office going through the pile of mail, reports and miscellaneous items that had accumulated. On the way in the secretary told him that Eric wanted to see him upon his arrival. Would he be suspicious of him for seeking but not getting the MRI files from the Hospital? He didn't know but worried nonetheless. He had no idea of all that had happened behind the scenes; his father had never taken him into his confidence on his paranoia about Dr. Eric Rhodes activities and Discovery.

Upon walking into Eric's office, he was greeted with a big smile, a pat on the back and a request to be brought up to date at a meeting Eric had set for 10:00am.. After that, Eric walked to Mr. Johnston's office, greeted him with heartfelt pleasantries, closed the office door and sat down to talk for a few minutes. Eric told him his plans; he would move ahead quickly on reviewing the project's in progress through his office, both new and old, and would want to hear the administrative thoughts on them and their priority. And next, he wanted Mr. Johnston's thoughts on the practical side of setting up the Conference where he intended to announce and present the Paper they had discussed and Mr. Johnston had read.

Mr. Johnston said he had been told, and he agreed as well, to give Eric free rein on setting up the whole event. The Chairman urged that this be done at a level and with such a style befitting, and adding to, the reputation of the Medical Research Center as a major institute. There was always a subtle, behind the scenes, competition and comparison among these organizations to gain an advantage in terms of prestige and grants. On the matter of size, Mr. Johnston made it clear that 200 would be too small and 1000 would be unwieldy and to great in size. He then volunteered to contact the University President and try for use of the Great Hall, generally used for many large meetings; he guessed in this case, this would be around 400 to 500 attendees. Eric was to be in charge of the guest list and issuing the invitations. Mr. Johnston would let him know this afternoon of the date(s) available; then they went on to discuss other timing issues. Eric urged sooner rather than later in that he was anxious to go public to get the 'threat' monkey off his back.

There was one other key point, and that was keeping the Paper confidential and secret until its distribution at that the Conference. Mr. Johnston promised to do this with his copy, locking it in his office safe. Beyond that, it was up to Eric to take care of its printing and publication. Eric would also 'artfully' come up with a minimal title for the subject to be 'presented' at the Conference; he would wrap it around a characterization of the Discovery, in order to promote broad interest.

Eric left for the 10:00 am review meeting satisfied that it was all on track. In the interim, before the catch-up meeting, Dr. John Howard, had just enough time to call his dad, Dr. Alex Howard, and give him the surprise news that Eric was back at work, fit and healthy, with all his faculties in order and that he would let him know more later. Dr. Alex, after this short call, sat back shocked and dismayed. This was not supposed to happen. He had paid for this not to happen. What would he do now? What could he do now?

About an hour later, while they were still in the meeting, the door opened and Mr. Johnston called Eric out in the hallway. He said he had the date all set up now and that it would be on the Friday afternoon, three weeks from last Friday. Eric indicated that this date would be a 'push' but that he would see that all was done to get a selected audience there. They shook hands on it and Mr. Johnston said:

"Thank God your back Eric;" to which Eric smiled, snickered a little, and with a wink of his eye, answered:

"I think you have that one right." and went back into the meeting.

The meeting went on for a little while reviewing ongoing project matters; at which point Eric interrupted and said:

"I have some big news for all of you; something that will now put us under immediate pressure; we are going to host a Conference (and he named the building) three weeks from last Friday at which time I will announce and present a major Paper that I have written; it includes a Discovery made right here in our lab, that bears upon the physical make-up of the human body.

That's all I can say about it at this time.

I am going to select three of you to take on the list of invitees. And at the same time I want all of you to find and come up with your own list of those in the scientific community that should attend. We are dismissed for now. I will get back to the three of you right away on compiling the list of those to be invited. Clearly, this list is needed right away. Turnaround will be only one day. The invitations must be ready for mailing quite quickly."

And the meeting ended with talk buzzing all around as they left for lunch.

Dr. John Howard hurried to his nearby apartment. As soon as he got there, he called his father again:

"Dad, dad, it was just announced by Eric; three weeks from last Friday, we are having a Conference on campus, where he will announce and present a Paper on a Discovery made in our lab on the physical make-up of a certain part of the human body. I'm sure it has something to do with the Project he closed just before taking the sabbatical leave and going to Israel. You remember; this was just before I tried to get the MRI's from the Hospital for you."

For Dr. Alex Howard, this was even worse news than learning of Eric's return to work at the MRC. He had worried all along that something like this might happen. Now it was taking place. Sullen, and deeply drawn, his only reply to his son was:

"See if you can obtain for me beforehand, a copy of that Paper; and make sure that I am invited as a fellow scientist. I have to see and hear this, for myself."

After his meeting with Janice and Eric, Andy Cardwell withdrew the request for a confession in the deal to be made with Jeff Sullivan. It would be enough that Jeff enters a guilty plea to the various charges stated in the deal and testify against Dr. Alex Howard at his trial. Any confession that failed to state specified acts that directly caused the coma, would in the end do more damage than good. The defense for Dr. Alex would seize on this absence and make the most of it. Andy would avoid making this an issue as much as he could and let the timing of the coma, that followed immediately after the money was wired, speak for itself in drawing the needed conclusion.

Additionally, in that this would be a trial where the guilt of Dr. Alex would be determined based on circumstantial evidence, the coma would necessarily follow as a part of all that had happened. And, Jeff and his attorney would know from their discussions, that if any of this became an issue during the trail, Andy would attack the credibility of this ex-CIA agent on this issue claiming him to be a liar. Why wouldn't someone like Jeff deny having caused the coma, being the most culpable act to take place? If he hadn't caused the coma, how could it have happened on its own? Furthermore, given traditional Doctor- Client privilege, the lawyers for Dr. Alex would not be able to obtain the medical tests on Eric detailing his 'condition'. As with all matters in the trial, it would come down to whose story the jury believed.

He would have to work around whatever developed at that time.

Thus, the deal was now in place, including the understanding that part of Jeff's penalty would be the time he served in jail before entering his guilty plea, following his testimony against Dr. Alex Howard. This would be in addition to paying restitution to the government of one-half of the amount recovered from the sale of the property on the Eastern shore of the Chesapeake Bay.

Andy was now prepared to seek an indictment from the grand jury. In this case, Andy would use a 'closed' grand jury. He did not want any word of this case leaking out to the media, potentially resulting in Dr. Alex Howard 'running' in order to avoid arrest and prosecution.

A few days later, standing before a recently convened Grand Jury proceeding at the Federal Courthouse, Andy freely used the testimony of Jeff plus bank and the other 'collected' evidence in support of the charges requested within the indictment. He did this knowing full well that the record of this type of proceeding was not accessible to opposing counsel nor the media.

With this all in place, the indictment was handed down in short order by the Grand Jury, charging the

defendant with Conspiracy (to commit murder) and
Attempted Murder.

It was now time to arrest Dr. Alex Howard. The
timing and opportunity to do this was falling into place
and Andy would be there to take him into custody. Andy
always found it interesting how a person reacted at the
moment of arrest. Sometimes there were some very
damaging remarks made that he could use at the trial. He
would be there.

Would that be the case this time?

CHAPTER 48

Eric awoke this Friday morning feeling good, very good, hoping that it was going to be a great day. He reached over and gave Janice a tender whack on her bare backside and said;

"Get up, get up, this is the big day."

Dazed and groggy, Janice lifted her head and said:

"You mean its Christmas already; I didn't know its Christmas."

"All right, all right;" Eric smiled: "let's get ready."

He was right; this was going to be a big day. It was the day of the Conference and he was going to be at the MRC early to make sure everything was in place and ready. And, in private, he would go over his presentation once again, probably, for at least the fiftieth time. He did not want to be embarrassed in front of all the scientists, professors, technical magazine editors and colleagues that would be there.

Even with the relatively short time they had, his office had been successful in issuing and booking acceptances for attending the Conference. It certainly helped that a large community of academia lived, taught, researched and worked in the vicinity of the University-Medical Research Center- Hospital complex. Furthermore, with Washington, D.C. being not that far away, this allowed for scientific and administrative professionals from the government to join with them. Also, they had made a good effort to secure the attendance of one or more writers from applicable technical publications in order to promote coverage with a broader audience. And, even the local newspaper would be sending over a reporter to cover the meeting.

In addition to the announcement and presentation, the MRC was going to include a tour of its facilities and showcase some of the ongoing research projects under way. This would be the first part of the day, followed by a luncheon, then Eric's program, and a follow-up reception. Eric had been very careful to keep the Paper secret from everyone, including all persons at the MRC. He had the Paper duplicated privately, at his own expense, at a shop in a nearby town and picked up this printing the previous day. Many had been frustrated by not having had a chance to read the Paper beforehand; but, in the end, this secrecy added to the buzz and growing mystery of what was about to be announced and presented. The Paper would be distributed to each registered attendee, after they entered the Hall and took their seats for the presentation. It would be passed out beginning with the arrival of Eric on the stage.

In looking over the registered guest list, Eric noted that it included Dr. Alex Howard, as arranged by his son. Dr. John Howard, Eric's assistant. Eric made sure that Justin, the investigator that had helped him so much, knew of the planned attendance by Dr. Alex Howard. Eric also invited Justin and Andy to attend and would feel safer knowing that they were in the audience.

About one: thirty p.m., Mr. Richard Johnston, the MRC Chief Administrator, took the podium. He promptly made the introductions for Dr. Eric Rhodes and Dr. Janice Westphal, describing that together, they were responsible for the work stated in Part 1 of the Paper now in the audience's hands and entitled:

"A BRAIN DISCOVERY: The finding of a human language Code deep within a physical part of the Human Brain." By Dr. Eric Rhodes and Dr. Janice Westphal, and the Medical Research Center and Hospital.

Naming this title brought a brief reaction from the audience; this quickly quieted down as Eric and Janice began and the presentation. As they had practiced and prepared, step by step they walked through the first snippet from Barney's thalamic brain area and the rest of the 'live' samples listed within the Paper. When they shared with the audience the mystery and wonderment at finding 'blank' DNA test results from these snippets, all seemed greatly surprised believing this to be impossible within the human body.

Eric followed Janice at this point, indicating that the 'blank' results made him more curious than ever, so he decided to have the same snippet(s) tested further, using the Hospital MRI. At this point, he flashed on a large screen the results of such an MRI test. To one and all, it seemed to show nothing. Picking up a pointer, he then picked out a very faint line on the screen, and then two additional lines just below the first line. This he said caught his attention, and with the help of a Hospital technician, they magnified these lines. Then, Eric flashed on the screen the first, second and third lines, all magnified 5000 times. This magnification presented a strange Code, a mysterious Code, clearly appearing to be human in origin, probably ancient, definitely unknown to Eric and the genetic world of DNA syntax combinations.

The audience buzzed with reaction and comments among themselves. They were quite literally astounded. Even so, Eric went on, detailing finding this same result in the other 'live' samples tested, but always absent where the patent had *died* in the interim. He made it clear that there was no Code whatsoever, when the patient was deceased at the time of testing. He then spelled out the consistent patterns found: patient alive when tested – Code found; patient dead when tested- no Code. Even with the limited number of samples, this pattern was consistently repeated.

Eric went on to describe the dilemma of whether and how to proceed from there; and some of what happened leading up to the momentous moments of discovering the nature of the strange Code while in Israel;

and the subsequent translation of the three 'region' words found in all four of the 'live' samples tested by MRI and magnified to show the Code. Then he presented the four translations of the Code pertaining to the patient donors.

At this point, Eric turned the podium over to Janice, who separately took the translation of Barney's Code and compared it to her write up from interviews of his friends, family and ex-wife. She carefully drew the correlations as close as she could from the story of his real life to the summary Code listing, setting aside any reading of the slashes. And further, she stated that she had found similar correlations between the Code and the life history for the other three patients studied.

Concluding, she allowed as how she had no idea or explanation on how all this happened; it was simply that this was what had been Discovered by her and Eric's efforts. The audience continued to buzz with excitement on what they had just seen and heard.

Eric then stepped up and said that it was now time for Part 2, noting:

"That Part 1 was all science plus assistance from the translation of encrypted words from the ancient Coptic language. This, he qualified for the interviews Janice had made by way of patients, relatives, friends and acquaintances of the 'live' sample patients.

Now, by way of Part 2, he was going to give his interpretation of the meaning of what had been discovered."

At this point, he became exceedingly careful, as he had been in the Paper, to spell out that:

"What he was about to say was not offered as science, nor as the sole interpretation of Part 1, and that others may well scoff at what he was about to say, or offer their different view of the meaning of the strange Code."

At this time, Eric went on with the reasoning stated in Part 2, on what we know (from Part 1); what we think we know and therefore take notice of via religion, science and history; and then by way of a conclusion, what he drew from the Code 'by extension', and its "context,' being: *that, it represents a 'window on the Human Spirit (the Soul)' of each Patient tested..*

Before there could be much reaction, he unequivocally stated that he refused as a scientist to offer any further insight upon what this Discovery may or may not mean in other areas of human endeavor. Everyone knew at this point that he meant religion, natural science, the humanities and so on. He would leave that to others better qualified and suited than him to answer.

As Eric ended, the audience burst forth with thunderous applauds, hoorays, cheers and expressions of approval from almost one and all. It was a moment of great elation and joy for Eric and Janice who embraced each other upon the stage and started crying. Mr. Johnston and the Chairman were around and about them giving accolades and pats on the back. Eric was so relieved that the Discovery was now public that he was visibly shaking.

It was time to celebrate and that is what took place at the reception that followed. It was to be a grand party.

As the audience filed out two tall well built men wearing nondescript black suits slipped up behind Dr. Alex Howard in line; one of the men whispered into his ear that they were Federal agents and that he was under arrest and unless he wanted to make a scene, he was to come with them. Dr. Alex looked over his shoulder and the man on his right flashed his badge as a deputy of the U.S. Marshall. Easing themselves away from the crowd heading to the reception, they entered a side room.

At the door, they stopped just long enough to tell Dr. John Howard that he was not to enter and that his father was under arrest. Inside the room, Andy Cardwell was waiting at the table; he immediately read Dr. Alex Howard his rights. He also informed him that at this same time, at his home in the Boston suburbs, search and seizure warrants were being served in connection with his Conspiracy and Attempted Murder of Dr. Eric Rhodes. Did he want to say anything at this time?

With bitter contempt burning in his eyes, Dr. Alex Howard said:

"You don't have anything on me; I demand a lawyer; I won't say anything more."

Whereupon Andy replied: " Fine; Have it your way; I think you will have even less to say when your friend 'Charles' gives his testimony against you. We had a preview of this when he testified before the grand jury that indicted you. Take him away."

Dr. Alex sputtered: "What, how; I couldn't even find him." as he was taken out the door.

Meanwhile, at the reception, Eric was the star attraction. Everyone wanted to ask questions? The MRC would have to address that in the near future.

It was a momentous time.

Later, much later that evening, feeling more than a little tipsy, Eric and Janice fell into bed and congratulated each other in deep and sensuous ways. Their love had endured this difficult and unusual time in their lives and they wanted it to never end. They were meant be together now and for the rest of their lives. Yes, they promised each other to marry soon. Down with 'committed but not married,' or living together. Eric would not move out anytime soon.

PART 6

'KNOWING ENDS'

CHAPTER 49

The month following the Conference was a whirlwind of activity. Immediately, the media was all over the story, captioning it in their usual style of overstatement: "Geneticist Discovers Human Soul." They went on to state many things well beyond the findings in the Paper distributed at the Conference. The story was further sensationalized by coupling it with the arrest and charges against Dr. Alex Howard, publisher and prominent spokesperson for the 'evolutionary science' movement. Somehow this story had leaked out at the same time. All of this took on a life of its own.

Notwithstanding this notoriety, the Discovery and Eric's story was publicized and reviewed in many religious, scientific, medical and technical journals all over the world. Eric and Janice literally became instantly famous; and generally, he was well respected for the professional way that he separated the Part 1 'facts' from the Part 2 'finding' of the Human Spirit (the Soul) encapsulated by the Code, whether one agreed with him or not. And, not surprisingly, the upshot was generally more and more questions on the ramifications to be gathered from the Discovery than disbelief. To a certain degree, it seemed that there was some sense of 'relief' that actual proof existed for the presence of the Soul. By the end of the first year, their Paper was so well known and their acclaim so wide spread, rumor had it they would be nominated for an international award for the advancement of medical science. Because of this, the MRC received constant requests for Eric to speak at many venues to all kinds of organizations.

Meanwhile, planning for the new year, the MRC announced the promotion of Eric to Vice President, Project Research and Development. In this position, he would be in charge of all 'genetic' science issues for the many Projects at the Center. With this reorganization, he would have two Project Directors reporting to him as well as the Lab Director, who was in charge of all testing conducted by the MRC. In addition, Eric would be responsible for the Capital Budget for the ever expanding and changing process equipment. Moreover, and likely most important, he became the lead person that would greet, meet and discuss proposed Projects with grant making foundations, institutes, governmental bodies and others interested in seeking 'answers.' And, pleasantly, his salary was being doubled with bonuses promised at each year end. He was indeed a busy man.

Another matter that came up not long after the Conference was the continued employment of Dr. John Howard, son of Dr. Alex Howard. At a uncomfortable meeting for him, the MRC human resource officer pointed out the conflict of interest that now existed because of the arrest of his father. There was no doubt that Dr. Alex Howard, his father, was going on trial for actions taken as a result of information that he could only have obtained from his son in his work at the MRC. This would be an unpleasant matter for the MRC.

Thus, it would help if Dr. John Howard was no longer employed by the MRC at that time. Therefore, they urged that he resign for this and other reasons and before they decided one way or another on whether to terminate him. He was 'reminded' of the confidentiality agreement he signed at the time his of employment. Three days later he submitted his resignation. He knew he was in a bad position; and that he would have to step in for his father on the 'evolution science' publishing business that was still active. This made for a graceful exit, eliminating a problem for Eric, who quickly moved to promote a bright in-house project scientist to Project manager.

On a more personal note, it became clear that Eric was not going to move out of Janice's place and back his condo. They loved each other more than ever and so they decided to marry. As he had said before, it was time to end the 'committed but living apart' status that went on for many years. There's was a true love story and it was time to make their union 'official.' So, in one of Eric's meetings with Mr. Richard Johnston, Chief Administrator for the Center, they agreed to some year-end Christmas time 'off' before Eric assumed his new duties and responsibilities.

Together, they set the wedding date quickly, inviting friends, their small remaining family, close colleagues from work, Justin and Andy, and a few others. Because it was important to Eric, the ceremony was held at the church where his father had been pastor and he had attended his entire life. And so, on a bright and sunny Saturday afternoon, a week before Christmas, Janice and Eric became Mr. and Mrs. (Drs.) Rhodes, blushing and beaming with pride and joy at their union.

This was followed by an overdue honeymoon vacation traveling all the way to Moorea, Tahiti, in the Society Islands, of the South Pacific. There, they spent many hours in the 'on the water' hut, wearing little or nothing in the way of clothes, sunning themselves and doing all the things honeymooners love to do in private. It was a glorious, well deserved time. A real 'break' for them after the trials and tribulations of the last few years.

Rejoining the University environment with the newly arrived year, Eric went on with all of his many duties and responsibilities. In an entirely incidental way, on a blustery winter mid-January day, he strolled over and casually began a lecture to the second semester medical students on genetic research. They knew, of course, all about Eric and the Discovery, his landmark Paper and the Conference that had given him such acclaim. They were not going to let this meeting pass without getting in some questions of their own. Near the end of the lecture, the students started with their questions:

Student Rodger: "Dr. Rhodes, many of my fellow students and I have read your famous Paper; we know of the 'Window on the Soul' finding and the correlations with the Code words and Patient lives; how can this conclusion be a metaphysical one, i.e. the Soul, instead of determining a scientific one?"

Eric, smiling: " Well, you students go right to the heart of it, immediately, don't you? Before I give my answer, let me make clear that the Paper itself poses this very sort of thing. If one questions or disagrees with this finding, it is incumbent on this person to suggest or bring forth his or her conclusion. So, what do you think is a better, more scientific finding?" and the rest of the students all smiled and chuckled.

Student Rodger, reacting and stammering a little: " I kn...ow, I knn...ow, thats a tough one, I am only a graduate student. From the established facts, we have words .... words... and an investigative report of the 'live' persons history. Seems to me, it is entirely possible that the Code words are too general, and lack sufficient definition to make a clear connection to the subject person."

Student Glenn: "Rodger, aren't you forgetting that the word connection here is uniquely clear; they come from the persons body, deep within that body, being the thalamic region of the brain. That's pretty impressive, isn't it?"

Student Andrea: "And, let me suggest that, when one thinks of the life of a person, over many years, doesn't it largely take on a general nature as opposed to a hard edged character. I think so."

Eric: I think you can see from these exchanges that one and all may see this thing in different ways. Let me go on and add some underlying thoughts here. First, factually, it has been clearly established that the Code leaves the body; it is no longer present; it goes away, at such time as the person dies. Why do you suppose that happens ---- what is the suggested explanation for this over the history of civilization? Next, why are the same words always present for the three regional areas? Repeated for each of the 'live' patients.

Decoded as: Morals, Intellect and Values. What do these words mean separately or together, to you and your colleagues, and, do they fit together in any logical or meaningful way? What makes good sense here? And finally, are we to just throw up our hands and forget about all about this? Is it not better to postulate an answer, make it known and ask for better answers? I think so. It isn't enough for me to be the one to present the only answer. I do not claim a pride of authorship for this conclusion. Only through time will we see if this hypothesis holds up or if the reasoning of others find a better solution! How's that?

The room of students then buzzed with reaction back and forth among each other. Then:

Student Charles said: " Dr. Rhodes, with all due respect, and not intending to be insolent or over critical, I want to say that it was hypocritical to find the conclusion of a 'Window on the Soul' and just end it there. I mean, if you are going to go out on the limb with a metaphysical 'answer', does it not follow that you may have more insight to offer on what this all means. After all, it would not have been a stretch as a scientist to observe what it may mean for medical science. Stepping away from its significance for religion, humanities and other areas of natural science is understandable. But at least, speaking about its meaning for medical science is within the expertise and purpose of the MRC. Is it not?"

Eric answered: " Yes, Charles, I suppose so;" and at just that moment, the class bell rang and the students started to file out, and they failed to hear the last words coming from his lips: " but I do think, and am troubled by, the realization that once one starts down the road of speculation, where will it all end and how much damage will it do while moving in that direction?" and quietly he said to himself: " its a slippery slope, that's for sure."

Eric was not happy with the way this lecture to the medical students had ended. As he walked home that day, he contemplated his uneasiness; reasoning and testing in his mind why he was feeling this way. The solace of his 'church of the walking feet' was not working. He was troubled. This wasn't the first time he had left a 'talk' on the Discovery and the Paper with a 'downer' feeling from the questions and answers that had followed.

He knew what was at the heart of it but just didn't want to face it.

It all came down to the 'meaning' of the Code and what happens to the Soul. This was a multifaceted subject. The more he thought about it, the more he knew he had just taken an expedient way out in the Paper. He had 'buried' it, pure and simple. Was he a coward? He didn't know. Was he limited by the MRC? Did they control him on this subject indirectly? He didn't think so. Did he just do the prudent thing? Probably! Should he do anything about it? He didn't know. He would have to think about that. He would talk to Janice, and get her thoughts. He hoped this would help. He doubted the issue would just go away.

CHAPTER 50

Just like many others, and despite Eric's best intentions, he never got around to talking to Janice about his uneasiness with the limitations adopted within their Paper. Each time he prepared to speak to a group about the Discovery, the Code, its translation, and its prospective meaning, he was forced to revisit these self imposed limits. And additionally, there was the matter of the 'add-ons' Eric had found upon touching the patients MRI Code listings. To this day, he had no idea how this could have caused him to have the insights realized at those moments. Other than one brief disclosure of this to Janice, this had not come up again between them.

These things became a frequent distraction for Eric since he was in demand for speaking engagements with various types of organizations, i.e. genetic, medical science, religious (and religions), 'evolution science'and creationist. Usually, these requests arrived at the MRC addressed to him in has capacity as a Vice President, and in one way or another, referenced the famous Paper: "A BRAIN DISCOVERY". Dutifully, with the approval of his boss and the MRC Board, he traveled to and delivered a restatement of his presentation at the Conference where it was all initially announced. This part usually did not bring about any difficulties. But, when a typical follow up took place with questions, it was inevitable that the questions posed would ask for answers well beyond the scope of the Paper. The audience would generally voice notes of dissatisfaction when Eric would decline to speculate of the meaning, use or purpose of having a 'Window on the Soul' of a person. After a while, one was left with the impression of having only half the story. It was starting to become a rather unwieldy exercise.

Understandably, in quiet moments, Eric would examine what he would say if he did have the freedom to speak on such matters. At such times, he realized that he would naturally shy away from commenting broadly on its 'meaning'. He was to reticent and too much the scientist to do that. Surprisingly, what came to mind though, were insights and views on life after death, heaven and what all that might entail. He did not know why or how he got all these thoughts. They were just 'there.' All he could think of by way of explanation was that he was the son of a pastor. Even though he was now in his late forties, he dismissed the thought that it was just one's normal contemplation of mortality. He was far to young for that.

However, he was certain that he 'knew' things and for whatever reason it had now become important to share them with others. The how, what, when, where and why he would have to work out. He would wait for the right opportunity to do so. The right occasion would make it clear. Never, for even a moment, did it occur to him that any of this was a result of the coma he had suffered.

Eight months after the arrest of Dr. Alex Howard, he went on trial at the Federal Courthouse in Raleigh, N.C.. Andy and his staff, worked closely with the FBI lab in connection with the search and seizure warrants served at the home of Dr. Alex Howard. In that raid, they had obtained his computer, bank accounts and other records that might have a nexus to the investigation. From this computer hard drive, even though deletions had been made, they were able to recover e-mails to 'Charles' the ex-CIA agent, a/k/a Jeff Sullivan, and establish a trail of evidence. The most damaging item was, of course, the 'barbeque' message sent from the secret cell phone the night Eric's coma started. When it was presented and admitted at the trial, there was an audible gasp from the jury and the audience attending. And, from the expressions on the faces of the jurors, it was clear that it made quite an impression.

Likewise, the bank records for Alex's publishing business led to the trail of money supplied to 'Charles,' that were corroborated in large part by and through the bank records of Jeff Sullivan. This evidence, was accompanied by the strong and clear testimony of Jeff Sullivan that he acted solely behalf of Dr. Alex Howard. When the defenses turn came, Dr. Alex Howard declined to testify, offering only character witnesses to support his alleged innocence. He even presented the testimony of colleagues from his 'evolutionary science' group of associates. Their point was that Eric had not discovered anything that would motivate a response by them, let alone a reaction against him. Nonetheless, Dr. Alex Howard was still convicted on all charges. Shortly thereafter, the Judge sentenced him to twelve years in Federal prison. This was a stunning blow to this proud but arrogant man. For Andy, Jared, the AAG, and their team it was a great success and notable within the Department of Justice due to its connection to the widely published Discovery of Eric and Janice at the MRC. With this threat behind them, Janice and Eric were able to end this sad and disturbing episode.

About a year later, it came to pass that Eric was asked by his Church to be a speaker at an evening gathering. This was the same church where his father had been pastor and preached many sermons. Furthermore, Janice had now joined this Church because Eric had asked her to do so in a most earnest way. With all that had happened, they were now 'celebrities' in a low key way and the pastor and members wanted them to share their Discovery with them.

Without thinking about it, Eric accepted this invitation and agreed to give his talk on a Monday evening. That night they sat down in a casual circle, with about thirty long standing friends and parishioners, and told the story of the Discovery, the Code, its translation and the announcement to the world of finding a 'Window on the Soul'. And then, without even thinking about it, and totally unsolicited, Eric went on to give the 'meaning' of the Code in life after death.

He stated without equivocation, that the Code was not the basis for Gods judgment and acceptance to Heaven and Eternal Life. He made clear that the Code, beyond its translation, included a persons special traits pertaining to their personality and character. He went on about how ones Spirit (Soul) linked with others and became that unseen, unheard, remote influence on the human mind and decisions. He related the nature of being a Spirit and interactions with other Spirits. He went on about Heaven actually being the Heavens and their unbelievable immensity. And finally, with a nudge from Janice's knee, he stopped, having gone into 'overtime' with the meeting.

The striking thing about it all, was the quiet, confident, knowing way Eric had presented all that he said. This had been given in a clear, distinct, credible, straight forward manner. Those present could tell that he 'knew' with certainty what he was talking about. He did not say it in the way a person 'guesses' about something or theorizes about unknown things. It was all stated in the way of 'knowing' these things to be true. Eric had now moved into a different element. Unwittingly, he had let go of the limitations and bounds that he had always followed. The look on Janice's face was astonishment. What was going on with Eric?

As the Church members filed out, the Pastor asked to speak with Eric in private in his office. Once seated there, the Pastor, a tall and deeply devout man, thanked

Eric for his talk. He went on to say that he was quite struck by many of the things Eric had said about life after death and Heaven. In a very careful way, he went on to say that his theological study and training had not revealed most of the things Eric had described. Carefully, he asked Eric if somehow the translations he had made gave him the knowledge and information he related during his talk.

By now, Eric was sensing that perhaps he had somehow gone to far in what he had said. On the other hand, inside him, he 'knew' what he 'knew' and did not feel a need to apologize for this. All he could do at this moment was throw up his hands and say:

" Pastor, I can't explain the how and why of it; I just 'know' these things and more."

Pastor: " Don't misunderstand. I am not being critical. In fact I am quite pleased. Our faith does not need a scientific foundation. It is enough that someone really 'knows.' The good news here is that *you, you alone, know more than all others*. Seldom, if ever, does one get to witness the kind of thing that happened tonight. I encourage you to go further with speaking out the way you did this evening."

Eric: " I am a bit embarrassed. I didn't plan that. I feel very comfortable in this Church, with my lifetime friends and my fathers history here; what I have kept bottled up just came out. I am sorry if I embarrassed you."

Pastor: "Now, now, no need for that; your missing my point, entirely; with all the apathy that exists today in our society, this Church and many other Church's, need to hear your message. I believe in the things you said. You simply 'know' these things. Our Pastors sermonize, theorize, and postulate; but even so, they don't 'know' as surely as you do."

Eric: " Thank you for your confidence in me. I best leave now, its getting late."

Pastor: " Thank you for coming and sharing. Please keep speaking out. I think I shall tell a few others. Thank you again."

With that Janice and Eric left the Church and began driving home.

On the road while driving, Janice said: " Eric, that was quite a performance tonight. What got into you?"

Eric: " I don't know; I don't know; with my friends there, in my lifelong Church, with my soul mate beside me, I just let go of the limitations that have been troubling me and started speaking from my heart. We need to have a talk tonight when we get home. I need to tell and share with you the frustrations I have been feeling for some time."

Janice: " Ok, lets do that. Lately, you seem to have the weight of the world on your shoulders. Let see what we can do about it."

CHAPTER 51

Later at home, after changing into some comfortable clothes and sitting down on the loveseat in their bedroom, Eric and Janice had their talk. At first, Eric was himself, describing the troubles and frustrations he was encountering during the aftermath of the many presentations given in the last year. Janice listened carefully and asked why this was so difficult. After all, he was the one that had initiated the limitations in the Paper.

Eric: " Yes, I know; and I shouldn't feel the way I do. I can't help it; there are things in me that I 'know' and feel deeply and they struggle to come out. What's happening to me, Janice? I just don't know." and he started to sob a little. He was breaking down. She could see it on his face and in his tears.

Janice put her arms around him and hugged him tenderly, saying: "Now, now Eric, I love you and I am here for you. We will work this out; find a way to make it right for you; just have confidence and we will get thru this as we have always done."

Eric: " Janice, tonight, as I went on with this Church group of friends, and for the first time in a long while, I felt some relief; it felt right at the time and I do not regret speaking about these things."

Janice, sitting back a little, said: " Eric, I am glad this happened for you. Lets look at it; where did this all come from; you and I both know that the Code and its translations did not give rise to even a small part of what you 'know' and described in your talk." Carefully she worked this around to: " where did all this come from?"

Eric: " That's the strange part; I can't explain it in the normal way; its just there, when the question comes or I am prompted in some way, I can give my 'take' on what follows from having a 'Window on the Soul'; I utterly and simply 'know' the answer. I don't even have to think about it, its just there; I 'know' it but can't explain how I came to 'know' it.

Janice, deeply thoughtful, asked: " Eric, I recall the time you showed me the add-on you could see by touching the MRI Code for , I think, patient Barney. Are the things you 'know' anything like that?; remember, you described this to me?"

Eric: "Well, yes and no; it differs because I don't need to touch anything for this recall; its just there, not relating to a particular person or patient; the things I 'know' seem like memories or experiences one remembers due to having been there or lived it; yet, you know my whereabouts, day in and day out for the past few years; I haven't died; I haven't been in Heaven, nor experienced Eternal Life; I am still here and have been all along; its all very puzzling; how can this happen?"

Janice: " It's a mystery for sure; instead of trying to over analyze it, lets try just accepting it as part of you for

367

whatever reason and go with wherever it takes you; even thinking of it as a 'gift'; although, you might be careful picking out the right setting; following along the lines of what you did tonight; but nonetheless, follow thru with what you 'know'; I can tell you without a doubt, setting aside my clear bias for you, that when you speak as you did tonight, you are very believable, persuasive, and credible. Definitely, well beyond my minimal knowledge of theology and things metaphysical, or maybe even supernatural."

Eric: "You said persuasive, and that is the thing; I am not trying to persuade anyone of anything. Somehow, I truly 'know' these things to be true; and if anything, the only thing one should take away from such a session, would be an interest in caring for the development of one's Soul. This comes right back to the very thing we discovered, 'a Window on the Soul'."

Janice: " Eric, your getting to deep for me at this hour. Lets go to bed. I have a procedure tomorrow morning and I need my sleep."

Eric: "I know; I agree; I will think more about it and likely do as you said."

And they kissed good night and went on to sweet blissful sleep.

Early he next day, the Church pastor took the notes he had jotted down the night before and used them to prepare a memo about the 'talk' Eric had made. He knew that his Church was aware of the Paper given at the MRC finding a 'Window on the Soul.' Clearly, this gave new support to the long standing biblical references to the Human Spirit and Soul.

And now with Eric's 'talk' there was much more to think about. Having the very person that made the Discovery give further meaning and insight into life after death, (i.e. Eternal life) and Heaven, in such an authoritative way, was an entirely different matter. He had read the Paper by Eric and Janice as a result of the widespread publicity it received following the MRC Conference. Surprisingly, he came to realize that Eric was a regular member of his Church and his father had even been the pastor there before him.

After the memo was done, he called his District Supervisor and reported the gist of the prior evenings gathering. This led to a request for his memo which he promptly attached to a brief e-mail. This, in turn, was passed up the line within the Church hierarchy. It arrived later that day at the office of the Church's chief executive officer. Additionally, he was a Bishop, a soft spoken man, cordial, friendly, outgoing and quite in touch with the pastors and the lay councils of the Church.

With the memo in front of him, having read it three times, each time more carefully, he called the

Church Pastor to hear from him firsthand what he had witnessed, and get his 'take' on the words used and the speakers demeanor. He learned of the MRC Conference and Paper , and obtained an immediate copy, and read it thoroughly. The more he thought about it, the more he realized this to be an exceptional circumstance. He wondered what should be done, if anything? He rolled this around in his head the whole day.

In doing so, he called a close friend that had been a fellow religious head that had retired about two years ago. Together, they had served on a key committee for the World Ecumenical Council. This organization was well known for its promotion of unity and cooperation by and between Christian denominations. It served to bring together millions of Christians from the worlds major faiths. It worked on developing mutually recognized theology, as well as toleration and respect for each religions different points of view.

Following a brief description by the Bishop, he forwarded overnight copies of the Pastors memo and the Paper announcing the 'Window on the Soul.' The friend had vaguely recalled reading of this Discovery although he had not looked into it due to his 'retirement.' With the urging of the Bishop, he quickly read this information and called back three days later. Promptly, they got down to it, acknowledging that the kind of things Eric 'knew' at the evening church gathering were well beyond that which could be derived from the scope of the Paper. Furthermore, they both agreed that no matter how much one studied the Bible, or read between the 'lines' of the

Bible, one could not 'know' the things about Eternal Life and Heaven that Eric had described.

Jointly, they placed a conference call to the Pastor to ask a few further questions. Their inquiry was along the lines of Eric's mental state, veracity and credibility. This process didn't take long; the Pastor made it clear that Eric was well known and respected, a key person at the Medical Research Center, highly educated, without the slightest hint of any mental instability, unbiased and believable beyond measure; moreover, he is generally regarded as truthful, accurate and correct about the points he makes. In conclusion, he said:

"If, your looking for a 'crackpot' to have stated the things repeated in my Memo, you have the wrong man. Eric is not such a person at all."

Bishop and his friend: "You mean you believe the things he said?"

Pastor: " Yes, I surely do; I have no idea how or why he has this special knowledge, but without question, I believe him. I think you would too."

After hanging up the Bishop and his friend talked further; even about the Pastor and his training and experience within the Church. All of this turned out to be good. He had a doctorate in theology, substantial experience on behalf of the Church, including missionary service; he is beloved to the various congregations he has served, and long overdue for a promotion because of his excellent record. He is a stalwart and highly believable. He was creditable, definitely creditable.

This was enough. They had to go and see this for themselves. Being Church leaders and highly motivated Christians, they had to witness the words, demeanor and knowledge of Dr. Eric Rhodes, and hear firsthand the things he spoke about. For this to be real to them, they needed a face to face Question and Answer session with Eric. They both knew that if he was as 'real' as was being represented, it was high time that the world should hear from him. So, by and through the Pastor, they arranged a meeting at the Pastors office at the Church Eric had attended his entire life.

How would this turn out? Would this support or destroy what they had learned of Eric? What would all of this turn out to mean in the long run if it were true?

CHAPTER 52

Two weeks later, in the very room at the Church where the fateful Monday evening gathering had taken place, the Pastor, Eric, Janice, the Bishop and his friend all sat down to discuss the 'talk' made by Eric. The Pastor had asked Eric for this meeting citing their office discussion, his Memo, and the level of interest it had sparked at the Church headquarters. Eric had been apprehensive about doing this session but softened after Janice had encouraged him, pointing out their in depth conversation about his ongoing struggles with the limits adopted. Additionally, they were curious about why the head of his Church wanted to talk with him.

The introductions were brief, followed by thank you's to Janice and Eric for taking time out of their busy schedules to attend, and then they all sat down at the table. The Bishop took the initiative and began with the obvious, being the Paper about their Discovery, the Code, the 'Window on the Soul,' and the acknowledgement that all present had read it. The visitors congratulated Janice and Eric for this amazing advance in Medical Science.

He went on to say that this was only background for the reason he and his friend were there today. What had really brought them was the 'talk' Eric had made that Church evening, expressing what he 'knew' about the meaning of the Code, its use and purpose during the Eternal Life of ones Spirit (Soul) and there time in Heaven. This, they had to hear for themselves as well as for the religious organizations they represented and served. Eric was now squirming in his chair, when the Bishop asked:

"Eric, please tell us about how the Code serves one's Spirit (Soul) in Heaven?"

Eric, drew a deep breath, and calmly, picking his words with care, answered:

" The Code gives an ongoing means to assess the 'state' of one's Spirit (Soul), by way of its core Code regions, being: its morals, intellect and values, and the personal traits possessed; and, in turn, this reading bears upon that Spirit's (Souls) subsequent activities and travels in and about the Heavens, including placement, associations, projects, scope of communication, linkage, and other connections, direct and indirect."

Bishop: " Please tell us why this would be important?" Eric responded:

"Because, Spirits can and do choose these things to bring them happiness in their life in Heaven; moreover, they can also choose to engage with other Souls in various ways that give them challenges, purpose and value. This comes from the nature of their Soul, as disclosed by the content of their Code and the Spirits 'one of a kind' unrecorded character.'

Bishop: " What can you tell us about Heaven?"

Eric: " Well, its certainly not a country club or golf course resort, that's for sure. 'Judgment' must have taken place for one's Soul to be 'accepted' into Heaven. It must be 'worthy' of life after death, i.e. Eternal Life. The Heavens are vast, immense beyond all physical concepts known to mankind. In that Spirits (one's Soul) are non temporal, having no physical needs or desires, they can and do move and exist over and above and around all the physical planets in the Heavens. It is from this vantage point that they indirectly influence humans and other life forms on inhabited planets. "

Notwithstanding the unusual other world concepts, the Bishop looked at Eric and saw a man in full command of his faculties, believable, competent, confident, and assured; and, it appeared that the longer he talked the more relaxed and engaged he became. With that, the Bishop asked:

"Eric, how do you 'know' these things? It's as if you have been there? Do you claim such a thing?" To which Eric replied:

"No, I claim no such thing; I am not a nut or anything like that; I do not know how to answer your question other than to say that I just do. Somehow, someway, I 'know' the answer to these kinds of questions. The answers are just there. It is not a stretch for me to give the answer. That's all."

Bishop: " I know of you and your fathers long history with this Church. Being my Church as well, to be sure. Would you say these things you 'know' are purely an expression and an extension of your faith?'

Eric: " Of course not; while I have faith, as you and those present do, that is separate and apart from what I 'know.' As I have already said, I plainly 'know' the answers to the questions you have asked. If I didn't 'know' the answers, I would just say so. I can understand why this whole thing may seem 'off based' to you and others; I can't help that; I am being honest and straight forward the best that I can? I have no agenda in what I say. In fact its quite the opposite. Being at home in this Church makes all the difference for me. I seldom volunteer spontaneous comment."

At that point, they took a fifteen minute break. After a restroom visit, the Bishop and his friend quietly disappeared into the Pastors office for a few minutes. Once there, the Bishop looked to his friend, trusting his instincts and judgment as much as his own, and said:

"Well, what do you think?" clearly referring to Eric and his answers.

" He is even more believable in person than our original 'take' on what we learned about him in the Memo." the friend answered.

Bishop: " I agree. Never in my lifetime have I seen or heard such things. Shall we go ahead with what we discussed earlier?"

" You bet." the friend said.

With that, they rejoined the group in the meeting room.

The Bishop began: "Eric, I have heard enough for today; in fact, we both have heard enough; as you can no doubt tell, our presence today was solely to hear from you and the kind of 'knowledge' you uniquely possess. We have done that and we are more than satisfied by what we have observed and confirmed. You are indeed 'special' in all that you 'know.' The question now becomes, whether you are willing to share this 'knowledge' with others of our faith. We think the things you 'know' are well beyond the science of genetics, the field within which you work. Your 'knowledge' appears to be a gift, likely from God. It is very important. Maybe we are all to 'know' these things and maybe not. We encourage you to join with us and share with others who would like to hear what you 'know' and listen to your answers about our fate beyond that which the Bible provides."

Eric: "What do you mean? I am a scientist and a good one. I work for a leading center in the United States at the cutting edge of advances in genetics. What are you saying? More specifically, what are you asking me to do?"

Bishop: " Together, my friend and I are much like you. We are part of the leadership of two of the most major Religions in the Christianity. And, we are part of the World Ecumenical Council. We implore you to find a way to bring that which you 'know' to the attention and theology of our Religions and the World Ecumenical Council."

Eric, feeling and looking stunned:

" Please understand, I am in general a shy and retiring man. I don't seek the spotlight or the supposed glory of the twenty-four-seven media. Its just the opposite, I prefer being left alone. Knowing this, what is it that you want?"

Bishop: " Eric, we know these things about you. We do not seek to thrust you out there for the media to do the kind of things you worry about. We are asking for a few verbal sessions to begin with, the kind you had with the Pastor at the evening gathering. Only, in this case the sessions would be with an invited and select group that we would carefully choose. There would be no media or press coverage. We would do everything to keep it all private and confidential."

Eric: "Thank you for showing this sensitivity. I refuse to be put out there as a kind of circus attraction. On the other hand, I have been searching for a way to say the many things I 'know' and feel but have set aside because of self imposed limits. Lets do this; I need to think about what you have said and discuss it with Janice, my wife and soul mate. This won't take long; when we are ready, the Pastor and I will call and talk further with you. How's that?"

They readily agreed, pleased that Eric would at least think about it. The meeting ended at that point, each party going their separate way. Eric and Janice went back to work agreeing to talk later at home in private. They all left together with smiles and friendly handshakes. Mutually, there was warmth and a good feeling by and between each other. They were all on the same side.

After finishing work for the day, Janice and Eric met for dinner at their favorite Chinese restaurant. They liked to have oriental food once or twice a month, switching back and forth between Thai and Chinese. In a silly mood, Janice always insisted that the words 'in bed' should be added to the little sayings in the Chinese cookies. They always left laughing after reading and comparing their separate little notes with this appendage applied.

And this evening was no different. They were in a light and happy mood, pleased with the days activities, relaxed and ready for a good evening. They agreed to talk about today's meeting at the Church, but promised each other to keep it upbeat. Janice started:

"Well Eric, have you thought about it? What's going on in that deep mind of yours?" giving him that big smile she possessed.

Eric: "I don't know. This is a tough thing for me. My life has been so definite up to this point. My education, my work at the MRC, my love of the science of genetics, the advances that have taken place in my lifetime, it goes on and on. But I do have to admit that the Discovery, the Code and the Paper, have changed the whole equation. And all of that, I sense, 'pales' when I let myself think about this 'knowledge' within me. What do you think?"

Janice: "Eric, my love, my dearest love; I feel for you and I am always here for you. You are so rich and special. Your inner person goes beyond anyone or anything I have ever known. I know you struggle with these conflicts that seem to find you. Let me offer this; they are not asking you to quit who you are or what you do; they are only asking you to go a little further. And, by that I mean, it seems that they are asking you to share this unique 'knowledge' at a few group sessions of specifically invited colleagues. That's all; being as devoted as you are to your Church, you would likely do this anyway, if asked, without even thinking about it. Right?"

Eric: "I suppose so. But what if they want more? This always seems to happen."

Janice: "Then we will cross that bridge if and when that happens. Ok."

Eric: "Ok, I'll give it a chance."

CHAPTER 53

A week later, having rolled their request over in his mind again and again, Eric and the Pastor contacted the Bishop to go forward. In their conversation, it was agreed that Eric would try this out via three or four groups, at the rate of one a month. The Church would pick up his travel expenses as well as those of Janice if she were to accompany him. Eric absolutely refused any thoughts of compensation for himself. He would receive advance information on those attending and there would be no publicity. He would give a 'talk' with questions and answers but no speeches or sermons. The size of the group was to be limited to 30 - 40. It was Ok with him if what he said was taken down by a stenographer as long as he could edit it afterward without further changes by others. The attendees would receive in advance a synopsis of the Paper given at the MRC Conference and a short bio about him. These points were more than acceptable to the Bishop. This would strictly be extra-circular for Eric; not on behalf of the MRC. It was all set and Eric made his first appearance in this program two months later.

Coincidentally, his Church was having a nationwide retreat at this time at a beautiful setting in Southeast Colorado. This was a casual affair, with various speakers and sessions, all taking place at an outstanding hotel. Eric's 'talk' was not a part of the regularly scheduled program. This would be a private and confidential session that the Bishop personally supervised and directed. Those invited to attend became a rather fluid matter with the Bishop. Eric did not see the group list until the day beforehand. It turned out to largely be the other leaders of the Church, some Pastors and a few guests from the World Ecumenical Council, totaling thirty-eight people and the Bishop. Curiously, it followed the retreat, being the day afterward.

The Bishop did as Eric asked, introducing Janice and Eric in a quiet and understated way. You could feel a shudder of surprise from the group when they realized they were about to hear from a scientist. Eric began by using the background statement given to those attending, as a means of moving from the Discovery, the Code, and its translation, to the leap of finding a 'Window on the Soul.' From that moment, he went on to the realm of the special 'knowledge' he possessed and would now share.

He started first with the nature of a Soul (Spirit) and its life in Heaven. He expanded on this by explaining how one's Code bears upon the various aspects of this afterlife, including the types of possible connections, linkages, activities and purposes. He revealed the Spirits insights into the glory of Nature, seeing this first hand in travel about the Heavens and by other means. He did this all in a way and manner that set every one at ease. He took questions as he went along and readily moved quickly across the spectrum of things he 'knew' with certainty. At times, he simply responded to some inquiries stating that he did not 'know' the answer to that question, thereby establishing that he was not claiming to 'know' all things about one's Spirit (Soul).

It did not come as any surprise, that sooner or later, considering the nature of the audience, someone said:

"I have read and studied the bible thoroughly in the Seminary, and otherwise many times over the years preparing for sermons and church functions. I know for sure that much of what you have said is not part of what's there. It's not in conflict with what's there; but its well beyond what's there and what we have all known and preached over the years. How do you answer for this?"

Eric, after thanking him for his question, answered:

384

"Yes, your are right, its not written there. I know this. I grew up the son of a Pastor of this very faith. He was my beloved father. And, I have followed a different path than him, as you heard from my introduction. All I can say by way of explanation, is that something has happened to me. When I think about it, it seems to have occurred about the time I prepared the science based Paper presented by us at the MRC Conference. Ever since that time, the Papers limitations have pressed forward on my mind. Yet, beyond that, I 'know' the things I have said today. I can understand your skepticism; I 'get' that myself; but, everyday, this all resurfaces within me. I have shared some of this 'knowledge' with the Bishop and others; and they still wanted me to do this and other talks. I don't have any other thing to add to what I have just said; Its just there, within me; believe it or not; its beyond anything I can explain further. I hope that helps."

Before the words were even out of his mouth, the audience burst forth with unrestrained applause. It was a spontaneous acceptance. It went on for three or four minutes. The Bishop was standing, applauding. This was not a recrimination of the man that had asked the question; it was just a moment of clear support for the person standing before them and the message he was delivering; The man that raised the point stood up with the rest of the people, and joined in the applauses enthusiastically.

It was the kind of moment that one hopes to have at least once in a lifetime. Janice was so proud of Eric she began crying. Eric had reached a new level of being. An exalted moment to be sure.

Later that evening, in the quiet of their room, Eric and Janice talked about this huge moment. For the first time in a long while, Eric could honestly say that he was happy and pleased with the way things went that day. He felt a unique satisfaction with the talk given and the response received. There was now a sense of relief within him. He couldn't say exactly why, only that he felt good about opening up and sharing. Janice joined with him in feeling good about the 'talk' and the event as it took place. She went on to say:

"Eric, I must say that this was the first time I ever heard you mention the time when you first sensed possessing or 'knowing' the special kinds of things you do. I don't think you ever told me about this. To my recollection, there was an early sign of this even beforehand, when you briefly told me of 'seeing' and 'knowing' the character traits of Barney upon touching his MRI readout. Remember?"

Eric: "You know, I do; I think you are right. I should have realized something was going on then. Especially since it continued to take place with the other patients we were studying. You're right; what do you think this is; what's going on with me?"

Janice: "Eric, your a strange case, that's for sure. But I still love you. Lets try not to think too much about it and just 'go' with it for as long as it lasts. You know, this may not last forever. And, furthermore, I think it would be bad to name it or attach any kind of label to the things you 'know'. These things, labels, just end up being demeaning 'put-downs'. And, we don't want that to happen to my loveee, now do we Eric?" and she gave him a big kiss.

This type of gathering set the pattern for what was to follow over the next five years. The meetings would all be carefully arranged by and through Church and World Ecumenical Council. If there was an essential message to what they were doing it was kept behind the scenes and controlled, although not emphasized as a secret. Eric was satisfied with the way it was all handled and taking place and he participated in his own diligent way.

He went out of his way to keep this separate from his work at the MRC. Often times, he was able to coordinate trips on the Centers behalf with a Saturday or Sunday talk session somehow related to his travel route. It seemed the MRC projects, grant solicitations, report meetings and visits to other important organizations frequently kept him on the road. Plus, by way of vacation periods and short leaves ostensibly for special travel, he was able to meet and give talks set up by the World Ecumenical Council at various locations around the world. Eric was indeed a busy man.

One day, perhaps out of a sense of guilt, he sat down with Mr. Johnston, saying:

"Mr. Johnston, I have a bit of a confession to make."

Mr. Johnston: "Oh, Eric, what could that be? I hope it isn't about some sexual harassment issue; I have heard enough of that lately." ending with a big smile because he always enjoyed his time with Eric.

Mr. Johnston: "I haven't been entirely candid with you and the MRC on something over the past few years. This being, that I have given some quiet talks within my Church's structure at various locations. The foundation for these talks came from the project and Paper delivered at the MRC Conference. You remember that, I'm sure."

Mr. Johnston: "Eric, how many years have we known each other? And furthermore, with all the time this covers, you and I should be on a first name basis; so call me Richard from now on. And, of course, I remember that Conference and all that led up to it and followed from it. It was a great thing for all of us."

Eric: "Ok, "Richard," I'll try, but this will take some getting use too; what I was getting at was that somehow I developed a certain 'knowledge' about the meaning of the Code pertaining to one's Spirit (Soul) and life after death. I couldn't keep this bottled up inside me. And, it didn't feel right to mix it in with my work here at the Center. So, it was with great relief that this became something I could and did share with my Church. Richard, that's what I wanted to say."

Mr. Johnston: "Eric, Eric, my good man; if that's the most difficult issue can hand to me, I have nothing to worry about. And, neither should you. Its your Church; the Center has nothing to do with this; and as far as the Centers concerned your conduct and work has always been and still is exemplary. Now go on, keep doing what you do so well; and call me Richard the next time we are together."

Afterward, Eric was pleased with this conversation. He went home and shared it all with Janice. He felt a sense of relief that his behind the scenes work was now in effect 'licensed' by the MRC and he was no longer hiding the other major thing that he was doing. He could go on in good conscience with these 'talks' for the Bishop and his Church. Furthermore, in some way, reaching this point seemed to tell Eric, that he and Janice had come thru an incredible period and time in their lives. They were happy and should be contented with being in a good place at the moment sharing their love for each other.

Their life together had survived as difficult a time as any married couple might endure. They had no idea of what may happen to them next. Nonetheless, they would come thru whatever that may be.

CHAPTER 54

One month later;

It was now Saturday and Eric was free for the first time in a long while from the duties and responsibilities that usually kept him so busy. Janice and Eric went about doing those catch up errands we all put off to the weekend. Starting late morning, going on thru mid afternoon, they shopped, had lunch out, looked at some new furniture, and so on. When they arrived home, at their front door was the latest Fed-Ex package from the Church's stenographer.

The weekend before Eric had given one of those group 'talks' that he was becoming known for among a limited circle. It was his practice to carefully edit the stenographers regular transcriptions of these meetings. When completed, this one, when added to the others, would total thirty separate writings that encompassed the full scope of his special 'knowledge.' The Bishop had approached Eric with the thought of publishing these reports in a book format. Eric didn't know whether he wanted to do that and in his usual manner promised to think about it.

Taking his leave from Janice for a little while, he went into his den, sat as his desk and opened the package. Placing the report in front of him, he leaned over and started to read and work on editing. Usually this was an easy thing for him to do. His special 'knowledge' just kicked in and there was complete recall of that which he had spoken about in and during the 'talk.' Not just simple memory but also that one and only ability to 'know' of what he was speaking.

However, at this very moment, there was nothing there. This was the first time this had happened.

It was only the words that he must have said, that were recorded at that time. Eric was shocked. He was quite taken back. He was stunned. He staggered from his den to Janice in the living room and said:

"Janice, its gone, just like that, its gone."

Janice: "Eric, calm yourself; what's gone?"

Eric: "You know. All that special 'knowledge' I have been sharing with the Church groups. Its gone, its not there anymore."

Janice: "Are you sure? How do you know?"

So he described to her his attempt to work on the latest report in the way and manner that he had followed each time before. He told of separately trying to say out loud what he had been able to recall and could say from the recesses of this 'knowledge.' He couldn't do it. He knew for sure that it was no longer there. It was over. There was no more.

The next day, Sunday, Eric tried once again to access this special base of 'knowledge.' He was right, it was no longer there. He did not know whether to be happy about this or not. Anyhow, it didn't matter, since he no longer had the 'knowledge.'

After Church, later that Sunday afternoon, he called the Bishop. He apologized profusely for calling him on the Sabbath. Then, he told him of the loss of what he 'knew' and drew upon for the Church 'talks' he had been giving. The Bishop empathized with him and asked if he thought he had covered the most of what he had 'known'

392

with the sessions held over the years. Eric answered that he had and realized as much after completing the recent 'talk', being their thirtieth group meeting. The Bishop couldn't thank him enough for all that he had done. He went on to observe that he was happy that these meetings were all a matter of record, referring to the completed reports. Eric agreed and added that he would do what he could with this last one and send it back. The Bishop was happy with what Eric had shared and the Bishop promised to stay in touch with him.

Eric, the Bishop and the others interested in this phenomenon must now realize that this thing with Eric was finished. Over, Over, Over. They would have to carry on with the record from the thirty 'talks' Eric had given to them. They had in writing Eric's special 'one of a kind' insight into one's Spirit life. It described the nature of the afterlife of the surviving Soul of each previous living being. It was all there. What more could one ask of one man as a temporal legacy? He had made his gift for posterity.

<u>EPILOGUE</u>

One year later;

This fine Saturday afternoon the sun was beaming, the birds were singing and all was well at the home of Eric and Janice. Eric had thrown open the patio doors to his den and reveled in the scent of the blooms and flowers upon the arrival of Springtime. Meanwhile, Janice was away on an emergency situation It seemed that she was trying to put together some poor fellow that had been severely injured as the result of a motorcycle accident. In her absence, Eric thought he would attend to some things on his desk and clean up his office. He was quite relaxed and in a great mood.

He was feeling this way because the day before he had a long talk with Mr. Richard Johnston, the Chief Administrator for the Medical Research Center. He had known 'Richard,' his colleague, his entire career and Richard was now reaching retirement age and their conversation turned to this point. Mr. Johnston said:

"Eric, before I can retire the Board wants me to find and name my successor. In this connection, I told them that in-house, which is what they always prefer, there is only one choice, and that is you. You would be perfect in this role. You are of the right age, the right background and have spoken on our behalf and represented us with all of our key constituencies'. Moreover, the entire Board is well acquainted with you as a result of the many presentations you have given over the years. What do you think?"

Eric: "Well, I am pleasantly surprised and deeply appreciative of your vote of confidence. Of course I would like this promotion. Before I can say yes, though, I need to talk it over with Janice. Thank you, beyond all measure," ....and they shook hands and ended the workweek.

Eric was greatly elated with this development and so was Janice. He would definitely take this next step. Hence, he was in the process of putting things in order at home at this time.

Sitting there on his desk was a recently delivered copy of the thirty 'talks' Eric had given at the Church sponsored events. This publication even included an appendix of the names of the various Church and World Ecumenical Council attendees and their respective titles. It was a virtual list of who's who in the broad spectrum of Christian religion. In a recent conversation, the Bishop indicated that this was being circulated to these people for them to add their thoughts and comments about your 'talks' and meetings.

The Bishop went on to explain that his Church and other Christian religions, by and through their relationship with the World Ecumenical Council, followed a united process in taking a position on and characterizing the life and words of people 'knowing' things as Eric did. He asked if Eric, as part of this process would allow an in depth interview with him, his wife and others about his life history. It seemed that all of this would need to be studied. Eric did not see any problem and would help, if he could. The Bishop assured him that this would be a long process and that more than likely he and the Bishop would be deceased by the time it was all finished.

Eric realized that the question left for one and all would be the conclusion to be made at the end of this process. Would this be lost within the dim memory of history. Or, would it gain prominence and recognition for all time. And, if so, what should that be. This would be left for those who witnessed Eric in his 'talks.' This would be left to the Church leaders to debate. This would be left for philosophers and thinkers to come. It would take its rightful place in time, one way or another. Who could know at this point? Eric was satisfied to leave this whole matter alone. Now that his unique 'knowledge' was gone, it was hard for him to focus on this period of his life.

Moving on, he picked up this publication and put it in his ongoing file named "the Code." In doing so, while thumbing thru the accordion folder, he happened upon and placed on his desk, the one page copy and separate translation of the: *The Cure of the Soul: the Place & the Legend* *by: Jacoby, Assistant to the Head Librarian, Library at Alexandra.* As he looked at it, his mind flowed back to his time in Israel. He remembered that as a consequence of finding this document, he had gone to the library at the Hebrew University of Jerusalem, and while following an article note, he found the Errata reference where he learned that the wall carving at the Library of Alexandria was in the Coptic language.

He smiled thinking back to this enormous moment. It had made all the difference. His quest had paid off. He had finally been able to make translations of the Code.

This had colored the rest of his life. He picked up the translated copy and read once again the enigmatic words of the inscription placed above the hallway in the Library at Alexandria on that strange and fateful night, being:

"The Place of the Cure of the Soul"

Eric's eyes drifted down the page to where Jacoby concluded:

*"me think it **Yahweh:** the night and carving; left mystery for all; me no know answer- me guess; answer inside; within carving!"*

Eric, smiling again, thinking to himself:

"Jacoby was right, the answer *was* inside the carving. My guess is that this was a moment of self congratulation by **Yahweh**. Clearly, this announced that the Code had now been placed within the human body and this was a kind of celebration. The hint was the use of the Coptic language for the inscription. The very language used within the internal human Code!"

"This enigma survived all attempts to understand its meaning. It would seem that this carving was not placed there for the age within which it was created. It was put there as a challenge for all time.

Somehow I backed into unraveling this mystery."

"I now believe this was intended and inevitable!"

With this, Eric placed the document back in the file and put it all away. He was smiling to himself, and chuckling a little, but with a small tear of joy in the corner of his eye.

The END

www.ingramcontent.com/pod-product-compliance
Lightning Source LLC
Chambersburg PA
CBHW060143260626
47160CB00001B/103